THERE IS A LEGEND OLDER THAN KING ARTHUR'S . . .

A story of great wizards and evil warlocks, battling for the fate of a kingdom. The Isle of Celydonn, once plagued by the monstrous powers of the Wild Magic, is darkened by the shadows of a terrible conspiracy. And only the wizard's apprentice, Teleri, can stop the growing evil through the secrets she must uncover in ancient, magical books. Books which tell of a secret grove, where the Green Lion speaks . . .

THE GREEN LION TRILOGY

This magnificent new series brings all the action, magic and excitement of a medieval world vividly to life. An epic tale that will stir your imagination and capture your heart . . .

Book Two
The Moon in Hiding

KING & KINGDOM OF
YNYS CELYDONN

THE MOON IN HIDING

TERESA EDGERTON

ACE BOOKS, NEW YORK

THE MOON IN HIDING

An Ace Book/published by arrangement with the author

PRINTING HISTORY
Ace edition/September 1989

Ace Books by Teresa Edgerton

THE GREEN LION TRILOGY

CHILD OF SATURN
THE MOON IN HIDING

THE WORK OF THE SUN
(coming in March 1990)

DRAIGHEN

CUAN

leth scathach

CAMBOGLANNA

CELLIWIG

❧ Ynys ❧ Celydonn

KING & KINGDOM of
CELYDONN

YNYS
PRACHE

YNYS
OARRE

FINDIAS

CUAN

DRAIGHEN

SKELL

leth scathac

COBLYNAU
HILLS

COILLDORCHA

TREGALEN

DOL TAL
CARREG

CAMBOGLANN

CAER CADEIRY &
TRELEDIG

DINAS EMRACHWYR

TEIRWAEDD
MORFA

REGUIN

CAMBOGLANNA

ST.
CUBI

CASTELL
ABERLYN

YNYS
ABERLYN

DINAS MOREN

MURIAS

DUN
FIONN

GORLAS

DUAN
DESSI

YNYS
MOREN

YNYS
CABIR
CARREG

YNYS
GLASTIG

YNYS
MORAS

GORWYNION

CELCYNNON

RHIANEDD

MOCHDREFF

PERFUDD

GWYNGELLI

WALGAN

Ann Meyer Maglinte

PERFUDD

GWYNGELLI

PENNGAREN
PEFYN'S GRAVE
PENNEFYNN
CADIR CERI
R. DYFERDALIBEN

DINAS SPAGEN
ST. MADDIEU
CASTELL MAELDUIN

WALGAN
ABERDALIBEN

FFYNOG

25   50   75   100
A SCALE OF MILES

TRUFFIN & FFLERGANT

ARFONDWY

CEILYN & TELERI

Ann Meyer Maginte

A GUIDE TO THE PRONUNCIATION OF THE NAMES OF PRINCIPAL CHARACTERS AND PLACES MENTIONED IN THE GREEN LION

Generally speaking:

c and *g* are always hard.
f is pronounced like *v* in English.
ff is just *f*.
ll is the Welsh *ll*, except in Draighenach names.
dd is a soft *th*.

Vowels are usually the same as in Welsh, except where the names look Irish, or where I decided to pronounce them differently.

With only one exception that I can think of, the accent is on the penultimate (second to the last) syllable.

Specifically:

Teleri ni Pendaren (Tel-AIR-ee nee Pen-DARE-en)
Ceilyn mac Cuel (KAY-lin mac KILL)
Cynwas fab Anwas (KIN-wass vab AN-wass)
Sidonwy (Sid-ON-wee)
Caer Cadwy (Kair KAD-wee or Kair Kah-DO-ee)
Camboglanna (Kam-bog-LON-nah)
Diaspad (Dee-AH-spad)
Calchas fab Corfil (Kal-kass vab KOR-vill)

Fflergant fab Maelgwyn (FLUR-gant vab MEL-gwin)
Tryffin (TRIF-fin)
Garanwyn (Gar-RAN-win)
Gwenlliant (Gwen-HLLEE-ant)
Glastyn (GLASS-tin)
Tir Gwyngelli (Tear Gwin-GELL-ee)
Mochdreff (MOCK-dreff)
Rhianedd (Hree-ANN-eth)
Cadifor (Kad-EE-vor)
Llochafor (Hllock-AH-vor)
Daire mac Forgoll (DARE-eh mac FOR-goal)
Derry (the way you think it is pronounced)
Morc (Mork)
Prescelli (Press-KELL-ee)
Caer Celcynnon (Kair Kel-KIN-non)
Manogan fab Menai (Mann-OH-gan vab MEN-ee)
Gwdolwen ni Dyffryn (Goo-DOHL-wen nee DUFF-rin)
Arfondwy (Are-von-DO-ee)
Tiffaine (Tiff-ANE)
Anwe (AHN-wee)
Castell Maelduin (CAS-tell MEL-doon)
Dyferdallben (Duff-ur-DALL-ben)
Teirwaedd Morfa (TIRE-wayth MOR-vah)
Celydonn, Celedon (Kel-UH-don)
Donwy (Don-OO-ee)

A note for the linguist: The Celydonian tongue and its dialects are not intended to represent any real-world Celtic tongue or dialect, nor any mixture which would be historically or linguistically possible. Rather, it is an intentionally fanciful combination of Welsh, Irish, and pseudo-Celtic elements, which derive any coherency or consistency they may have by a loose adherence to a pattern of migrations, intermarriages and inter-tribal cultural exchanges which could only have taken place on Ynys Celydonn and nowhere else.

CONTENTS

0.

The Alchemy of Change

Teleri ni Pendaren grew up one year, from a child of twelve to a young woman of eighteen all in the space of a single summer. Until that time, her misdirected talents as a Wizard kept her young, allowing her to move past and through calamity, around and beyond uncomfortable emotions, allowing time to flow over her without actually touching her, so that she remained always the child: innocent, scatheless, and sometimes unintentionally cruel.

Then Ceilyn mac Cuel came into her life . . . Ceilyn who was all the things that Teleri was not: eager, passionate, and determined to make his mark on the history of Ynys Celydonn. Yet not so different from Teleri, either, for Ceilyn had his own magic, shape-shifting magic that he feared and loathed.

When the ardent young knight conceived an odd, inconvenient infatuation for the ice-locked little sorceress, both of them were changed by it. Together, Teleri and Ceilyn thwarted the schemes of the flamboyant and ambitious Princess Diaspad, together they stood fast in defense of Queen Sidonwy. But more importantly, Teleri and Ceilyn made the first steps toward forging an alliance of mind and heart.

Alike and unlike, having much to learn and much to teach and much to share . . . through the interplay of such forces of opposition and attraction, earth and air, fire and water, male and female, sun and moon, through these Nature works her Alchemy of change. Teleri was both Alchemist and Wizard and should have known it, but she chose to forget what she knew. No matter—Time and Circumstance stepped in and transformed her all the same, with Ceilyn acting as the catalyst.

The season moved on toward Michaelmas. A magic mist, an

enchanted falcon, a chest of ancient bones . . . each offered a different challenge and in meeting that challenge Teleri changed in spite of herself. But then came autumn and—though she did not know it—Teleri still faced greater challenges and the greatest transmutation of all.

1.

Daybreak at Caer Cadwy

The castle was in an uproar. Clothes chests were opened and the contents all tossed out, beds overturned, storerooms and pantries ransacked—one enterprising guardsman even sifted through all the hay in the stables—but the casket containing the bones of the ancient kings of Rhianedd could not be found.

In the King's bedchamber, a breakfast of beef and bread and ale lay untouched on the table, and the Queen (looking ill and unhappy) took no more than a sip of wine before sending it away.

"I will hear your story again," King Cynwas said wearily, "from the beginning, if you please."

His two young kinsmen, Fflergant and Tryffin fab Maelgwyn, shifted uncomfortably, exchanged an anguished glance.

"We were walking in the Lady's Garden, a little after midnight," Fflergant began, only to be interrupted by the King.

"From the very beginning, I believe I said—and you have not yet explained what it was that you were doing just outside the Mermaid Tower at that hour."

Fflergant blushed. "Begging your pardon, Lord, but that isn't a question we can honorably answer," he replied stiffly.

"Which means," the Earl Marshall of Celydonn interjected dryly, "that there were women in it somewhere."

"Were there . . . young ladies of the Queen's household involved?"

Fflergant hesitated; he and his brother exchanged another uneasy glance. "We went there in the *expectation* of meeting two young ladies," Tryffin admitted at last.

This time, the King and the Earl Marshall exchanged a glance. "Very well," said Cynwas, with what might have been a faint suggestion of a smile, "we will let that pass, for now at least. You were walking in the Queen's Garden—alone or in company—and then . . . ?"

"We discovered one of her guards lying unconscious in the little maze, with a great purple lump on one side of his head. As the fellow showed no signs of reviving, we were about to go for Brother Gildas, when sounds of a fight taking place in the little garden behind the Chapel of St. March attracted our attention.

"We ran to the gate, but that slammed shut in our faces, and someone on the other side dropped the bar into place," Fflergant continued. "So we had to go through the chapel, down the little stair at the back, and break open the door at the bottom. By that time, the fight was over and there was no one in sight. We searched around until we discovered that someone had broken into the grand new sepulchre and removed the casket. It was lying there closed, beside the tomb, amidst all the scattered bricks."

"You did not open the casket to see if the bones were still inside?" the King asked.

Fflergant shook his head. "No. I was just about to do that, when Tryffin—"

"—that was when I realized there was more at stake than we had originally supposed," Tryffin interjected smoothly. "After a little discussion, we decided to go for the guards at the Main Gate, and we did so at once."

The King frowned thoughtfully, picked up his knife, and prodded the cold slab of beef lying on his plate. "You did not remove the casket when you left the garden? You did not put the bones anywhere for safekeeping?"

The two young princes from Tir Gwyngelli both shook their heads emphatically. "We left everything exactly as we found it, thinking that was what you would want," said Fflergant.

"Then where," said the King, "are the bones of the ancient kings of Rhianedd now?"

Fflergant did not reply; nor did Tryffin, though his deceptively mild brown eyes rested, for a moment, on Queen Sidonwy. She sat at the far end of the table, and all her pages and handmaidens clustered around her, attempting to offer comfort; but one member of her household was missing, and it was obvious that the Queen felt his absence keenly.

"Where is the faithful Ceilyn?" whispered Tryffin. "Not at his usual post, anyway."

"And what are we to say or do," replied Fflergant, also in a whisper, "if he's taken it into his head to go off questing again, or disappeared entirely?"

. . .

And the Princess Goewin took the young man by means of a back stair into a large, fair, upper chamber. There was a charcoal fire upon the hearth and cushions of fair brocaded silk and samite and bliant upon the bed. And the Princess Goewin said, "Here you may rest until your hurts are healed."

Then it came into the mind of the Princess that the young man (though already she loved him well) was indeed a stranger. "My honor is in your hands," said she. "If you are, as you say you are, my true friend, you will respect me as you would your own sister."

"As God is my witness," said the young man, "you are my lady and my love. Neither by word or deed shall you obtain any harm from me."

—*From* Goewin and Ellwy: The Death of Goewin

. . .

Ceilyn woke with an odd, unexpected sense of well-being. Teleri's bed was soft and warm, and her sheets and her pillow, like all her things, were fragrant with bittersweet herbs. A fire blazed on the hearth, Teleri's cloak was draped over a stool, and his own boots were lined up by the fire. There was something very cozy and intimate, Ceilyn decided, in the sight of his things and her things laid out together.

He tried to sit up, but as soon as he lifted his head a few inches off the pillow the room spun madly around him and he discovered that he was as weak as water. He lay back down again, allowing the room to settle into place.

Very gingerly, he examined his wounds. His side, under the bandage, was still tender; his right hand, though stiff, was no longer painful. His dizziness he blamed on Teleri's potion—opium she had said, hadn't she?

Turning his head, he looked around the room again. Teleri was gone and there was no indication where or why. His contentment ebbed at finding himself thus deserted.

After a while, he tried to lever himself up again, this time with greater success. His head whirled, but he was able to sit up, throw off the scarlet coverlet, and dangle his legs over the side of the bed. Save for the bandages around his middle and his blood-stained linen breeches, he was naked. He searched the room for the rest of his clothing. He could not find his shirt or his tunic but his hose lay spread out on the floor beside his boots, his swordbelt hung on a hook by the door. Picking up his hose and his boots, he wobbled back to the bed.

He was fastening his points when Teleri came in, pale and inconspicuous as always in a grey dress and a faded blue tartan shawl. Remembering some of the things he had said to her during the early morning hours, he was suddenly terrifically embarrassed.

Teleri closed the door behind her, and crossed the room without meeting his eyes. Perhaps she was also thinking that she had revealed more about her feelings than she had ever intended. Though neither of them recognized it, they were both as self-conscious as if they had spent the previous night in bed together.

Teleri reached under the tartan shawl and produced a bundle of familiar clothing: a white linen shirt, a knee-length cyclas of forest-green sendal, and a cincture of flat copper links. "I brought these down from your room in the Seraphim Tower. I'm afraid that your other things were past saving, and I thought it best to burn them."

She allowed herself one sidelong glance in his direction. "How do you feel? You looked so much better this morning, I thought it would be safe to leave you alone. And I thought, also, that it might be useful to learn what others are saying about last night."

"I feel amazingly well, under the circumstances," he said. "Almost as good as new. What did you hear? What does everyone say?"

She took off her shawl, spread it across the foot of the bed. "It's all rather confusing—so many different stories! And I've still not heard your version, you know."

While Teleri was busy laying and lighting a fire, Ceilyn reached for the bundle of clothes. "Of course," he said, "I imagine I was just about incoherent when you found me."

As he dressed, he told her how Morc and Derry mac Forgoll (magically disguised to resemble the Queen's brothers, Cadifor and Llochafor) had attacked the guard outside Sidonwy's door, and how he had arrived to find the man unconscious but still alive. "Derry and Morc were down in the garden by the tomb by then, but I dodged out of sight when I heard footsteps approaching from the opposite direction. It was the Princess Diaspad accompanied by Calchas, so naturally I followed them down to the tomb. They were after the bones, just as we had suspected, planning to place the blame on Cadifor and his brother.

"As soon as I knew what they were about, I'd have been off looking for help as I promised you when we parted, but the bones betrayed me. I don't know why—God knows, *I'm* not the rightful King of Rhianedd—but something in the relics . . . some residue of power, maybe, reacted to my presence. The Princess felt it, and guessed that someone was watching her.

"Morc I eliminated easily—a broken collar bone and he was out of the action—but I scraped my hand on that damned silver brooch. Silver being poison to me, I was sufficiently weakened that Derry got the better of me.

"I lost consciousness for a time. The next thing I remember, Fflergant and his brother were there and I was bleeding like a pig. I convinced them that I was capable of taking care of myself (a mere scratch, I said, and made certain they didn't look too closely) and that nothing would be gained by telling anyone they had seen me there. After that, they went for the guards and I tried to make it up the stairs . . . which is where you found me."

He pulled on his boots, reached for his swordbelt, suddenly realized that the scabbard was empty. "Jesu! I never thought until now. My sword . . . it will be down in the garden still— or in the hands of the guards. How am I to explain that?"

Teleri threw open the chest at the foot of her bed, took out a gleaming length of steel. Ceilyn released a profound sigh of relief. "My sword. You went out this morning to fetch it?"

"I never thought to do that," said Teleri. "But I found it lying on my doorstep this morning."

Ceilyn slipped the sword into its scabbard. "But who—"

"Fflergant or Tryffin?" Teleri suggested.

"Possibly. I did indicate I might come here if I found myself in need of a doctor. But why would either of them choose to deliver the sword in such a mysterious manner?"

"The Princess Diaspad, then, or one of her people?"

"I think the Princess would be inclined to keep the sword, in

order to frighten me, or send it to the King, in order to incrim-
inate me, or else return it along with a warning," said Ceilyn.
"But what would she—or anyone—stand to gain by leaving it on
your doorstep?"

"Unless there was someone . . . allied with the Princess's
household who wanted to do you a good turn without you knowing it?" Teleri suggested, carefully avoiding his eyes.

Ceilyn felt the ready color rising in his face. "Prescelli . . .
Yes, that's possible. Though I'm inclined to think she would
keep the sword for a while, to see what she might gain by it."

He settled the swordbelt around his hips. "Could you help me
with this?" he asked, deceptively casual. "My right hand is still
a little stiff."

For a moment, he thought she would refuse. Even Teleri would
know what such a request meant: To gird a knight's sword on
him was an honor reserved for the Queen, a close kinswoman,
or his own chosen lady. Under the circumstances, it was a del-
icate compliment, implying at the same time some degree of
intimacy between them. And perhaps he was asking too much
of her, perhaps the hopes kindled by her words and actions when
he lay apparently dying were utterly unfounded.

Then she stepped forward to assist him, and he knew from
the faint tinge of pink rising in her cheeks that she understood,
and was not offended.

Indeed, she was well aware of the implications, and uncharacteristically conscious of other things this morning, too: his
warm breath on her hair as she fastened his belt, his hard, tense
body so close to her own. He could sense a change in her, but
said nothing, did nothing, for fear of endangering this new understanding between them.

To cover her confusion, she began to tell him of her own
adventures the night before. Ceilyn sat down on the bed, listening to her account: how she had discovered the real Cadifor and
Llochafor in a drugged sleep, how she had run to fetch Brother
Gildas, the Royal Physician, to help her to revive the men and
their servants and to bear witness on their behalf, should it prove
necessary later.

"How do you suppose she did it?" Ceilyn asked. "Gave their
faces to Morc and Derry, I mean?"

"There is a spell," Teleri said, "for capturing a man's reflection in a mirror. The Princess might have caught Cadifor's and

Llochafor's images at any time, then kept the mirror in a dark place until she needed them.''

Ceilyn had an uncomfortable thought, and spoke before he remembered to whom he was speaking. ''God help me! There was a huge ornate mirror on the wall of her bedchamber. I remember looking into it the night Prescelli and I . . .''

Teleri picked up her cloak, folded it over one arm. ''I shouldn't worry about that, if I were you. I would imagine that the Princess might find your reflection rather elusive.''

''I do *have* one, you know,'' he said indignantly.

''Still,'' said Teleri, placing the neatly folded cloak in her clothes chest and closing the lid, ''you aren't just exactly what you seem to be, either, and that would make bespelling you harder.''

Ceilyn nodded. ''This business of *naming* things, again, I suppose.''

''Yes,'' said Teleri. ''But you know . . . it works both ways.''

Ceilyn sighed. ''Yes, I know. You've said so before. And in the light of recent events, I'm beginning to think you are right. This ignorance of mine may well prove perilous.''

By noon, a dozen wildly implausible tales had circulated through the castle and the town below, growing more fantastic with every repetition. The guard from the wall-walk regained consciousness with no ill effects—or any memory of the men who had attacked him—and the guard at the Queen's door, obviously addled by the blow to his head, told an incoherent tale featuring the Queen's brothers, goblins, witchcraft, and the Dragon of Ildathach—though the latter had been dead for a period of one hundred fifty years. The Queen was sick with apprehension, recalling the months of family discord that had marred the first part of the year, and terrified that a similar ordeal was before her now.

Amazingly, the King remained perfectly calm. He had somehow conceived the idea that the whole complicated plot surrounding the bones was nothing more than an elaborate prank perpetrated by some of his esquires or younger knights. To this comforting theory, he became increasingly attached as the day went on. After all (he reasoned), if the bones had merely been spirited away as a prank, then no one was guilty of any crime more serious than poor judgment and worse taste, and, therefore, neither the stability of the realm nor of the Royal Household was actually threatened.

Then, too, he had remembered his early resolution not to lend credibility to the bones as a symbol of Rhianeddi independence by making too much of them.

Nevertheless, the matter could not be completely glossed over; somebody had to be blamed and punished. Suspicion rested heavily on Fflergant and Tryffin. The two boys spent an uneasy day confined to quarters in the squires' dormitory with a guard posted outside the door. But their uncle, the Marshall, spent several hours closeted with the King; Sidonwy's handmaidens, Fand and Finola came forward to confess their presence in the garden, and Fflergant and his brother were released early the next morning.

Meanwhile, the two young princes entertained some suspicions of their own—and Ceilyn mac Cuel was the object. Though they were relieved to find that Ceilyn had not disappeared, they still felt that he owed them a better explanation of his activities the night of the theft than any he had offered them before. Unfortunately, Ceilyn was far too busy to answer their questions, and three days passed before an opportunity to speak with him privately finally presented itself.

They found him in the practice yard, lightly armored, bashing at the pells with a blunted practice sword. "Saints preserve us!" exclaimed Fflergant, pausing by the gate to watch. "You have to admit that he is fast."

"He is that," agreed Tryffin. "And you have to admire the man. A partially healed wound in his side—and I hold it was something more than the scratch he said it was—yet he's out here practicing as though there wasn't a thing amiss with him."

They watched for a few minutes longer, awaiting a good moment to approach him. When Ceilyn stopped to adjust his shield, they crossed the yard and joined him by the pells.

"Good morning, Cousin," said Fflergant most politely.

Ceilyn returned his greeting coldly. "Has no one assigned you any useful task this morning?"

"Well, no, they haven't," said Fflergant, "but we were—"

"Then don't you think you ought to put on some armor and join me?" Ceilyn suggested.

Fflergant flushed. It was just like Ceilyn to put them at a disadvantage by implying that they ought not to be idling about

"Perhaps later," Fflergant temporized. "But we have a few questions we would like to ask, if you can spare us a little of your time."

"Have you?" Ceilyn said, apparently much absorbed in the strapping of his shield.

"You do owe us an explanation, you know," Fflergant insisted. "We trusted you the other night, despite appearances, and we'd like to know now whether we made a serious mistake."

Evidently satisfied with the strapping on his shield, Ceilyn picked up his sword again. "I thought I explained myself adequately at the time. Correct me if I am wrong. I did swear an oath—did I not?—that I was there in the interests of the Queen and those near to her, that nothing I had done endangered your interests or those of your family."

Fflergant and Tryffin exchanged an exasperated glance. "That was before the disappearance of the bones, you will remember," said Tryffin. Then, putting the question bluntly: "Where are they now? Who has them?"

"That's odd," said Ceilyn, testing the weight of his sword. "I've been wondering whether or not I ought to ask the pair of you that same question." He motioned them aside, took another series of lightning-swift swipes at the wooden post.

"You were with them last," Fflergant pointed out, backing away.

"It seems I was not," said Ceilyn, "since I've not got them and somebody else has. And how do I know that the pair of you didn't come back for them after I left the garden?"

"How do we know," said Fflergant, "that you didn't take them with you when you left?"

Ceilyn was clearly amused. "The size and shape of the casket—if not the weight—would argue against that, I think. And I wasn't just at my best on that particular occasion, as I recall."

"Perhaps you had help," Tryffin suggested.

"I was forgetting," said Ceilyn. "This whole thing is supposed to be a plot between Prescelli and me, isn't it? Quite naturally, she was able to supply the muscle that I lacked."

"You know," said Tryffin, at his blandest and most reasonable, "it would be simple enough to lay our suspicions to rest, simply by telling us what you were doing there and exactly what happened. We've kept your secret thus far—you might trust us with the rest."

"I'm sorry," said Ceilyn, continuing to rain blows on the pell. "But I don't think that would be wise. And not just for my own sake."

"Is that supposed to be a threat?" asked Fflergant.

"Not at all," said Ceilyn, a little breathless by now.

"Because if it is," continued Fflergant, "I'll just remind you that we can go straight to Cynwas and tell him all that we know—and then *he* can ask the questions."

"I think," said Ceilyn, "that you might regret doing that. You've been allowed your freedom, but your position is still doubtful if not precarious. And you would have a difficult time explaining why you waited so long to mention my name—and a more difficult time still proving that I was anywhere near the tomb, if I choose to deny it."

"There is blood on the flagstones and on the steps," said Tryffin, "and a ten- or twelve-inch cut in your right side to show where it all came from."

Ceilyn removed his shield, transferred the sword to his right hand. "Sheep's blood—I think that was what the King decided, was it not? A dramatic embellishment by some prankster with a morbid imagination.

"As for the cut in my side: I wasn't so badly hurt as it might have appeared. These flesh wounds *will* bleed at a terrific rate. And I heal very quickly, Cousin," he added, executing the same dazzling movements as before, this time right-handed. "I think that you would find, if you examined my right side, that it was impossible to determine whether the injury had taken place four days . . . or four weeks ago."

In fact, the rapidly fading white scar resembled a much older injury, and he was by no means eager to display it, but Ceilyn was reasonably certain that they would not call his bluff.

"Still," said Fflergant, "if Cynwas questioned you, you would have to admit that you were there, or swear to a lie."

"I wonder," said Ceilyn, sounding amused, "how you can imagine me capable of stealing or concealing the relics and not just as capable of lying to the King?"

Fflergant frowned. "Are you saying that you did take the bones?"

"Not at all," said Ceilyn. "I'm only trying to point out that either my word is good, or it isn't, and you may find out that much by carrying your story to the King, but perhaps not much else. And either way, you might not be entirely pleased with the results.''

Fflergant's scowl deepened. "There are more ways than our word against yours to settle the question."

Ceilyn lowered his sword, put down his shield. He looked Fflergant over from the top to toe, his gaze lingering longest on the plain brown leather belt and silver spurs, insignia of a squire. "But you're not in any position to avail yourself of those means, just at the moment," Ceilyn pointed out, from his own lofty position as Knight of the Order of the Lion of St. March. "Why don't we discuss this again, when you are?"

"Which will be never, I wager, if *you* have anything to say about it," Fflergant retorted hotly.

Ceilyn merely shook his head. He picked up his shield and headed for the armory, but paused for a moment within the arch of the doorway, looking back at Fflergant. "You are wrong, Cousin, if you imagine that I'm the source of your problems."

"Well," snorted Fflergant, as Ceilyn disappeared inside the tower. "It certainly seems as though he is guilty of something!"

"Either that," said Tryffin, "or he just doesn't care to explain himself to the likes of us."

Fflergant leaned against the wooden post. "I suppose you are right, damn it! It would be like Ceilyn and his stiff-necked northern pride to refuse to answer—whether he had done anything to be ashamed of or not!"

"*Especially* if he had done nothing to be ashamed of," said Tryffin.

Fflergant ground his teeth in frustration. "So what do we do now? Just take him at his word, be good little squires, and attend to our own business?"

"We take him exactly at his word," agreed Tryffin, "and we bring up the matter again later. When, as he said, one or both of us is in the position to challenge him."

The Philosopher seeks Wisdom in old books and ancient tracts. He wanders far in search of Truth, over the mountains and into strange lands; if his courage fails him not, he ventures down even into the dark womb of the earth. Always he asks the questions of everyone he meets: "Who knows the Truth—who will teach it to me?"

But verily I tell you: The Truth may be found in none of these places, and in all of them. And only the Wise Man knows it when he finds what he seeks.

—From The Mirror of the Ancients

2.

A Royal Inquiry

The weather turned cold and wet. Rain spattered on diamond-shaped window panes, leaked in under wooden shutters, and puddled on flagstone floors. Up in the Solar, where the Queen and her pale-faced women sat sewing, the pages drew thick red velvet draperies over all the casements to keep out the cold and the damp.

All morning long, the ladies sat sewing, silent and subdued. At mid-day, the King and his step-sister arrived, to sit by the fire at one end of the room and play a game of Nine-Men's-Morris. The Princess played with ingenuity and great enthusiasm, but the King was listless and dull. The Queen's brothers lounged gracefully in, stationed themselves by the other fire, and began to pick half-heartedly at the nuts and sweetmeats laid out upon a gilded table. Then Fand took out her harp and attempted to play a tune.

It was Finola who precipitated the crisis, by accidentally running a needle into her finger and uttering a bloodcurdling shriek. That caused another lady to drop the handful of pearls she had been sewing onto a sleeve, and send them bouncing and rolling across the floor. Little Gwenlliant, painfully sensitive to the uncomfortable emotions around her, burst suddenly into tears.

Fand stopped trying to play. Finola sat as if turned to stone, watching the bright blood drip onto the white linen in her lap, and Gwenlliant covered her face with her hands and sobbed uncontrollably. The King looked up from his game and met Sidonwy's anguished gaze.

"This cannot continue," he said grimly. He signaled to Fergos fab Neol, who was stationed by the door. "It is time we settled this matter, once and for all. Bring me the men who built the tomb."

The stonemasons and the bricklayers were still encamped down in the courtyard, unable to leave Caer Cadwy until the King dismissed them. And that Cynwas was determined not to do until someone explained to him why a seemingly impregnable tomb had been so easily entered and despoiled.

"All—all of them, Lord?" stammered Fergos, for the encampment was a large one.

"The men that I spoke with before: the journeyman stonemasons and the bricklayers."

The King turned to Ceilyn, who stood in his usual place by the Queen's side. "I'll want Gildas the physician, and the little sorceress as well. No, don't go yourself," he said, as Ceilyn moved toward the door. "The Queen wants you here. Send Goan or one of the other lads instead."

As Fergos picked his way across the muddy courtyard, he met Fflergant and Tryffin, looking bulkier than ever under several layers of wool and sheepskin. Briefly, he told them what was afoot, then continued on his way through the slanting rain.

"Well?" said Fflergant to his brother.

"I reckon you're right," replied Tryffin. So they went up to the Solar, shed their outer layers, and found a place by one of the fires.

The stonemasons and the bricklayers arrived soon after. They bowed awkwardly to the King, ill at ease in such elegant surroundings and painfully conscious of the muddy water they were dripping on Queen Sidonwy's polished oak floor.

The men repeated the story they had related twice before: how a fortnight or so before Michaelmas a man in a green cloak and the golden spurs of a knight had called on the Master Mason, how the man and the mason had talked for an hour or more, called for wine, then continued to talk until midnight. In the light of subsequent events, there could be little doubt that this unlikely visitor had bribed the Master Mason to lay the bricks on the eastern face of the tomb without the use of mortar. Unfortunately, no one could describe the stranger exactly, because of the hood which shadowed his face.

He was a man of slender build, that they could agree on, about medium height, and he spoke with a "foreign" accent.

"And then," the journeyman was saying, "the northern gentleman—"

"When I asked you before," the King interrupted him, "none of you could agree on the accent."

The journeyman ducked his head and looked embarrassed. "We talked about it since then, Lord, and we're all agreed. And Ffodor here ought to know. He spent two years in the north when he was a lad."

Cynwas addressed the burly mason previously identified as Ffodor fab Fearn. "And it was you, if memory serves me, who poured wine for your master and his mysterious visitor?"

"Begging your pardon, Lord," said Ffodor, shuffling his feet. "It was I that brought the wine, but the gentleman insisted on serving himself." He cleared his throat nervously. "I remember because he stained the cloth, pouring left-handed, you see, although he—"

A soft cry escaped Sidonwy's lips. She reached for Ceilyn's hand and clasped it tightly. Cadifor nearly choked on a piece of walnut, much to the consternation of the squire who had shelled if for him. Fflergant and his brother exchanged a significant glance. And seated on the floor at the Princess Diaspad's feet, Derry mac Forgoll snickered nastily and was silenced by a vicious slippered toe in the ribs.

The King, too, was disconcerted. "I do not remember that you mentioned this before. The knight who called on your master poured wine with his left hand, you say? We must be very sure on that point, you understand, because it is rare—indeed practically unknown—for a left-handed fighter to attain the rank of knight."

Ffodor nodded knowingly. "Ill-luck they call it, though the common-folk have it that a left-handed fighter brings bad fortune only to his opponents. But what I was *going* to say: I fancied the time that the gentleman had injured his right hand somehow, and that would explain his awkwardness."

The Queen relaxed and summoned up a weak smile, and Tryffin and Fflergant decided to hold their tongues a little longer. In five years serving meat and drink to the King and Queen, no one could remember a time when Ceilyn mac Cuel had ever spilled anything.

Nevertheless, the King thought it necessary to ask the question. "Ceilyn?"

"Yes, Lord?"

"Ceilyn," said the King, "I should like to hear you say that you had nothing to do with this."

The young knight did not reply immediately. "I didn't do it," he said finally. "I will swear on or by anything you name, that I was not the man they speak of."

Cynwas addressed the masons again. "Do any of you recognize this young man?"

Two of the men denied it immediately. "It may have been him," said the journeyman, "but I couldn't say for certain."

"Begging your pardon, Lord," said Ffodor, who had been listening carefully while Ceilyn spoke. "But this young lord comes from Rhianedd, I think?"

Ceilyn's fixed stare become indignant. "From Gorwynnion," said the King.

The mason shrugged, as though the distinction were of no importance. "Well, Lord, I don't know much about the *far north*, and never could see any difference between the Rhianeddi and the Gorwynnach, saving the young lord's presence. But I did spend two years working for a cousin in Dun Fiorenn when I was a lad, and I've considerable family up in Draighen. I'm willing to swear that the man who called on the Master Mason was Draighenach, born and bred."

Now it was Derry mac Forgoll's turn to squirm uneasily, and the Princess Diaspad was moved to ask a question of her own. "Draighenach, you say? You are quite certain of that?"

"Yes, Lady."

"And yet," she continued in her soft, melodious voice—so much at odds with her hard, predatory face—"you spent but two years in Draighen and that not recently. And by your own admission know nothing of Gorwynnach or Rhianeddi."

Ffodor cleared his throat again. "I know how the Draighenach speak—yes, and I know a Draighenach oath when I hear it, too!''

Diaspad sniffed. ''As for the 'injured' hand—sheer conjecture! If the man hurt himself, surely he would not wish to call attention to the fact. No, he would take great pains to hide his disability, lest it be used to identify him later.''

''Well, Lady, I've been thinking,'' said Ffodor. ''Perhaps he hadn't hurt himself, perhaps he just wanted it to appear he was left-handed—out of spite toward that young lord there, maybe— only he was too clumsy to carry the thing off.''

''Or perhaps, being left-handed, and thinking he had already given himself away, he tried to cover his tracks by a deliberate act of clumsiness,'' suggested Diaspad sweetly.

The King looked to Ceilyn. ''Is there anyone here at court who bears you a particular grudge? Someone who would like to see you in an awkward position?''

(''Is there someone here who wouldn't?'' Fflergant asked under his breath—purely rhetorically.)

Ceilyn's bright hazel eyes rested for a moment on the Princess Diaspad, but all he said was: ''I'm not very popular here, Lord. I think you know that.''

The King sat silently, considering all this. Some of the others began to stir restlessly; the Princess stifled a yawn. ''Really,'' she said, ''this line of inquiry seems to be yielding little or value. All we have been able to determine is that the mason's visitor was a youngish man of average size, attired in a green cloak and golden spurs, who spoke with an indeterminate northern accent, and that he may—or may not—have been left-handed In fact, he might have been any one of a half-dozen younger knights, or even one of the squires or serving men borrowing his master's cloak and spurs. He might have been . . . practically anyone.''

(''But not, thanks be to God, either one of us!'' Tryffin murmured in his soft southern lilt.)

''But really, the identity of the young man is not important,'' she continued. ''I know, dear Brother, that you persist in regarding the whole matter as a childish prank, but you are overlooking one thing: Someone bought off the Master Mason—and that took gold. A great deal of gold, for a skilled craftsman to disappear, abandon his craft, and begin a new life elsewhere.

''The mysterious visitor was not acting on his own, but as the agent of another man: a man of wealth and position, a man with more than a passing interest in the bones of the ancient kings of Rhianedd.''

The King sighed. "Perhaps you are right. I would like to think otherwise, but . . .'' He singled out the journeyman again. "Did you not think it odd when the Master insisted on laying the bricks on the eastern wall entirely by himself? Is it customary for a master-craftsman to perform such menial tasks?''

"No, Lord, not customary,'' said the journeyman. "But our master had his little freaks and foibles, as you might say, and we none of us felt it was our place to gainsay him.''

"And no one made any connection between the man who called on your master, and his sudden and unexpected desire to lay bricks?''

"Well, Lord, in a manner of speaking. We understood there was to be another commission. A grand tomb in the north. Very full of it he was, and could speak of nothing else. He spent a fair bit of time down in Treledig celebrating, and came back tipsy the day we worked on that section of the east wall, pushed the rest of us aside, and insisted on laying the bricks himself.''

The King brooded on that for a time. Then he dismissed the masons. "You may break camp when the weather clears, for it is plain that you have nothing useful to tell me.''

He beckoned to Fergos. "Is Brother Gildas here?''

The tall solemn physician told his tale: how he had retired early on Michaelmas, only to be roused shortly after midnight by Teleri ni Pendaren, who begged him to accompany her to the bedchamber of Cadifor fab Duach. There, he discovered the Queen's two brothers in a drugged sleep. He was familiar with the soporific; if Cadifor and Llochafor had imbibed a large dose, as he supposed, it was impossible that either of them had been anywhere or done anything anytime that night.

"But might they not have walked abroad before the drug was taken?'' murmured the Princess. "No one seems to know exactly when they downed the wine.''

The monk permitted himself a small, tight smile, amused by her evident ignorance. "The drug, though potent, is slow to act. Drowsiness comes on gradually, followed by sleep and deeper sleep. When I first examined them, their pulse was slow, their breathing scarcely detectable—the potion had been in their blood for hours. They slept until mid-morning,'' he continued, "for it was impossible to rouse them sooner. But the men and the boys, having swallowed a smaller dose, woke several hours earlier.''

The King dismissed the physician and summoned Cadifor's squire. The boy, a fresh-faced lad of about thirteen, stopped cracking nuts for his master and knelt before the King. He patiently told the same story he had related many times before.

"Yes, Lord, as I told you, it is customary for my lord and his brother to drink a flagon of wine every night before they retire. The butler always sends the wine at the same hour, but not always by the same servant. I don't know the man who delivered the wine at Michaelmas, and I haven't seen the fellow since.''

The butler, when questioned, declared that he had received word—apparently through the same man—that the wine was not to be delivered, because Lord Cadifor had already imbibed heavily at supper.

"I believe," said the King, turning his attention to the squire again, "that you and the other boy—and the manservants as well—each drank a small quantity of the wine?"

"Yes, Lord, we always did that," said the boy. "I was his taster, you see, and the other fellows always took a sip or two as well—to encourage me, they'd say. By way of a jest," he concluded morosely.

"And you found nothing wrong with the wine?"

The boy looked uncomfortable. "I've not been properly trained as my lord's sewer—the position came to me unexpectedly. The wine tasted fine to me. I poured a cup for Lord Cadifor and another for Lord Llochafor and I left the flagon—about half full it was—for them to serve themselves later.''

"And you felt no odd effects from the wine?"

"I know we were all uncommonly sleepy, Lord," said the lad, "but the hour was growing late. And no one was thinking of a *sleeping* potion, not even Lord Cadifor. I was employed to look out for poison.''

Cynwas nodded. It was customary for men and women of rank to employ sewers, or tasters, for fear of assassination, but Cadifor fab Duach's dread of poisoning was proverbial. Rumor declared that he ate a small quantity of arsenic daily in order to acquire an immunity, and it was well-known that any twinge of indigestion sent him into a panic. His last sewer had been sent home merely for bringing up wash water that had not been properly treated with alicorn, or unicorn's horn, and it was likely that this boy would have been dismissed as well, were he not nearly related to Cadifor's lady, and previously a great favorite.

The King lapsed into a brooding silence, and the room was still except for the steady sound of the rain beating on the windows.

Cynwas sighed. "Where is Teleri ni Pendaren? Is the child here?"

Ceilyn left his post by the Queen's side long enough to lead Teleri into the room. "You have nothing to fear," he whispered in her ear. "No one is accusing you of anything."

Teleri made her curtsy to the King, and another to the Queen. Then she stood quietly, waiting to be questioned. Sidonwy smiled on her kindly.

"Only tell us, my dear, how it was that you came to feel concerned for my brothers that night. Had you some presentiment of danger? Did you foresee some peril?"

"Yes," said Teleri, very low. "That was how it happened." That was not the whole truth, but neither was it a lie.

All this while, Cadifor and Llochafor had held their peace, but now Cadifor was moved to speak. "But no one has yet explained *how* it was that this young woman and Brother Gildas gained entrance to my bedchamber. The boy always locks the door in the anteroom and brings me the key before he retires."

Teleri hesitated; she appeared about to dissolve or evaporate rather than face so many pairs of curious eyes. Then she began to solidify around the edges.

"I don't need a key," she said, just above a whisper. "Glastyn taught me to open locks without one."

Those few quiet words elicited general and horrified astonishment—shrieks from some of the girls and indignant protests from the Queen's brothers. By nightfall, branches of rowan and other charms would appear over doors throughout the castle, intended to keep Teleri out.

In the meantime, the King silenced the outcry with an uplifted hand. "A somewhat disquieting skill, to be sure, but one to be expected of a pupil of Glastyn's." He waved Teleri away and called for a goblet of wine. It seemed that he was growing bored.

"But what," said the Queen, looking sadly worn and weary, "can all this possibly mean?"

"Mean?" said Cadifor, surging to his feet. "What can it

mean except that the whole scheme was not a practical joke at all, but a plot intended to discredit Llochafor and myself?''

"If that is so," said the King, "it still remains impossible to fix the blame."

"Impossible?" exclaimed Llochafor. "But you need not look far to find one capable of such infamous schemes, one who makes no secret of her hostility to Cadifor and me, one who, by slander and ridicule, has ever sought to work our ruin." He waved a slender beringed hand in Diaspad's direction. "There she sits beside you, Cousin, and that boy from *Draighen* sits at her feet!"

Diaspad only laughed and settled herself more comfortably in her silver chair. "I cannot believe that I am the only one under this roof who can be counted among your un-friends. Indeed, a man so fearful of poisoning must have many enemies.

"So if—as I continue to doubt—*if* there is a plot against you, I would advise you to look elsewhere for the culprit. For someone less open, less honest in his or her dislike."

Cadifor bridled. "You say you doubt there is a plot against us—but what other explanation can you possibly offer?"

Diaspad smiled. "Who, in all of Celydonn, had any reason to steal the wretched bones? Why, no one but yourself. To further your ambitions, style yourself King in Rhianedd, the bones would be of inestimable symbolic value. But to anyone else—even my brother—of sentimental value, no more.

"Oh, I don't say that you actually soiled your hands or stooped to the deed yourself," she continued. "We have all seen that you could not possibly have done so, the mad ravings of that poor guardsman notwithstanding. But you might have ordered it done, then drugged your own wine in order to divert suspicion.

"Moreover, it seems to me that the Celcynnon boy still remains suspect in the matter of the bribe."

"But Ceilyn mac Cuel," said Llochafor haughtily, "is no man of ours to do our bidding."

"There is the matter of a blood tie, as well as that allegiance he owes your sister," said Diaspad, smiling now on the Queen. "He might have been induced to act on your behalf, out of loyalty to her."

A horrified silence settled over the room. But this time, in her malice, Diaspad had finally gone too far. Cynwas had patched up his own quarrel with Sidonwy, and still feeling guilty because he had doubted her in the first place, he was not about to let anyone question her integrity now. "Am I to understand," he said frigidly, "that you are accusing the *Queen* of some part in this plot of yours?"

Diaspad recognized her mistake too late. "Not at all," she said quickly. "I merely meant to say—"

"Madam—" began Cadifor.

But the King, disappointed by his failure to clear the air and outraged by Diaspad's insinuations, interrupted them both. "Nothing can be gained by the sort of wantonly irresponsible accusations we have heard here today. Nor will I permit the Queen to be tormented by doubts and insinuations any longer."

He stood up, and the rest were obliged to stand, too. "The relics are gone. Lost, stolen—it matters little, for this is not the first time they have disappeared. I will remind you that I and my father kept this realm together—and largely in peace—for fifty years *without* the bones of the ancient kings of Rhianedd. And so I shall continue to do.

"And until someone comes forward to confess his or her part in the disappearance, or can offer me convincing proof of the guilt of any other person, I do not want to hear anyone mention the relics again. The subject is forbidden—on pain of banishment!"

And with that startling declaration, he crossed the room, offered an arm to his Queen, and nodded a curt dismissal to everyone else.

"Old man," cried Diaspad, the daughter of the Queen, "all the days of my life you have labored to do me hurt. I do not know why this should be, for I have never done you any harm. Your grudge against my mother is an old one, and perhaps it is just—but to what end should the sins of the mother be visited upon her child?"

"Not the sins of the mother," replied the wizard, "but the passionate willfullness of the daughter!"

—From The Life of Anwas
(attributed to Glastyn)

3.

A Fine Tissue of Cobwebs

"You made a fine mess of things, didn't you?" the Princess taunted Derry, later that afternoon. "Thought you were so clever and ended up outsmarting yourself!"

"I don't see how it was my fault," muttered Derry. "You might have enhanced the resemblance with a little magic, you know. Close enough to pass for Ceilyn in a dim light, you *said*, and didn't want to take the trouble, but look what came of it. And how was I to know I would end up talking to the one peasant in all of Camboglanna who knew anything about Draighen or the Draighenach? And that's another thing . . . That fellow didn't think or talk like any common laboring man that I ever heard of."

The Princess and Derry, along with Calchas and Pergrin the giant, were exploring the unused parts of the castle. They were two floors above the kitchens, in the round tower adjoining the Hall, climbing a precariously steep circular staircase to the top floor. Calchas and the giant brought up the rear, the latter car rying a lighted torch. When the stairs creaked ominously under Pergrin's weight, Calchas skipped a step or two ahead of him.

"Anyway," Derry went on, pouting, "I don't see what difference it makes, considering what a disaster the whole thing was. And that was no fault of mine. In fact, it was I who took care of *our* mysterious intruder."

"So you say," said the Princess, "but I have my doubts. How can you be so certain that you killed him?"

"I felt the impact when my sword sliced into him. A deep wound like that, just below the ribs, is always fatal—you should know that."

He skipped nimbly over a tread which had rotted almost entirely away, and offered Diaspad a hand. She stepped across the gap and they both continued on, more cautiously than before.

"But there was no body, Derry," the Princess said testily. "Dead men are not in the habit of picking themselves up and walking away—at least, not immediately."

"Well, I don't say that he was dead when I left him," said Derry. "But he couldn't have lasted many minutes or hours longer. And as for getting up and walking away—impossible! Whoever it was took the casket and the bones must have cleared the body away as well. It must have been Fflergant and Tryffin— though why they bothered with our friend the corpse, I really couldn't say."

"Quite a lot for the two of them to do in such a short time, don't you think?" said the Princess. "To hide the bones and the body—which they could scarcely have anticipated—was hardly the work of a moment. And then to declare their presence at the tomb by running off to tell the guards all that they had seen and heard, when they might just as well have slipped off to bed and pretended not to know a thing. Better for us if they hadn't been so conscientious. Then Cynwas would never have conceived his fantastic notions about boyish high jinks. But I must admit, they've scarcely behaved like young men with something to hide . . . at least, not since the matter of the young ladies was explained."

At the top of the stairs, they faced a long, drafty corridor, lined with doors on both sides. Diaspad took the torch, approached the first door, and flung it open. Finding the room too small for her needs, she pulled the door closed and tried another. This was locked, but the giant forced it open.

"I don't see," said Calchas, trailing after his mother as she proceeded down the dusty corridor, "why you don't just hang up some rowan over your door, like everyone else is doing. Why go to all the trouble to hide your things up here?"

"Rowan," said Diaspad, "has it uses, but would hardly prove effective in this instance. There is no reason to suppose that the girl isn't as human as you or . . . as human as anyone in the castle. And it is not only the little apprentice who worries me. The year is dying and our enemy grows stronger. You remember what the Old Ones said: *between Beltane and Samhain.* That time is almost past, and before long he may be back to trouble us. Though by then," she added, "I hope to have accomplished all my ends. Still, it pays to take precautions, and in Glastyn's case, a branch of rowan would simply serve as an invitation."

"But won't your comings and goings here be noticed?" asked Calchas.

"Not at once, I think. I want a quiet, out-of-the-way place to perform the rituals, and one of these rooms will serve me for the time being."

She opened another door, pushed aside the fine tissue of cobwebs that obscured the interior. Finding the chamber on the other side more to her liking than any of the others, she shook off the last clinging threads and the brittle little husks of insects that adhered to them, and stepped inside to examine the room more carefully.

A pile of moldy straw and disintegrating cloth was heaped in one corner of the room—the remains of a mattress, perhaps. Diaspad prodded the mass experimentally with one toe.

"This will do very well," she pronounced, glancing around the room. "I will tell Bron to change the lock on the door. An unfamiliar lock for the little apprentice to try her skill on—we'll see how well she succeeds."

"Is Bron a locksmith?" Derry asked idly. "I didn't know that."

"Bron has many talents," said the Princess. "Many unexpected talents. He was apprenticed to a blacksmith when I found him. Dwarfs like Bron often find work at the forge—some folk believe they have a special affinity for metalwork. The muscular forearms prove useful, and no one cares, there, if a man is as ugly as mortal sin."

She began to wander around the room, inspecting it minutely.

"But who, I wonder, has the bones now?" she mused. "That is what I would particularly like to know. Who knew or guessed what I was planning and made plans of their own to step in and spirit away the bones?"

"The Old Ones?" Calchas suggested.

"Why?" asked Diaspad. "Why would the Old Ones deliver the bones into my keeping, only to take them away again?"

Calchas shook his head. "I can't begin to guess. But then . . . I never understood why they were willing to give them to you so cheaply at the start."

Diaspad shrugged. "They have little love for Cadifor. They wouldn't like to see him rule, here or in Rhianedd. You know how they live in the north, in constant fear of discovery and persecution, in Rhianedd quite as much as in Gorwynnion or Cuan. They aren't ignored there as they are here, or allowed to practice their rites under the guise of May Festivals and Harvest Celebrations, as they do in—

"By all the gods!" she breathed. "I *have* been a fool! I thought that I was using them, when all along they were using me to further their own ends." She turned to Calchas, extended him her hand. "Of course the Old Ones would prefer you on the throne over Cadifor or his brother—given that choice and that choice only. But why should they not attempt to create a king of their own . . . as Glastyn did so many years ago?"

She took Calchas's clammy hand affectionately in hers. "It seems, my precious boy, that you were right from the very beginning. And I—yes, I admit it—I was wrong."

"How?" asked Calchas, finding her reasoning hard to follow. "How was I right?"

"Who is it," asked his mother, "that the Old Ones and the Hillfolk honor above all men? Who is notoriously tolerant of the Old Religion in his own land? And who is it stands as close to the throne as Cadifor according to the ancient law—the old pagan law—of Mother-Right?"

"Maelgwyn of Gwyngelli!" exclaimed Calchas. "You think that the Old Ones are scheming, not only to put an end to Cadifor's hopes of a northern crown, but also to put Maelgwyn fab Menai on the throne of Celydonn when Cynwas dies?"

"Yes, I do," said Diaspad, grinding her teeth. "Maelgwyn ab Menai, or else—as he is a few years older than Cynwas—

one of his sons.'' She kicked savagely at the pile of debris on the floor. ''One of his big, beautiful, golden-haired sons!''

''That would certainly explain why they were down at the tomb that night,'' volunteered Derry. ''Yes, and Fflergant and Tryffin were right there, too, when the bones were first 'discovered' in the wall!''

''And they were serving at the banquet the night we all discussed plans for the tomb.'' Diaspad was restlessly pacing the floor, the train of her black velvet gown twitching in the dust behind her. ''Yes, they've been everywhere all through this, and I never noticed or wondered what it might mean until just now.''

''But you were convinced that they weren't interested in succeeding Cynwas,'' said Calchas. ''You were certain that Maelgwyn's own lands and titles were sufficient to satisfy him, and his sons, too.''

''Yes, yes, it seems that I was wrong about that as well. I should have thought before: Maelgwyn has two promising boys and only one crown to bestow between them!''

Derry wandered over to the window, unlatched the shutters, and pushed them open. The rain had slowed to a drizzle. He dusted off the window ledge and seated himself.

''But why should they need the bones to further their plans?'' Calchas asked.

''Because of Maelgwyn's lady, Gwdolwen—or rather, because of her father, Dyffryn fab Drwst,'' Diaspad explained, with exaggerated patience. ''The very same Lord Dyffryn who enjoys such popularity throughout the north, the very same Lord Dyffryn who holds such a prominent place in the King's affections. Had our plan succeeded, had Cadifor and his brother been convicted of treason, their lands and properties confiscated, the heirs of their body barred from the succession here and in the north—who would be Lord in Rhianedd then?''

Calchas nodded vigorously. ''Of course—Cadifor's Uncle Dyffryn! And Dyffryn could make the same use of the bones that Cadifor could—better, because he already enjoys considerable support in the north. That's supposing it came to that. . . . Cynwas might just as well create Dyffryn King of Rhianedd out of hand, because he loves and trusts the old man as he never trusted Cadifor.''

''Indeed,'' said Diaspad. ''But with or without Cynwas's consent, so long as he possessed the bones—proof positive, as the Rhianeddi might see it, of his right to rule—"

"And Lord Dyffryn has no sons to succeed him," interjected Calchas. "Now, isn't that convenient? Because he does have grandsons, and can choose among them according to the law of Mother-Right. Fflergant's the eldest, of course, but Tryffin may be the favorite—so there you have it: one crown for each!"

"And with two such extensive *degfeds*, two crowned and anointed kings in the family," said the Princess, "no one could hope to withstand Maelgwyn if he chose to take on the other eight portions. As the kings of Camboglanna styled themselves emperors of Celydonn in the old days, so one day Maelgwyn or his heirs might lay claim to all of Ynys Celydonn!"

"They might," offered Derry, from his place in the window. "But not if you have anything to say about it, I fancy."

"Truly," said Diaspad. "Not if I have anything to say about it!"

"And so," said Glastyn, "you have chosen names for the child, and the christening will be tomorrow?"

"She is a sweet babe and favors her father's people—though of course her hair may darken," said Gwenalarch. "And because she is healthy and strong, we saw no reason either to hasten or delay her christening."

Just then, Gwenalarch's small son came into the room. He was six years of age, light-skinned and pale-haired, remarkably fair even for a Rhianeddi. Glastyn smiled on young Garanwyn, and into his mind came an image of the boy's new-born sister as she would someday be. "The babe will remain as fair as her brother. She will grow to be very beautiful, and her hair shall be like the waters of the Arfondwy during the time of the White Flood."

Now, Gwenalarch had great respect for the wizard, and taking his words for a fair omen, she said, "She shall be named Gwenlliant, for the White Flood, and Ellwy, for the daughter of Goewin—as I had originally intended—and also Branwen, which is the white raven."

4.

The Parliament of Rooks

Tryffin fab Maelgwyn was far from satisfied. He inserted the "goatsfoot" into his crossbow, cocked it, and dropped in a bolt. Raising the bow to his shoulder, he took careful aim. An instant later, the popinjay burst apart in an explosion of brilliant feathers.

Wordlessly, Tryffin went through the entire process again. This time, he aimed at one of the painted targets lined up at the far end of the archery range. He squeezed the trigger mechanism and sent another bolt flying. It landed, with a decisive thud, in the heart of a ramping crimson tyger.

"Something is bothering you," said Fflergant. "Something is on your mind. I can always tell."

"I've been thinking," said Tryffin, inserting another bolt. "We leave in two days' time for Eisiwed's wedding, and we'll be gone for nearly a month. Who knows what might happen or come to light during that time? If we only knew what really happened at Michaelmas, I might feel easier in my mind."

Another bolt landed in the target, this time in the tyger's fierce golden eye. Tryffin put down his bow and walked toward the targets, Fflergant following in his wake. "But you are the one who always says—"

"I *know* what I always say," Tryffin interrupted him. "Wait and watch—but has it never occurred to you that I might occasionally be wrong? And I think there might be someone—someone besides Ceilyn—who isn't telling everything she knows about the bones. The only problem is, I don't know if we can convince Garanwyn to allow it."

They had arrived at the earthen butts backing the targets, and Tryffin began prying his bolts out of the tyger.

"You want to ask Gwenlliant?" Fflergant bent to retrieve the popinjay's gaudy crested head and the ball of variegated feathers that served as the body. "Yes, I see. She might know something at that." He glanced at his brother's set face and asked shrewdly, "Just what, precisely, did Garanwyn say when you asked him?"

Tryffin slipped a handful of bolts back into his quiver. "I haven't asked—because I already know, precisely, what Garanwyn will say. And I don't like to go behind his back to question his sister on the sly."

Fflergant deftly reattached the popinjay's head and wings. "Well," he said, setting the bird back atop its perch, "as she's the only one we can ask, we'll just have to convince him to permit it."

But Garanwyn, when they found him in the pantry arranging dates and goblets on a silver platter, was not easily persuaded. "I just don't want to encourage her. She has to forget all that nonsense, if she is going to lead any decent sort of life. And she can't do that if you keep taking notice of her . . . eccentricities."

"We promise we won't be making a habit of it," Tryffin said

soothingly. "But just think about this," he added, lowering his voice confidentially. "We aren't the only ones who saw and heard how Gwenlliant behaved when the relics first came to light, and maybe we aren't the only ones who are wondering what she knows, now the bones have disappeared. So maybe we, who love her, ought to find out how much she does know, before other people start asking questions."

"But the King said the matter was not to be discussed," Garanwyn pointed out virtuously.

"That he did—last week," said Fflergant. "But we'll not be here a week or a fortnight hence, when he changes his mind again. And even if he stands firm for once in his life, he can't stop folk from talking privately."

Garanwyn was forced to agree. "Very well," he said, putting down the tray. "But I'm coming with you. And mind what you say to her!"

They found Gwenlliant in the Hall, playing a game of Prisoner's Base with the other young ladies. They took her aside for a private word. "Tryffin and Fflergant have some questions," said Garanwyn. "They would be vastly obliged if you would answer them the best you can, but I want you to know: You needn't say anything if you would rather not."

Gwenlliant looked up at her big cousins expectantly. "Gwenlliant," said Fflergant, choosing his words with care, "when the men found the box in the wall . . . you felt something, didn't you? Just by looking at the bones, you knew what the rest of us could only guess at." The child nodded her head. "Now that the relics are gone," Fflergant continued, "do you have any idea at all what might have become of them?"

Gwenlliant looked around her in all directions, to see if any one was near enough to overhear. "I think," she said, with a great air of mystery, "that they just went back where they came from."

"Back where—you mean someone put them back in the outer curtain wall?" Garanwyn asked incredulously. "That doesn't make sense!"

Gwenlliant giggled. "Not back in the wall. That would be silly! I mean," she lowered her voice again, "that they just went back again where they belong."

"To Rhianedd, you mean?" asked Fflergant.

"I don't know," Gwenlliant answered vaguely. "Maybe."

Garanwyn raised a skeptical eyebrow. "You see?" he said to Tryffin. "It's all utter nonsense. She knows nothing."

"Oh yes," said Tryffin, "I reckon she knows a good deal. But we're a bit slow to understand her, lacking her gift." He went down on one knee, in order to talk to her more confidentially. "You feel quite comfortable about the bones, don't you? So you don't believe they were stolen at all. You think they just went back—or somebody took them—to a place . . . a place they were kept at sometime in the past. That is what you are trying to tell us, isn't it?"

Gwenlliant nodded delightedly. "Yes, that's right."

"But *who* took them back?" Tryffin asked her. "Can you tell us that as well, dear heart?"

"Does it really matter?" Gwenlliant asked ingenuously. "After all, the bones *belong* to them. And perhaps it isn't nice to say so, but it was horrid of Cynwas to bury the kings here, so far away from home."

"That it was, now that I come to think of it," Tryffin agreed. Like all Gwyngellach, he held a deep reverence for his own native soil, and could imagine no fate more pitiful than to die and be buried far from home. "That it was. But I don't suppose Cynwas ever thought of it that way."

"But who do the relics belong to," Garanwyn asked, unable to keep up with them, "if not to the King or to Cadifor fab Duach?"

Tryffin shook his head, and Fflergant, without thinking, blurted out, "Not Ceilyn mac Cuel, in any case."

"Ceilyn mac Cuel?" Garanwyn asked indignantly. "But *surely* you don't believe the Princess's insinuations about the man in the green cloak."

Tryffin shook his head. "Naturally not. But we do have our own reasons to wonder . . . Suffice to say, we have our reasons. Gwenlliant—"

"No!" Garanwyn broke in. "You're not to ask her. I don't now what quarrel it is the two of you seem to have going with Ceilyn, but I'll not have you drag Gwenlliant into the middle of ."

Fflergant groaned. "For the love of God! He was only going ask—"

"Because if she did know anything . . . if she sensed anything amiss about Ceilyn, she ought not to tell it to *you*," Garanwyn went on. "It would be disloyal."

"Why would it be disloyal?"

"Because," said Garanwyn, bringing forth the one argument he knew must carry weight with his kinsmen from Gwyngelli, "Ceilyn is our first-cousin, Gwenlliant's and mine."

Tryffin and Fflergant had the grace to look ashamed of themselves. "We were forgetting," Tryffin said humbly. "I do beg your pardon, Gwenlliant."

But though he was forced to set his questions aside for the time being, he was not about to abandon them altogether.

It was a fine day for travel, so clear and cool and bright that Ceilyn found himself regretting his decision to stay at Caer Cadwy, found himself wishing that he might be one of the party leaving that morning for Castell Maelduin in Tir Gwyngelli. Indeed, as he crossed the courtyard and passed through the Gamelyon Gate, on his way to the stables to bid his kinsmen a safe journey, he entertained a half-hearted idea that he might still be able to change his plans.

A swift startled movement atop the crumbling tower where the rooks built their nest drew his attention upward, diverting him from his original purpose. Someone was moving around up there, someone pale and light, clad all in grey to match the stones of the parapet.

He found the door at the base of the tower unlocked. Inside, he mounted an ancient creaking ladder, climbed through a musty, fluttering dimness, and emerged at last into full sunlight upon the castellated roof.

Teleri had perched in a crenellation, seated with her back to the grey stone, absolutely motionless, staring down at the courtyard with the abstracted gaze Ceilyn knew so well. He joined her by the wall, leaned against the sun-warmed parapet. "What are you looking at?"

"Your kinsmen—over by the stables. They leave today for their sister's wedding, don't they? And Garanwyn goes with them."

She looked at him then, and the strange mood—the mood that always made a stranger of him—slipped away like water sliding over stones. "Weren't you invited?"

"I was invited," said Ceilyn. "Maelgwyn and his lady were most gracious in their invitation. And my grandfather, Meredydd fab Maelwas, wrote as well. I would have liked to go to the wedding, if only to meet Meredydd and all my mother's kin.

"My father and grandfather quarreled, you know," Ceilyn added wistfully, watching Garanwyn down below leading his horse out of the stable. "Long before I was born . . . But he sent me this sword as a gift the Christmas I was knighted. You know the custom in Gwyngelli? The swordsmith started to work the very same day that word of my birth arrived. My grandfather kept the sword all those years, and never said a word to anybody. Well, someone must have known; I was told that a sword would be provided, but I always imagined it would come from the Queen. I wrote, of course, to thank him for such a princely gift, but I wish I could meet him and thank him again."

"And yet you decided not to go," said Teleri.

Ceilyn shook his head. "I daren't go. At first, when I decided to send my regrets, I told myself it was because of the Princess. I would hate to be two hundred miles away, with Diaspad spinning her plots and you or Sidonwy perhaps needing my help. But the truth is . . . I just don't feel safe anywhere but here. I feel as if . . . if I left Caer Cadwy for any length of time, I couldn't answer for the consequences."

Teleri frowned. "The iron bracelet . . . ?"

"I wear it still. And the truth is, I've no real reason to fear any recurrence of my old problem. Yet I do fear it, and feel more apprehensive with every passing day."

Teleri sighed. "Sometimes," she said, "it's difficult, even for me, to tell the difference between a true presentiment and my own unfounded fears."

"You feel it, too?" Ceilyn asked, alerted by something in her voice.

"Nothing that need worry you," she said, still in that same tone that told Ceilyn that *something* was struggling to take shape in her mind. Two black birds landed on the merlon above her head, but she took no notice of them. "I was thinking of something Glastyn once said about Maelgwyn of Gwyngelli. He said that Maelgwyn was the most dangerous man in Celydonn."

Now it was Ceilyn's turn to frown. The man was, after all, his mother's first-cousin. "Oh, I don't mean that Glastyn thought him a wicked man, or ambitious," Teleri added hastily. "Only that Maelgwyn is so clever and subtle, and possesses such resources . . . if he ever chose to do a thing, it would be difficult for anyone to stop him.''

A single white bird, a pigeon or a dove, landed on the parapet among the black rooks, and the rooks started up with indignant cries, unwilling to accept the stranger in their midst. "Then it's on Maelgwyn's account that you're worried?" said Ceilyn.

"On Maelgwyn's account, or on his sons'. But the worst of it is, I don't know whether I am worried *for* them, or *about* them."

Down in the courtyard, a tiny blond figure clad all in peacock-blue and canary-yellow could be seen running toward the stables. "I wonder," Teleri mused, "how Gwenlliant feels, considering that her brother will accompany them on the journey?"

"Gwenlliant?" Ceilyn asked, startled. "What *should* she feel?"

Teleri drew her legs up to her chest, rested her cheek on her knees. "She sees me sometimes, when she oughtn't to know that I'm anywhere near. You and she are the only ones I can never hide from. So I can't help wondering, sometimes, how much *else* that child sees, whether at times like this she shares my unease."

Ceilyn was genuinely amazed. "My cousin Gwenlliant— you're saying that Gwenlliant possesses some sort of second sight?"

Teleri nodded. "You didn't suppose, did you, that you were the only one of all your kin who still possessed the ancient gifts?"

"But little Gwenlliant . . . that innocent child—well, I did hear once that she was susceptible to nightmares, but that was before she ever came to Caer Cadwy," Ceilyn protested.

"That might mean a talent for prophetic dreams as well," Teleri pointed out. "At night, when the barriers of the mind are down, there are always things trying to get in—things both beneficial and inimical—and an unrecognized and undeveloped talent can be a weakness at times like that."

Ceilyn's scowl deepened. "But she is safe, here at Caer Cadwy . . . from those things you were talking about, those things inimical? So long as she remains under the beneficent influence of the Clach Ghealach . . . isn't it better that her talent—her gift, as you choose to call it—should remain unrecognized?"

A shadow crossed Teleri's face. "You think so? You still believe that?"

He looked up at the rooks, still circling angrily overhead, still agitated by the invasion of the white bird. He had seen the rooks in springtime, during the nesting season, tearing apart the nest of some hapless pair they didn't want in the rookery, and driving them out with a great squawking and a flapping of black wings. And he had seen men and women act exactly the same way when faced with any taint of the old wild talents associated with the Wild Magic, all banding together like a parliament of rooks to harass the misfit and cast it out. "Who should know better than you or I," he asked gloomily, "that abilities of that sort can be a mixed blessing?"

"All gifts may prove to be so, all talents are subject to misuse—not only magical ones," Teleri countered. "Why should they alone be suspect?"

He could think of a dozen answers to that—all of which would offend her or sound hypocritical coming from him. "Because we don't—we can't understand them," he managed at last.

"It is amazing," Teleri said sadly, "how tenderly we each cherish our own ignorance."

"You've nothing at all to worry about," Garanwyn heard himself saying for perhaps the hundredth time. "And we won't be gone so very long. Start home the day after the wedding and be back here sometime the first week in November."

Gwenlliant did not answer. She only stood quietly watching her brother adjust the straps and the stirrups of his saddle one last time, looking, for all her bright plumage, utterly woebegone. Though she had never voiced any disappointment at being left behind—she was not and never had been a complaining sort of child—it occurred to Garanwyn now that she might, after all, have liked to go along.

"You are better here at home," he said apologetically. "This is no time of year for you to be traveling, with the weather so uncertain." A lame excuse and he knew it, for the weather these last few years was *always* uncertain—a howling blizzard the June before last and thunderstorms the following December. Garanwyn was old enough to clearly remember a time when season had predictably followed season, but he doubted Gwenlliant could.

But all she said, in a small voice, was: "*You'll* be out on the road, if the weather turns bad."

"We'll take the very best care of him," Fflergant promised blithely, as he completed his own adjustments and swung up into the saddle atop his sturdy roan gelding. "As devoted as a pair of old nursemaids, I promise you, and we'll see that he changes out of his wet clothes and always wears wool next to his skin."

Tryffin knelt on the ground beside her. "Give us a kiss for luck. That's the best kind of good luck where Fflergant and I come from: a kiss from a fair-haired maid."

Gwenlliant obliged with a kiss on the cheek, and Garanwyn bent over to receive his. "Now give me a smile," he said coaxingly, "and I'll bring you a gift when I return. What would you like? No, let me guess." He unknotted a lock of pale hair that had tangled in the fine silver chain around his neck, and held her a little distance away. He looked her over from top to toe, taking in the bright blue cloak and the yellow gown, and the tiny slippers with upturned toes. "I know what you would like! A new pair of shoes . . . red leather with fur to line them . . . to keep your feet warm all winter."

His reward was a tentative smile, though Gwenlliant was by no means certain he was not teasing her. She was fond of pretty things, silken gowns and gay ribbons, and was particularly vain of her footwear, her feet being small and well-formed, a fact which her brother and her cousins seemed to find inordinately amusing.

"You can't buy me red leather shoes," she said. "They would cost you . . . oh, ever so much! And even if you could, they would never be right. They have to be made to fit, you know."

"Just you wait and see," said Garanwyn, playfully measuring her foot against the length of his hand. He had been saving for a year for a new saddle—surely a pair of new shoes would not cost as much.

"And you will be back—when?" Gwenlliant asked tremulously.

Climbing into the saddle, Garanwyn made a quick mental calculation. "The third of November, weather permitting. Before nightfall on the fourth, at the very latest."

• • •

After Balor died, a shadow fell on Oonagh, his widow, and a great fear of old age and death came over her. She sat alone in her room for many days, in the grip of her fear, and nothing that anyone said could comfort her.

On the seventh day, Oonagh rose from her chair, put on the necklace Balor had given her, and left the hall without a word to anyone. She went to the hut on Magh Aeddon where her sister the witch lived, and she bartered her jewels for the secret of eternal youth.

When she returned to Balor's hall, Oonagh sent for Meis-Geghra, her oldest son. "Balor is dead," said she, "yet he might be living still, had he taken my advice." Then she showed her son a little box that the witch had given her. "Had Balor given me his soul to keep safe in this little coffer, then death might never have claimed him."

As Meis-Geghra listened to his mother's words, the desire to cheat death came over him. He begged her to take his soul and keep it safe inside the witch's box.

"That I will do, and gladly," said Oonagh. Then Meis-Geghra left the room, and when he returned he carried something in his hand, something that was small and trembling like a mouse or a black lizard. He gave his soul to Oonagh, and she put it inside the witch's coffer.

But later that evening, when everyone was asleep, Oonagh went down to the kitchen, and she took the little thing her son had given her out of the box, and she roasted it over the fire. And when it was cooked, she ate it.

Days passed, and Meis-Geghra grew weak and ill. At last he took to his bed. Within a fortnight he was dead and buried. But Oonagh, his mother, grew young and blooming again and the shadow of her death departed for a time.

—*From* The Book of the White Cockerel

• • •

"There they go," said Calchas, turning away from the window in his mother's sumptuous bedchamber. "And good riddance to all of them, say I!"

The Princess lounged in her silver chair, one hand languidly extended, while the dwarf-woman, Brangwengwen, applied gold leaf to the long curving fingernails. Derry sat on a velvet cushion at her feet.

"I think that I will rather miss them—Fflergant and Tryffin, at least," drawled Derry. "There's a certain pleasure to be had in ordering the future King of all Celydonn to polish one's boots.''

Calchas replied with a rude noise. "Anyway," he said to his mother, "now that you know what Maelgwyn and the Old Ones are about, how do you intend to stop them?"

Diaspad smiled sweetly. A change had come over her since the disappearance of the bones. Watching her influence at court continue to melt away—while, at the same time, the positions of the Queen and her two brothers became increasing secure— Diaspad had renewed her efforts to dazzle and impress: by the novelty of her dress and manners, and by the splendor with which she surrounded herself and her household. Thus the gilded nails and a dozen other affectations, thus the gaudy crimsons, plums, and tangerines that were gradually replacing the somber black gowns she had once preferred; thus, too, the extravagant slashes and patches, the ribbons and the dagging that character- ized the Mochdreffian fashions which—though she had popular- ized them—the Princess herself had rarely affected. These days, her lips and her cheeks were often the same mulberry or scarlet as her gown, and her eyes were rimmed with black—evidence that Brangwengwen applied the rouge and the kohl with a heav- ier hand. But the Princess's smile, the tender, dulcet voice, were, if anything, sweeter than ever before.

"The Old Ones have generously provided me with the means to accomplish all that I could wish," she said. "The Samhain sacrifice—from the very beginning, I was determined to employ the ritual to my own advantage, and now I know exactly how I shall go about that."

"And?" said Calchas.

"The rite is very old—of the greatest antiquity," replied his mother. "One of the central rites of the Old Religion as it was practiced in the south. It was always performed just past the hour of midnight at the beginning of the pagan New Year, when all the barriers between this world and the next grow thin and ten- uous. At the moment of sacrifice, it was customary for the pre- siding priest or priestess to ask a boon of the Lady, and the Goddess would listen and be well-disposed to any request that was made."

"You mean she will grant your wish—just like that?" Calchas asked incredulously. "But then . . . if the ritual confers such power, why did the Old Ones ask you to perform it?"

Diaspad shrugged her shoulders. "Someone must do it, and they dare not attempt it themselves. The appointed place, you see, is only a stone's throw from Caer Cadwy. Also, I once had some status among them—a sort of left-handed connection with the Draighenach cult."

Brangwengwen had gilded all the nails on one hand, and Diaspad paused to admire the effect. "Nevertheless," she went on, "I suppose they expect me to ask for something of benefit to all—fertility for the land, prosperity for the kingdom . . . you know the sort of thing—not supposing I would have the audacity to ask for anything for myself. But as for the Goddess . . . she may or may not grant my request, but most likely she will."

She extended the other hand to Brangwengwen. The old dwarf began to paint the nails with an undercoating of eggwhite. "I intend to ask," Diaspad said casually, "for the lives of Maelgwyn's sons."

"For the lives of . . . But you said they were under the Lady's protection! Why should she grant you a thing like that?"

"I said, once, that the Lady would be displeased were I to kill them by any means then available to me. It is another matter entirely for me to ask the Dark Mother to gather her favorites to her bosom for me." One gold-taloned hand slid down Derry's arm. "She is very fond of comely young men, our Lady Celedon."

A sneeze drew her attention to the other side of the room where Prescelli sat cross-legged on the floor, stitching feathers to one of the Princess's gowns. Diaspad glared disapprovingly.

"I can't help it," Prescelli protested. "I keep breathing in little bits of fluff."

"You have bits of feathers sticking in your hair, too," volunteered Derry. "You can't imagine how unbecoming it is."

Prescelli opened her mouth to speak. Like the Princess, Derry had taken to painting his face—his mouth very pink, his lashes very dark—though why he found it necessary was a mystery, for he was as pretty a lad as anyone might ever hope to see. Prescelli suspected that Diaspad encouraged him, recognizing that Derry's natural beauty only served to emphasize all that was contrived and artificial in her own. Prescelli was about to speak . . . but then she sneezed again.

"A lot of childish nonsense, masked balls," she said instead, crossly. "And that golden mask that Bron has been hammering on these last few days—it's bound to be dreadfully heavy and uncomfortable.''

"Never you mind about that," said the Princess, drumming the fingers of her right hand on the arm of her chair. "The conceit pleases me—that should be enough for you."

Prescelli looked from the Princess to Derry, from one mask-like face to the other, and she had a horrifying vision of Derry as he might be in twenty years' time: all his youth and beauty withered by years of depravity, artificially restored by Diaspad's Black Magic; and she was struck by an overwhelming nausea. *I'll never be like that,* she told herself. *I'll never let myself grow old and rotten and dissipated like that. I'd go into a convent first. I'd—*

"You were about to say something, I think?" the Princess asked, watching her closely.

Prescelli shook her head and bent low over her needlework so that Diaspad could not see her face.

But Calchas was not yet ready to abandon the subject of Fflergant and Tryffin. "They were baptized as Christians. Surely Caer Arianrhod is closed to them."

"Well, they were baptized, yes, and raised in that faith—after the Gwyngellach fashion," said the Princess, allowing herself to be diverted. "Like the Rhianeddi, most Gwyngellach are drawn to the trappings of the Christian religion, but they don't take it nearly so seriously, and there is something in the Gwyngellach soul that still responds to the old pagan rituals. And Maelgwyn has always preferred to keep a foot in both camps. So I feel certain that Madawc was on hand when Maelgwyn's sons were named, to whisper a word or two of his own at the ceremonies.

"But whether the Lady takes them for her own, or allows their own grim God to claim their souls, it hardly matters to us. *We* shall be rid of them, at least, and they have my leave to spend eternity in the paradise of their choice."

"Yes, but we *are* rid of them, just at the moment," Calchas pointed out. "They won't be here at Samhain—All Hallows Eve, I should say. How can you . . . ?"

"The hand of the Lady can touch them wherever they may be," replied Diaspad. "And—who knows?—the road from Castell Maelduin may be fraught with perils."

Calchas began to laugh. "Landslides and precipices in thei

own Gwyngelli Hills, and robbers and other hazards down in the lowlands. And dear little Garanwyn is with them, to share in all their adventures!''

"Now, now," said his mother playfully. "We mustn't be greedy!"

They arrayed him as befits a king, in white samite and yellow brocaded silk. They put a mantle over him and shoes of speckled cordwain with golden clasps upon his feet, and they laid his great sword upon his breast. Then they raised a mound over him as was the custom in those days.

The years passed, and the green grass grew over the grave of Sceolan.

—From *The Book of Dun Fiorenn*

5.

Of White Fairy Cattle and the Bull From the Sea

The King celebrated his birthday in mid-October. Every year, from the first week of that month until All Hallows Eve at the end, rare and precious gifts arrived at Caer Cadwy from all parts of the realm, as the greater and lesser lords of the land vied with each other, each hoping to procure Cynwas's special favor by sending exactly the right gift.

This year, the gifts began to arrive on the very first day of October, when a lovely silver-grey wolfhound bitch arrived from Gofynnion of Gorwynnion, and a circlet of ruddy gold from Rudraige of Leth Skellig. Lord Dyffryn (a man with much to celebrate after the miraculous recovery of his young wife and infant daughter) sent his from Glynn Hyddwyn in Rhianedd: an intricate timekeeping device of marvelous design. And Maelgwyn fab Menai, though engrossed in preparations for his youngest daughter's wedding, took the time to send a dozen rolls of silk and a chest of rare foreign spices.

But the most magnificent (and certainly the most unexpected

gift of all came from Forgoll of Leth Scathach, the father of Derry and Morc.

It arrived under escort on the morning of the King's birthday, and entered the castle amidst great commotion and general amazement, for it was a beast such as few in Camboglanna had ever been privileged to behold: an enormous Draighenach bull with great polished horns gleaming like crescent moons and a hide as white as seafoam.

Now it happened that the King owned a large herd of cattle, that kept the castle supplied with beeves and cheeses, but he took no interest in breeding them or improving his herd, leaving all such matters in the capable hands of his Steward.

"This is certainly—certainly an impressive gesture on the part of your cousin," he told his step-sister, when the two of them wandered down to the Lists where the beast had been temporarily penned. "Truly a—a princely gesture. But what does Forgoll expect me to *do* with it?"

"My dearest brother," gushed the Princess, "you can scarcely have any idea what a wonderful gift this is. Even I, half-Draighenach as I am . . . But probably your own herdsmen could explain it better. The bull will prove a boon to the entire local breed."

"Hmmmmmm," said the King. "Yes, indeed. But you know, I have never been particularly interested. . . ."

"Why a few hundred years ago, it was forbidden by law for any but the King of Draighen to breed such cattle as this. And in Leth Scathach, you know, they are nearly as attached to their cattle as they are to their own children. It really is the most elegant compliment," she trilled, "that my cousin Forgoll has paid you."

Now, Derry mac Forgoll, who had trailed along behind the Princess, could scarcely believe his ears. He knew perfectly well that such generosity—no matter *what* he might expect to gain by it—was quite unlike his miserly father, as were compliments, elegant or otherwise, and he was wild to know by what means Diaspad had coerced Forgoll into sending the bull. But if Derry had good reason to believe that Forgoll of Leth Scathach would part with his two youngest sons far more readily than he would relinquish even the scrawniest and weakest calf in all his vast herds, the boy managed, for once, to keep his thoughts to himself.

"Well," said the King, scratching his head and staring blankly at his new acquisition—which, taking exception to the Saracen in the middle of the yard, was pawing up great clods of turf from the Lists—"I suppose we have an empty field somewhere in which to pasture it—him."

"Oh no," protested Diaspad, pretending to be shocked. "Just any pasture won't do! You will have to build a stout fence to keep this magnificent creature in, and you must put him to graze where the right sort of grass grows.

"Why not allow Morc . . . or better yet, young Daire . . . to advise your Steward on the care of the beast?"

Cynwas stared doubtfully at Derry, and Derry stared doubtfully back. "I was not aware," said the King, "that Daire counted animal husbandry among his many—er—interests."

"But of course," the Princess laughed merrily. "The boy is Draighenach born and bred. Though he is far too modest to say so, he knows all about cattle and horses."

And so it came about, that very afternoon, that the guards on the castle walls and the peasants working in the fields were treated to the sight of a disgruntled Derry mac Forgoll, in the unlikely company of Cynwas's cowherd, daintily picking his way across the meadows below the castle, searching for "the perfect spot" to pen the bull.

But Diaspad's words produced one outcome she had not foreseen, and the King—convinced that the bull was of incalculable value—decided to set a guard on the beast day and night, for fear of cattle thieves.

As the Princess had predicted, the local farmers and herdsmen were able to appreciate the bull as the King could not. For days, the countryfolk could think or speak of little else. If the bull's virility in any way matched his size . . . if he was able to pass on his own characteristics of his offspring . . . if they, in turn, bred true . . . The little thatched cottages for miles around buzzed with excitement and speculation, and in many a heart was kindled a desire to make the pilgrimage to see this prodigy, to observe at first hand the creature and his habits and determine if the bull was—could possibly be—all that he was reported.

While the bull remained corralled on the Lists, the country-folk maintained a respectful distance, but the day he went out to pasture, the meadows below the castle resembled a country fair, as crowds of rustics in their Sunday best gathered around the newly constructed enclosure to gaze and to marvel.

For the next three days it continued the same. Whether the bull was strolling majestically across the field waving his great tufted tail like a banner, pawing up great divots of turf in a sudden spectacular rage, or peacefully cropping the long yellow grass, there were always a dozen or more sturdy farmers and herdsmen surrounding the pasture, shaking their heads in admiration, or reverently pointing out the bull's manifold virtues for the benefit of their wide-eyed sons and daughters, wives and sweethearts.

Among the onlookers, one warm and windy afternoon, was a solitary young woman. She arrived alone and stationed herself at some distance from the farmers, perched on the lowest rail of the fence, and remained for some time staring raptly at the bull. Barefoot and dressed in homespun like any herdsman's daughter, with her ash-blond hair in a single long braid, she was largely ignored by the guards, for the figure under the loose grey gown was slight and almost childishly flat and the face beneath the broad-brimmed hat was pale and rather plain. She was able to watch the bull undisturbed until Ceilyn rode by.

He was returning to the castle after a solitary morning ride. Ceilyn had not been happy these last weeks. Since the end of his affair with Prescelli, in August, he had returned to a sober, temperate, celibate life. That had been easy at the beginning, before the first glow of virtue wore off, but as time wore on he was increasingly troubled by that same dissatisfaction with himself and life in general that had precipitated his earlier fall from grace—as well as those darker stirrings he had mentioned to Teleri, that caused him to examine the iron band circling his wrist a dozen times a day, as if seeking reassurance that it was still there. To make matters worse, there had been a heavy frost on the ground this morning, reminding him that the first snow might fall soon, and with the snow . . .

This afternoon, however, sunshine, fresh air, and exercise had worked their healing magic, and he was relaxed and relatively at peace with himself. Spotting Teleri from a distance, he tethered Tegillus to a hedge by the road and trudged across the meadows.

He joined Teleri on the fence. "This is no ordinary bull, you know," she said, after they had exchanged a few words.

"So everyone says. Remarkably ill-tempered and aggressive, too. I don't know much about cattle, myself," he added. "They don't raise such beasts where I come from. Even I can see that this creature is enormous, near twice the size of anything you see in these parts, but beyond that . . . ?"

Teleri nodded. "They raise few cattle on Ynys Aderyn, and those they do are not like this at all, but small and shaggy like our ponies.

"But I opened a book this morning," she went on, and Ceilyn could detect an undercurrent of excitement in her voice, "a book of old tales, bound in blue leather, that I hadn't thought about in years. It was the bull, I suppose, that reminded me."

"And what," Ceilyn prompted her, when it became apparent that she was not going to continue, "did you read in that book to bring you down here this afternoon?"

"Tales of harpers and heroes," she said. "Of milk-white fairy cattle wearing sweet, chiming, golden bells, and bulls from out of the sea." Her gaze became rapt, her voice dreamy. "There was a king in Draighen, once, who kept just such a bull as this. He found it on the beach one morning, grazing on seaweed. A stray it was from Dylan's own herds."

"Oh," said Ceilyn flatly. "Fairy tales."

"Yes, fairy stories," Teleri agreed, a trifle wistfully. "Bed time tales for small children. Draighenach grandmothers an storytellers recite such tales—much as nursemaids up in Go wynnion and Rhianedd, I believe, tell tales of selkie folk an werewolves."

"Yes, I see." The sidelong glance he gave her showed tha he was amused at his own expense. "I deserved that. And you tell me that *this* bull is some eldritch hybrid of earth ar sea, it would be unbecoming in me to doubt you."

Teleri returned his smile. "No, I'd not go so far as to say tha But I've learned that there is always a grain of truth in the o tales. In this case, the meaning is not difficult to find. Whi cattle were once sacred to the old gods, you know."

Ceilyn frowned. He had a proper Celcynnon-bred horror the Old Religion and everything pertaining to it, and Teler words conjured up some sinister pictures: bloody rituals carri out beneath a baleful full moon, terrible old men wielding gold scythes, monstrous wicker effigies consigned to the flames.

But these, as Ceilyn told himself, were all horrors out of t dead past. There were no more pagans in Celydonn, not any that he knew of, except maybe among the Hillfolk and a scattering of dirty old men and women up in the north, who practiced their nasty rituals on ducks and chickens and died wretched deaths themselves whenever they came to the attention of the authorities.

"First fairy tales, and now ancient history?" he asked.

"Maybe," she replied. "And maybe not. I think you would find, if you knew what to look for, that the Old Religion still survives in some surprising ways and in some unexpected places."

Her thoughtful grey gaze rested on the castle on the hill for a moment, then wandered northward. "There is a line—a track they call it—between Brynn Caer Cadwy and the stone circle at Dol Tal Carreg. And another track leads from Pefyn's grave in the south, to the Holy Well at Tregalen. There is a force, some kind of a power, that flows along these lines."

"A track? Is that what they call it?" said Ceilyn, beginning to be really interested. "I've always wondered." Then, seeing that she was staring at him in wide-eyed astonishment: "I beg your pardon. Did I say something wrong?"

"You knew?" she said. "You already knew?"

"Well, of course," he said. "That power—whatever you call it—makes crossing the line rather like wading a river, doesn't it? Only there's no physical resistance—only a kind of pressure in the mind. And once, when I was riding back to the castle a little after sunset, I found myself following a trail of silver that stretched before me in the moonlight like . . . Do you mean to tell me that *you* can't see or feel them?"

Teleri shook her head. "I only know that they exist because Glastyn told me so, and I can calculate, knowing where they begin and end, where they ought to be."

Ceilyn began to feel uncomfortable. "I thought that everyone could feel the power when crossing a line. I assumed it was just one of those things that it's not polite to mention—like the rowan that people hang up over their doors, or the charms and amulets most everyone wears."

"These tracks turn up everywhere," said Teleri, "crossing each other like threads in a length of cloth. I suppose you encountered others, when you lived in the north?"

"There is a place near Caer Celcynnon," he said.

"I know of it," said Teleri. "It runs between Pant Pwll Felyn and the old church of St. Teilo. All along these lines, and especially where two of them meet, you will find sites sacred to the people living near by. A church, perhaps, or the grave of some local hero, a spot dedicated to a patron saint, or even one of the old gods or goddesses under a lesser-known name.

"If I am not mistaken," she said, "the two lines of which I spoke converge somewhere near the middle of this very field. Perhaps over there, where the land rises a little."

She climbed down from the fence. "I wish that I had thought of this, three days ago, before the bull came to pasture here—and I had known that you could detect the lines. We might have investigated the mound quite safely."

"You really think that it's important to know?" said Ceilyn. He felt much better about the whole phenomenon since her mention of churches and holy places.

"Yes," she said. "But it would be too dangerous now—supposing the guards allowed it. What reason could we possibly give for wandering around out there now? No, we'll just have to think of some—"

But Ceilyn, all eagerness to be of service, ready to grasp this rare opportunity to perform a deed of daring before Teleri's very eyes, was not even listening. He looked toward the men guarding the bull, over at the farmers clustered on the far side of the field. He held up a dampened finger to test the direction of the wind.

Ignoring Teleri's protests, he untied the ribbons under her chin, snatched the straw hat off her head, and sent it sailing through the air, over the rails of the fence. It landed in the grass, where the wind obligingly picked it up and sent the hat rolling, exactly as Ceilyn had hoped it might, briskly across the meadow. Ceilyn hoisted himself to the top of the fence and dropped down on the other side.

"You can't," wailed Teleri. "What if the bull . . . ?" But Ceilyn was already following her hat across the pasture.

The meadow was wide, the bull grazed with his head pointing away from Ceilyn. For a time, all went well, and Ceilyn waited until he reached the hillock in the center of the field before he allowed himself to overtake the tumbling straw hat and snatch it up.

A faint humming sounded in his ears and a familiar sensation washed over him. But it was not that which caused Ceilyn to stand stock-still in astonishment.

Someone was buried under the hill.

He had no time to absorb that information or question how he knew it, because Teleri cried out a warning and the men gathered at the other end of the field shouted out also, attempting to alert him to his danger. He turned slowly to face the bull. The great white beast stared at him, massive chest heaving, nostrils flaring, heavy head shaking from side to side as if in annoyance. Ceilyn froze, clutching the hat to his chest to keep the brim from flapping.

He knew that many animals respond more readily to movement than to shape or color. One of his first lessons stalking game had required him to stand perfectly motionless until a grazing buck wandered within range of his bow. It was a trick that worked only so long as the creature did not scent danger.

It did not work this time, though Ceilyn remained perfectly still, though the men on the farther side of the pasture shouted and waved their hats in an attempt to turn the bull their way. The bull was not to be distracted. And Ceilyn recognized the attitude all too well: the lashing tail, the outraged glare—all his life, cats, dogs, horses, and hawks had reacted to him in the same hostile manner. He could feel his mouth go dry, the old familiar apprehension stiffening his limbs.

Damn! he thought. *He can't possibly scent me. The wind isn't even blowing his way. Whatever this thing is between me and the birds and the beasts, I wish to God it wasn't happening now!*

On the day he had captured the Queen's wayward peregrine, Ceilyn had learned to turn that special relationship to his advantage, but instinct warned him that any attempt to do so now would certainly fail. He knew all about falcons and hawks, even if he had never been able to handle them, but he knew nothing at all about cattle. This great creature was as alien to him as if it had truly emerged from the sea—more so, perhaps, because Ceilyn had lived his entire life within sight and sound of the sea, but he had never even seen live cattle or walked across the open land that bred them, until his sixteenth year.

The bull lowered his head, preparing to charge. Ceilyn took to his heels.

An eternity later, he tumbled over the top rail of the fence and landed in the yellow grass at Teleri's feet. A pounding of hooves and a mighty rending of timbers warned him that the bull had followed and was determined not to allow him to escape so easily.

Miraculously, the fence held. But Teleri offered him a hand up, and Ceilyn, deeming it prudent to remove himself, scrambled to his feet and followed her across the meadows.

He collapsed in a panting heap a safe distance away from the fence. Teleri knelt in the grass beside him. "You weren't hurt?"

Ceilyn shook his head, gulped air, and managed a reply. "You needn't tell me . . . how stupid that was. All the way across the pasture, I was wondering . . . what the difference was between a stake driven through the heart and one of those great wicked horns impaling my vitals."

Yet he was breathless and elated after his sprint across the field, his narrow escape from goring or trampling. Sprawled in the warm, fragrant grass, he felt the world spinning around, with himself as the axis—an odd fancy, that, since everyone knew that the earth was the one fixed point in the universe.

He propped himself up on one elbow and looked around him. The sky above was very blue and Teleri's eyes had captured some of that color. The air he was swallowing in such great drafts was intoxicating, and Teleri's own sweet scent mingled with that of the grass. Impulsively, he slipped a hand under her chin, tilted up her face to meet his, and kissed her.

The kiss was no more than a light brush across her cheek, a flickering of his tongue across her mouth, but Teleri stiffened and caught her breath sharply. Ceilyn pulled away, excitement fast turning to irritation.

Ever since that morning, three weeks before, when they had seemed to reach some better understanding, Ceilyn had believed that Teleri would welcome his advances, if he chose his moment carefully and proceeded very gently. Now it seemed that he had been mistaken—or that she had changed her mind again. "Apparently, I'm a bigger fool than I thought," he said bitterly.

A burning blush spread across Teleri's face. "Please don't be angry," she whispered. "It's not that I didn't want—"

"Not at all," he interrupted her coldly. "There is no need for you to apologize or explain. The mistake was mine, entirely."

• • •

Later, as they trudged up the long dusty road toward the castle, with the big chestnut gelding following obediently behind, Ceilyn told Teleri what he had learned. "Those two lines do meet there, just as you thought, but there is more to that little hillock than we suspected. A man was buried there—a great man, it seems to me—centuries and centuries ago."

Typically, Teleri solemnly accepted this amazing disclosure, without even asking him how he happened to know. "A royal burial, do you think?"

"Possibly," said Ceilyn. "I seemed to see a tall man wearing a golden torc around his neck, and a long bronze sword was laid on his breast."

"One of the early emperors, perhaps, Cadwy or Cynfelyn. Or even before that. A king or chieftain of the Camboglannach, maybe," Teleri speculated. "But it hardly matters. At least we know that the bull has been penned near a site of some significance."

"And that tells you—what?" asked Ceilyn.

"Lady Day . . . May Day . . . Lammas and Michaelmas," Teleri recited absently. "And now All Hallows Eve. There are older festivals roughly corresponding to all those holidays, which mark the waxing and waning of the ancient powers. Now I wonder," she said, "where the Princess Diaspad was at Midsummer?"

"On her way to Leth Scathach for a christening," Ceilyn volunteered.

"For a christening, yes. All the way to Dunn Dessi for the naming of Leam mac Forgoll's twins, and why should the Princess even care? Of course, there is always a power made manifest on such occasions—but children are named every day, right here in Camboglanna. No, she had other business in Leth Scathach, or perhaps along the way."

She stopped in the middle of the road to think for a moment. "Dol Tal Carreg . . . Tregalen . . . and any number of tombs and sacred springs and holy wells between here and Draighen . . . Where did she stop and stay the night on Midsummer's Eve?"

"But I still," Ceilyn reminded her, "haven't the least idea what you are talking about."

Teleri continued on up the hill. "Of course, I can't be absolutely certain. But she is always very busy on or around the holy days . . . I think it likely that the Princess Diaspad, like most witches, practices a debased form of the Old Religion.''

Ceilyn stooped to pick up a loose stone and pitch it down the hillside. "Debased?"

"Well, I mean that she performs the rituals at the appropriate times of the year hoping to gain favor with the Old Powers, enlisting their aid at her time of greatest need. But she may not perfectly understand what she is doing. The intent of the ancient rites, as well as the form—"

"And you, I suppose, know all about the proper form and intent of these heathen rituals?" The question was asked sarcastically, a churlish attempt (and he knew it) to pay her back for the disappointment he had suffered earlier. Much to his surprise, she took the question seriously.

"I'm not a witch or a pagan or anything like that, if that is what you are thinking," she protested, suddenly too busy unknotting and retying the ribbons of the hat hanging down her back to meet his eyes. "I was raised in the same faith as you—though not so strictly, I will admit."

The air was hot and still, the bulk of the hill cutting them off from the sea and the wind; the sun beat down on their bare heads. "I rarely see you in church," he said reproachfully.

"That hardly means anything," Teleri replied softly. "The Princess and her people are in and out of the castle chapels constantly. She makes quite a point of being seen at her devotions, I believe."

"Yes," said Ceilyn. "But I've never seen her touch the bread or the wine or any of the holy things—nor you, either, that I remember."

"I will take Communion this Sunday," she said faintly, "if you think that I ought."

"You shouldn't do it just to prove something to me," he replied primly. "Better not to do it at all."

They continued along the road, Ceilyn disapproving and self-righteous, Teleri lagging a little behind. Ceilyn stole a furtive glance over his shoulder.

She was the perfect picture of dejection and weariness, plodding along the road, her bare feet sinking into the soft dirt with every step, her ankles and the hem of her skirt dusty. It occurred to him that this was much too easy, that Teleri was too easy a target for his bad temper and disappointment. Abandoning the sport as unworthy of him, he suddenly relented.

"What I should have said . . . you don't have to do anything to prove yourself to me."

"Truly?" she asked softly.

"Of course," he said. "What kind of a friend would I be, if that weren't true?"

"The Gwyngellach," said Glastyn, "are a curious people. Good friends and dangerous foes, honorable liars, primitive folk who nevertheless excel in all metal-craft, lovers of the soil . . . especially lovers of the soil, for the land of Gwyngelli is very fair: the lowlands pleasant and fertile, the hills dangerous but picturesque. In the valleys grow sweet blue grasses and wildflowers of every color, and the sheep and the goats grazing there sometimes produce milk of remarkable flavor and startling hue."

6.

In the Hall of the Fairy King

Five days of uneventful travel brought Garanwyn, Tryffin, and Fflergant to the banks of the Dyferdallben. The river was dark and sluggish, easily forded, and the boys and their horses had no difficulty passing to Tir Gwyngelli on the other side.

Garanwyn looked eagerly around him, sizing up the landscape. The land differed little here from the country on the other side of the river: broad pleasant farmlands and gentle rolling hills, and over a little rise in the land, he spotted a prosperous-looking little village, just precisely like all the small towns and villages in Camboglanna and Walgan.

But this was not the *real* Gwyngelli, Garanwyn reminded himself, not the true hill country—the "Hidden Country" as it was sometimes called—where deadly landslides and flash floods waited in the narrow passes to surprise unwelcome travelers, where the people of the hills carried on their interminable bloodless feuds and lived according to all manner of quaint, archaic superstitions; where Maelgwyn fab Menai held court, like his counterpart the King of the Fairies, in underground chambers lined with silver and gold. They would be entering *that* country—if indeed it existed anywhere but in stories and songs—in few more days, and then . . . Garanwyn felt certain he would know the truth behind the legends.

All that day and the next, as Garanwyn and his cousins journeyed through the lowlands, the countryside gradually changed. The clustered farms and villages dwindled to a few tiny, isolated hamlets, the occasional drover's hut; the hawthorne and birch claimed more and more of the land. As the country grew wilder, the inhabitants were purer in blood: smaller, darker, and ruddier of complexion than their neighbors across the river.

Near the end of the second day, the forest of hawthorne and white birch thinned, and the hills loomed up, dark and forbidding in the failing light. Yet there was beauty, too, and gazing upon the hills of his mother's homeland for the first time, Garanwyn felt a tug at his heart, familiar yet unfamiliar, and something that might have been a memory stirring at the back of his mind.

"No one told me," he said a little reproachfully, "that it would be anything like this."

"No one could tell you," replied Fflergant, equally moved, though the sight was by no means new to him. "It's in your blood, you know. The blood of your mother and your mother's people."

Tryffin, typically, said nothing, but it was plain this was a sentimental homecoming for him as well.

They slept that night in a village named Trehilarien, and began their journey through the Hidden Country early the next morning, leaving the last vestiges of civilization as Garanwyn knew it behind. "You'll not see more than two or three dwellings grouped together until we come to Castell Maelduin," said Tryffin. "As for the people . . . I daresay you'll think them primitive enough, until you know more about them."

As it turned out, the only men they met were shepherds, and a party of fierce-looking fellows in goatskin boots and tunics, who became suddenly garrulous and tearfully sentimental in the company of Fflergant and Tryffin.

The Gwyngelli Hills—actually a rugged little mountain range in miniature—did not disappoint Garanwyn. The road took him and his companions along dangerous precipices and treacherous pathways, past hurtling waterfalls and steep rocky inclines. But there were also sparkling streams, pleasant valleys, and pools of pure silvery water. And Tryffin and Fflergant knew all the secret ways, all the hidden paths, the unexpected valleys and narrow passes that led to Castell Maelduin. What appeared, from the lowlands, to be nearly impassable country became surprisingly easy, and the journey was accomplished more swiftly than Garanwyn would have imagined possible.

Garanwyn would never forget his first glimpse of Maelgwyn's fortress: slender towers gleaming white against a soft October sky, the sun shining like a glory only a few degrees above the rooftops, and a magnificent silver eagle descending in splendor to light upon the highest tower and scream his defiance. For several minutes, the boy was absolutely speechless.

He looked back over his shoulder, to find his kinsmen looking inordinately pleased with themselves. "You look," he said, "as if you had arranged all this for my special benefit."

"I'll admit that we chose the hour of our arrival very carefully," Fflergant replied smugly. "But the eagle was a happy coincidence."

Viewed from a neighboring hilltop, the approach to the castle looked formidable, from the floor of the valley below, absolutely forbidding: an impossibly steep track looping up the side of the hill, so that every leg of the journey upward exposed the unwelcome visitor to attack from above.

"You're quite certain we were expected today—quite sure we'll be recognized from up above?" Garanwyn asked apprehensively as they dismounted and began to lead their horses up the path. His cousins only laughed.

"Do you know," Garanwyn went on breathlessly, as the ascent grew steeper, "I always fancied . . . you lived under the hill . . . not atop it."

"There are all sorts of rooms and passageways burrowing down into the hill," said Tryffin. "Mostly used as storerooms now, but there's an ancient chapel and a grand chamber which might have been a banquet hall once. We'll take you exploring in a day or two, if you like."

At that precise moment, a bloodcurdling wail issued from one of the towers above, a ululating cry like a banshee in mortal agony, that bounced off the rocks and echoed all down the narrow valley. Garanwyn immediately covered his ears, but Fflergant and Tryffin responded with ear-shattering cries of their own

"Oh yes," said Fflergant, when the unearthly racket finally died away. "We've been recognized, never doubt it."

The track became wider at the top, and the gates swung open to receive them. Just inside, pandemonium reigned: dark-haired children clamoring to see the horses, dark-eyed girls demanding to be kissed, a couple of rough-looking fellows (Maelgwyn's gate guards?) vigorously pumping Fflergant's arm and slapping Tryffin on the back; even the livestock took part in the excitement, honking and bleating and butting their heads, demanding their share of the attention.

Somehow, Fflergant and Tryffin managed to satisfy them all: dispensing hugs and kisses to right and left, affectionately pummeling the guards, lifting up the smaller children and placing them atop the gentle geldings, digging into their saddlebags and producing sweets for the young ones, and bread for the goats and the geese—while Garanwyn kept a firm grip on the reins and managed a bewildered smile. He had expected the Gwyngellach to celebrate the homecoming of their native princes rather differently, but he had to admit that the welcome he was observing made up in genuine enthusiasm what it lacked in pomp and ceremony.

"My nephew, Pwyll," said Fflergant, passing him a particularly grubby but undoubtedly robust urchin.

"Oh yes?" Garanwyn replied weakly as he gingerly accepted the infant.

After a time, the din began to die down. The older children took charge of the horses, leading them off toward the stables and taking the little ones with them. The guards and the livestock also dispersed.

There was a stir of excitement—a little more subdued this time—on the other side of the yard, and a tall man in a magnificent feathered cape emerged from the crowd; a man so like to Manogan fab Menai that he could only be his brother, Maelgwyn of Gwyngelli.

In a few long strides, Maelgwyn crossed the courtyard. He was an imposing figure, towering head and shoulders above his attendants who were forced to run in order to keep pace with him. It was easy for Garanwyn to imagine this darkly handsome man as he had been some thirty years before: splendid in his strength, his beauty, and his vigor, magnificent in his old-fashioned finery, one of the two "barbarian princes" who had caused such a stir at the court of Anwas II.

With tears in his eyes, Maelgwyn embraced his tall blond sons, then offered his hand to Garanwyn. "You are twice welcome," he said warmly, as the boy knelt before him. "Welcome and more than welcome on your own account, welcome again for the sake of your dear grandfather. You must regard Castell Maelduin as your home for so long as you choose to remain."

Garanwyn replied briefly but emotionally; it seemed impossible to do otherwise, here among the Gwyngellach and their outsize, outlandish emotions.

Maelgwyn led them across the courtyard and into the most imposing of the towers, then up three flights of stairs until they came to the pleasant rooms occupied by the Lady Gwdolwen and her daughters. There was another round of kissing and embracing, and before Garanwyn quite knew what was happening to him, he was whisked away to a seat by a window, where he found himself hand in hand with Princess Cerridwen, who stroked his cheek affectionately and plied him with questions about his sister, his family, and all the folk at Caer Cadwy.

". . . a pity the darling child couldn't come with you, for we all long to meet her. . . . And has she really hair so amazingly fair as yours? A grand place, Caer Cadwy, so they tell me. . . . And how did you leave my grandfather?"

Garanwyn blushed, answered as best he could, and looked the other way. Cerridwen was a statuesque woman, owing much of her beauty to youth, radiant good health, and a happy disposition, but she had other charms as well—attractions that were displayed all too obviously for Garanwyn's comfort.

She wore the short-sleeved lena, an ankle-length garment apparently worn by women of all classes in that part of the world, in this instance made of a thin, shimmering silk, that revealed an almost indecent amount of arm and clung to her figure in such a way that much else was revealed as well. Not that he supposed the lady had any idea how outlandish her costume appeared to him—her attire was clearly designed for comfort, anything else being incidental—and now that he came to think of it, he supposed that the Princess, were positions reversed, would be equally shocked by the low-necked gowns worn so often at court, and that immodest display of shoulders and bosoms that Garanwyn himself had eventually learned to take for granted.

Yes, it would be the height of bad manners for him to stare—yet it was difficult not to look, and looking, not to appear conscious, especially when the young lady leaned close and whispered confidentially in his ear. He sought relief in studying his surroundings, memorizing every detail so that he could recite them all to Gwenlliant when he returned to Caer Cadwy.

It was all very strange and wonderful. Bearskin rugs covered the floors, and the heads of pards, alffin, and other, more exotic, beasts were displayed above the fireplaces. The furniture, for the most part, was rough-hewn, unattractive to Garanwyn's eye, but contrasting with these primitive appointments were silken pillows, bright woven carpets and wall hangings, fair embroidered linens upon the table, everything, in short, that promised comfort, richness, and ease.

The glitter of gold and silver, the fire of precious and semi-precious stones fairly dazzled the eye. Everywhere he looked, there was wonderful jewelry: massive arm rings and pectorals on the men, jeweled girdles and bracelets on the women, golden fillets in the dark hair of the Princesses Eisiwed and Cerridwen. Even the servants had arrayed themselves with silver brooches, torcs, and finger rings, worked in the same designs: the dragon of Gwyngelli, the sunburst, the eagle, and all manner of intricate spirals. It was plain that the wealth—and generosity—of Maelgwyn fab Menai was beyond exaggeration.

With a start, Garanwyn realized that Cerridwen had stopped talking and was studying his face with obvious concern. The boy felt himself blushing furiously. "I beg your pardon . . . I didn't quite . . ."

"Are you ill, my heart? Tired after your journey? Shame on me for chattering on, when what you need is—"

"No, no," he stammered. "Really, you are very kind. It's all just a bit much, you know, to take it all in at once. . . ."

But Tryffin appeared at that moment, to rescue him and take him away to meet the Lady Gwdolwen. "You will feel more comfortable with my mother," said Tryffin. "She is a northerner, as you know, and shares your ideas of proper decorum."

"Oh, but really," Garanwyn protested. "Your sister is delightful. She—"

"—can be a little overwhelming, until you grow accustomed to her," Tryffin finished for him.

The Lady Gwdolwen put him at ease at once. She bore a striking resemblance to her father, Lord Dyffryn, though her hair was golden where his was silver, and her low sweet voice (very like to Tryffin's), combined with the familiar brogue of the north, sounded very pleasant to Garanwyn's ear.

Sitting at Gwdolwen's side, he was able to watch with amusement, when Fflergant and Tryffin fell into the clutches of their sisters.

"God, he knows you've a fine pair of legs, my heart—and now the world knows it, too!" proclaimed Eisiwed, inspecting the garments her brothers had acquired in Camboglanna, and pretending to be shocked by Fflergant's fashionable knee-length pourpoint and scarlet hose. "But haven't you anything respectable to wear to my wedding?"

"None of our old things fit us," Fflergant replied cheerfully. "We've both grown since we left home . . . or hadn't you noticed?"

"Noticed, bless your heart!" Cerridwen gave a little shriek. "And how could anyone fail to notice such a monumental wonder as our Tryffin? You had the better of him by an inch or two when you left, but I see that he's made good use of his time since. Were you made of stone, my love, you'd make a marvelous fortification!"

Supper came shortly thereafter, a sumptuous repast served on golden dishes and presented by proper squires, pages, and little handmaidens in velvets and silks—youths and damsels so neat, efficient, and respectful that Garanwyn was a long time recognizing the rowdy band of children he had met in the courtyard earlier. And could that angelic child with the fluffy brown hair, seated so demurely in Princess Cerridwen's lap, really be the disreputable Pwyll? It seemed that it was—and that his table manners were absolutely impeccable!

The next morning, Garanwyn lingered late in bed, savoring the privilege of an honored guest, the luxury of nothing particular to do: no wash water to be fetched, no armor to be polished, no duties in the stables, the kitchens, or the Hall. It was very pleasant just to lie among the pillows and sleeping furs. Remembering the festivities of the night before: the feasting and the music, the stories and the bits of epic poetry—especially the poetry, for the Gwyngellach were an eloquent people.

He must have drifted off to sleep again, for he did not hear a sound when Fflergant and Tryffin arose and dressed. The first thing that he did hear was Fflergant's voice, almost in his ear, saying: "A good splash of cold water ought to bring him around."

Garanwyn opened his eyes and glared up at his two cousins, who merely grinned amiably back at him. Fflergant deposited his bulk at the foot of the bed, while Tryffin lounged against the bedpost. "What shall it be? The passages beneath the hill, or a visit to your grandfather?"

Garanwyn sat up at once. "My grandfather, please." He eyed the two of them suspiciously. "You both look disgustingly self-satisfied this morning. I suppose you ate breakfast without me?"

"We made a good breakfast, thank you very much, and left you the crusts and the bones," said Tryffin. "We know you've no appetite to speak of before noon."

"No appetite compared to yours," Garanwyn retorted, climbing out of bed.

But as it turned out, they had left him more than the promised crusts and bones on the table in the antechamber. Garanwyn washed and dressed himself, broke his fast, and followed Tryffin downstairs.

In the yard, they found Fflergant there ahead of them, issuing some instructions to one of the serving men. The fellow replied in the same incomprehensible local dialect, but both switched to the High Celydonian at sight of Garanwyn. A matter of courtesy, Garanwyn noted approvingly, though he also had the distinct impression that the topic of conversation had shifted as well.

It was a fine morning for a ride, bright and breezy with a taste of woodsmoke in the air. "Is it far to Dinas Dallben?" Garanwyn asked, as they ascended the path on the other side of the valley.

"Not far. Two hours' ride at most," replied Fflergant. "It's not really a castle, you know, in spite of the name."

"But there was a fortification there once—I think my mother told me?"

"A thousand years ago," said Fflergant. "An old hill fort: earthworks and the like. And after that there was a watch-tower for five or six centuries. Your grandfather built a grand house, there in the ruins. You'll find that sort of thing here, even more than in Camboglanna and the north: the old wedded to the new—or more appropriately, the old wedded to the ancient.''

As they rode, Garanwyn's cousins explained many of the local customs to him. The Gwyngellach were a contradictory people, to be sure. So gay in manner, gentle in speech, kindly in attitude as they were, they nevertheless had earned—yes, even boasted of it!—a reputation for unbridled savagery when provoked. Indeed, their poetry, when it did not extoll the beauties of nature, celebrate the joys of family affection, or poke fun at the foibles of fallible humanity, was full of dark tales of revenge and hinted at other things not considered suitable for the ears of squeamish outsiders.

Known throughout Celydonn as creative liars, the Gwyngellach delighted in elaborate social fictions, principally designed to spare the feelings of others, though few (if any) were actually deceived—yet they would not lie for profit, or break their oaths, or bear false witness against their neighbors. And though they were an insular people, stubbornly clinging to their ancient pre-feudal tribal organization, their own language, they surveyed any other way of life with tolerant amusement, and were also the most generous and hospitable of hosts.

Their feuds often lasted for generations and embroiled whole families and communities, yet blood was seldom shed. "You see, it's like this," Tryffin explained. "Anywhere else you might go, if a man meets his enemy, if there is nothing restraining him, why he'd just as soon cut the fellow's throat as look at him. But the Gwyngellach, now, the Gwyngellach, would far rather *talk* the man to death if he could do it. But that's not to say that he is bluffing. You would be gravely mistaken if you supposed he was bluffing. You press the Gwyngellach too hard and he'll eviscerate you, take his time and do a proper job of it, and never feel a qualm of conscience afterward.

"Here in these hills, everyone understands that. Everybody knows the rules, so most of the time nobody gets hurt. But you bring outlanders into the feud—our neighbors in Mochdreff, for instance—and they don't know or don't care what is expected of them. They'll steal a man's property—rank stupidity on the face of it, for he'd give you his right arm just for the asking—dishonor his women, kill his brother—what's a man to do then? He has to respond in kind, and he does. But he doesn't like being in that position and he means to make certain that he's never imposed on again. So what does he do? He takes his time and devises something utterly devastating, a blow from which his enemy will never recover. Then he can go home and enjoy the company of his wife and children in peace.''

They came at length to another valley with a sparkling stream running through over smooth white stones. On one slope overlooking the valley stood an ancient drystone tower. At the foot of the tower, some shaggy white goats grazed among the short blue grass and late wildflowers, and an old man in brown sackcloth came out through a low doorway and scattered grain before a flock of small fowl.

"Madawc fab Garan, a sort of a cousin of your grandfather's.'' Fflergant gestured toward the white-haired figure on the hillside. "No doubt we'll visit him soon, when he takes it into his head to send for us.''

"*He* will send for *you*?'' Garanwyn asked incredulously, before he thought about it. He had long since accepted that his cousins from Gwyngelli never would display a decent dignity in their dealings with the common-folk, but sometimes his northern ideas about propriety got the better of him. "And you will come and go at his bidding?''

"Why shouldn't we go?'' Fflergant asked, surprisingly defensive. "We've a decent respect for old people, here in these hills, though you might not think so!''

"I didn't mean that,'' Garanwyn protested, bewildered by the heat of Fflergant's response. "I only meant—''

"Of course you didn't,'' interposed Tryffin soothingly. "I know what you meant, and so does Fflergant—if he'll stop a moment and think. You thought it would be a nice show of respect if Madawc were to pay us a visit. And so it would be, and so he might—if we chose to send for him. But he's a kind of a godfather of ours, don't you see, and so we choose to treat him with a certain deference.''

Garanwyn did not see. He had a good idea what "a sort of a cousin'' meant (born on the wrong side of the blanket, no doubt) but "a kind of a godfather'' was rather puzzling and aroused his curiosity. He thought that he has asked enough impertinent questions for the time being, however, and so he held his tongue until they came to Dinas Dallben.

• • •

Meredydd fab Maelwas turned out to be a raffish old man with a wicked sense of humor, a grand style of exaggeration, and a vast store of highly improper stories. Garanwyn found it hard to believe that this amusing old reprobate was actually the father of his own gentle, pious mother and his equally demure and god-fearing Aunt Merewyn. Oddly enough, there was something about the old fellow's slight straight figure and fierce hazel-eyed stare that did remind Garanwyn of his cousin Ceilyn—whom he had always before regarded as a near perfect copy of Cuel of Celcynnon.

"I thought I wrote you lads to bring *both* my grandsons from Caer Cadwy with you," he scolded Fflergant and Tryffin, as he and the three boys sat, eating honey-and-oat cakes and sipping spiced wine, in his many-pillared hall.

"We did our best to convince him, Uncle," said Fflergant, putting up his feet and basking in the warmth of a roaring fire. "But it isn't the easiest thing in this world to tear Ceilyn away from something he imagines to be his duty."

Meredydd snorted. "And I suppose young Cynwas fab Anwas can't contrive to run his castle or his kingdom without the help of my grandson?"

"I can't imagine what would become of the Queen's household if Ceilyn did leave for any prolonged time," said Garanwyn, before either of the others could reply.

Meredydd poured himself another cup of wine. "Well, well, be that as it may," he said jovially. "Don't imagine that I'm not delighted to see you, with or without your cousin Ceilyn. But there is something I've been meaning to send to the lad. Perhaps you will see that he gets it?"

He sent one of the servants off to fetch it, and the man returned shortly with a small wooden coffer. Inside was a slender golden bracelet set with milky white sidhe-stones.

"It belonged to his grandmother—my betrothal gift to her, after our custom. As Ceilyn is the oldest grandson, I thought he might wish to present it to his wife."

"Is Ceilyn getting married?" Garanwyn had never heard of any betrothal, but sometimes these things were privately arranged while both parties were very young and not announced until the wedding was imminent.

"And why shouldn't he marry?" replied his grandfather, closing the box and handing it over to Garanwyn. "He's old enough that's certain. . . . Won his gold spurs years ago and has already made an important place for himself at court, so you tell me. It's time he found a wife if he hasn't already.

"Or is there something wrong with the boy?" he asked suspiciously. "He has none of his father's fool notions about celibacy, has he?"

Garanwyn did not need to look at Tryffin or Fflergant to see that the old man's question had amused them. "There is nothing wrong with Ceilyn," he replied loyally. "In fact . . . well, I do believe that he is in love with a certain young woman. Quite . . . quite a virtuous young lady, I have heard, but unfortunately otherwise unsuitable."

Meredydd scowled ferociously, reminding Garanwyn once again of Ceilyn, in one of his tempers. "We don't hold such notions here in the Hill Country. The grace of a prince of Tir Gwyngelli—even a prince two times removed—is held sufficient to elevate any wife he might choose for himself. And we believe in love-matches unless necessity absolutely dictates otherwise. But Ceilyn is his father's heir, whether Cuel wills it or not, and he needn't look out for a woman with property or marry to please his father.

"You had better take a message along with the bracelet," said Meredydd. "You tell Ceilyn: If he truly loves her, if the girl be virtuous, and he can win her, though Cuel mac Cadellin oppose the match, he can rely on *my* blessing at least."

The Good Folk took him beneath the Hill, even into the Hall of their King, and that was a fair place the like of which few mortals have ever seen. And there he was feasted and entertained for many days and nights it seemed to him, and the Folk of the Hill made merry. All save the Lord of the Barrow, who sat silently on his throne as one in the shadow of some great grief.

—*From* The Book of the White Cockerel

7.

Beneath the Hills

Wedding guests continued to arrive at Castell Maelduin. The groom's family came, and kinfolk from Cadir Ceri and Ifarion, and representatives of all the major family-tribes of Tir Gwyngelli. But the Lord and his family continued to watch in vain for the one guest they most desired to see: Manogan fab Menai, the Earl Marshall of Celydonn, the uncle of the bride. It appeared that Manogan—cool, cynical Manogan—had not summoned the courage to face his brother, the woman they had both courted, and a wedding, all at the same time.

Though Maelgwyn grieved for his brother's absence, he took pains to insure that his personal sorrow did not mar his guests' pleasure. He kept them occupied by day with diverse entertainments and every night he held a banquet where the dishes were all flavored with rare foreign spices, and the crystal-clear wine of the hill country flowed like water.

But Fflergant, Tryffin, and Garanwyn preferred to spend their days riding about the countryside, through the hills and valleys surrounding Castell Maelduin. They stopped to gossip with cottagers, broke bread with shepherds and goatherders, and introduced Garanwyn to all the customs of the Hillfolk.

If the Gwyngellach were a source of wonder and amusement to Garanwyn, he soon discovered that he was no less an object of curiosity to them. From the Princesses Cerridwen and Eisiwed, right down to the lowliest scullion in the kitchen or chance-met herdsman in the passes, everyone plied him with the most probing personal questions. In Gwyngelli, it seemed, one man's business was every man's business. It did not take Garanwyn long to see and appreciate the very real concern and heartfelt good-will behind all the questions.

So he learned to answer them good-naturedly. He ate and drank with the cottagers, accepting their offerings of bannocks and blue-tinted milk, white grapes and thyme-scented cheeses, and he heard himself replying over and over again that no, he had no geasa, really and truly not even a single geas—it was no longer customary in Rhianedd, where he was born, for the godparents to enter a prophetic trance at a christening and utter the terms of a geas or geasa like so many reverse blessings. From Fflergant and Tryffin, Garanwyn already knew all about these often bizarre and invariably inconvenient prohibitions, which nevertheless seemed to confer some sort of status on those they were attached to—hence the curiosity of the cottagers and their amazement on learning that their princes' young kinsman had none.

The two young princes, of course, had a variety of geasa, and these the cottagers were fond of reciting, along with the names of the godparents who had "bestowed" them: Never tell an outright untruth (Tryffin, by the grace of Meredydd fab Maelwas), do not insult a lady (Fflergant, the gift of his grandmother's brother), never enter a church by the left-hand door . . . wear blue on a holy day . . . eat cheese with shoemakers . . . throw a stone at a raven . . . take iron from a corpse. . . . Garanwyn had always wondered how his cousins managed to keep it all straight.

One day, Tryffin and Fflergant took him down into the fabled mines of Tir Gwyngelli, where few outlanders had ever been permitted to venture. Far beneath the surface of the earth, at the very heart of the Gwyngelli Hills, in dark passageways silent but for the steady drip of water and the distant tapping of a hammer, the miners initiated Garanwyn into the mysteries of their craft.

The miners of Tir Gwyngelli were unlike the down-trodden wretches who labored in the mines of the north. Proud men, they not only mined the ore but refined it as well, achieving a nearly alchemical purity, and they cut gems and polished them as skillfully as any jeweler.

The mines themselves were places of great beauty and mystery, a realm of underground rivers, glimmering veins of gold, and the secret fire of gemstones. Especially there were the sidhe-stones: luminous gems ranging in color from a semi-transparent milky white to a clear pure blue—not so hard or brilliant as diamonds, to be sure, but often possessing the power to ward off evil forces or malignant magic. The Clach Ghealach, which guarded the High King, was a sidhe-stone, and the legendary Clach Grian, though a gem of another sort, had been discovered somewhere in these very tunnels.

Another day, Garanwyn's kinsmen introduced him to Mael-gwyn's swordsmith, a squat broad-shouldered man with a pleasant, homely face and muscular forearms like a dwarf. He welcomed the boys into his smoky forge and spoke long concerning his trade, hinting that his craft, too, had its mysteries, secrets long forgotten but recently rediscovered. . . .

Garanwyn caught his breath. "Magic swords, do you mean? Enchanted blades, as in the old tales? And you say that such blades are forged right here?"

"Ah well . . . as to that, I may not say," replied the smith. "But this I will say, for the fact is well-known: There are lucky swords and unlucky swords—or, at least, blades that prove so for the men who wield them. Here in the Hidden Country, we believe that swords are fated even as men are. The trick, you see, is matching the sword to the man, lest their destinies conflict. When such a misfortunate combination occurs, the consequences for all concerned must be unhappy."

And Fflergant and Tryffin took Garanwyn exploring, as they had promised, among the caves and passages beneath Castell Maelduin. Down and down a wide stone staircase they went, Fflergant and Garanwyn bearing torches, Tryffin carrying a ring of heavy iron keys. Whenever they came to a landing there was a corridor on one or both sides, and Garanwyn saw other corridors branching off of these, a regular maze of passageways beneath the hill.

"Storerooms on this level," Tryffin said at the first and second landings. "Prisons, if my father had any prisoners or the heart to lock them away down here," he said at the third. The corridor on the fourth landing led to some ancient tombs, which they would visit on their way up. After the fourth landing, Tryffin said: "We don't use the caverns down here anymore. The dampness gets into things and spoils them."

Indeed, the air felt very damp now, the walls and the steps were slick with moisture. They had to go carefully here and the steps narrowed, forcing them to walk in single file.

The steps ended before a low wooden door set into the rock. Tryffin took out his keys and unlocked the door, stepping aside while Fflergant pushed it open and thrust his torch into the cavern on the other side, testing the air. When the torch continued to burn as brightly as ever, Fflergant stepped inside and the other boys followed him into a vast chamber.

And here it was at last, exactly as Garanwyn had heard it described a hundred times: the Hall of the Fairy King, with fair alcoves and benches carved from the living stone, a deep firepit near the far end of the chamber, capable of consuming whole trees, and the ceiling aglitter with veins of crystalline ores.

"Pyrite and marcasite, from which the alchemists extract their Green Vitriol—so Glastyn told me once," said Fflergant. "No, not gold and silver as the story goes. Still, the effect is pretty, don't you think?"

"It's splendid," Garanwyn said fervently. "And it must have been glorious in the old days, with banners and a fire and music and feasting . . . though I pity the squires and pages, for it's a long way from the kitchens."

He walked to the brink of the pit. "Terribly close and smoky must have been with a great fire blazing here."

"There is a shaft above the pit, a sort of fissure in the rock," replied Tryffin. "Where the smoke went after that, I couldn't tell you."

They skirted the pit and passed through a natural arch in the rock, into a smaller chamber. "And this is the chapel."

There was a sort of dais at one end of the room and a low stone table upon it, which might have been the altar, and behind that a shallow basin carved right into the rock. There were no benches or alcoves here, but many niches carved high in the walls, which might have been meant for candles or small statues.

"This place is old . . . old," said Garanwyn, looking around him in awe. "Older than the castle up above? Yes, I thought so.

Older than the oldest ruins at Caer Cadwy, even. And the people who worshipped here—they were pagans, weren't they?''

"Long ago, this must have been a place of pagan worship," Fflergant agreed. "But it was consecrated and used as a proper Christian chapel in our great-grandfather's day, if not earlier. We still use it sometimes on high holy days, bringing the candles and the vessels with us. The altar cloths would rot and the metals all tarnish if we left them here.

"It's a very holy place, though you might not think so to look at it now," he added. "People have experienced visions here. Tryffin had one, once, when he was a little lad."

"A vision—truly?" Garanwyn asked, eyeing his big, placid cousin with new respect. He had never imagined that Tryffin was the sort of person who might be granted visions.

"Ah well . . . it wasn't much of a vision," said Tryffin, obviously embarrassed. "Only a light above the altar, and I thought I heard music, very distant, very faint."

"Nevertheless," said Garanwyn. He lifted his torch in order to inspect the altar and the basin behind it. He supposed that served for a baptismal font when the chapel was in use—what it was *before* he did not like to speculate. "I never knew anyone who experienced holy ecstasies before. Except Ceilyn mac Cuel, the Christmas he was knighted."

"As to that," said Fflergant, leading the way back into the great hall. "If you fast all day and stay awake all night, on your knees down in the chapel . . . likely you will see visions, too. The wonder is, it's not more common."

"Maybe it is more common than we think," said Garanwyn choosing to ignore his sarcasm. "Perhaps some of the others *have* seen visions during the Vigil, only like Tryffin they are reluctant to talk about it. I know Ceilyn was, and only told me about his own experience because I asked him."

"A wonder you lived to tell about it—asking personal questions of Ceilyn man Cuel," said Fflergant. "A wonder he didn't take your head off—speaking of holy miracles."

The day of the wedding finally arrived. Up in the tower bed chamber they shared with Garanwyn, Fflergant and Tryffin dressed themselves in a style befitting the sons of Gwyngelli Lord—for naturally their father, acting with typical foresight had seen that suitable garments cut to their measure were in the hands of his tailors and seamstresses long before his sons arrived at Castell Maelduin.

Garanwyn, whose own preparations were comparatively simple, sat cross-legged at the foot of his bed and watched his cousins put on their shirts of embroidered linen, their short wool breeches, and high kidskin boots. Over these, they slipped on long tunics of heavy crimson velvet and girded them with belts of massive gold links.

"I think I shall feel out of place," said Garanwyn, as they fastened on wristguards and pectorals and other pieces of heavy old-fashioned jewelry until it seemed impossible they could bear so much weight. "If everyone dresses like this for a wedding . . ."

"The lowlanders dress very much as you do. I expect they'll think you highly fashionable," replied Fflergant. "And for the festivities afterward, we'll change back into our other things. All this is much too heavy for dancing."

"Ah yes, the dancing . . . I thought, perhaps, you had your fill of the dancing by now." For Fflergant and his brother always contrived to be on hand in the evenings when the dancing began.

"You don't imagine—you don't really suppose that we do it all for our own pleasure?" Tryffin asked.

"You mean to say that you don't?"

"How can you think it?" Fflergant threw a fur-lined mantle over his shoulder and fastened it with a golden brooch of intricate design. "We do it for the sake of the young ladies, and for no other reason."

"For the sake of the young ladies?"

"Oh, aye. For the sake of the young ladies. All of them so eager to learn the new dances from the court of the High King— and who is to teach them, if not ourselves?"

As a final touch, the two young princes set golden circlets on their heads, and then they were ready to escort their sister the church.

The church, a venerable edifice built of the native stone, was located in a grassy valley about an hour's ride from Castell Maelduin. "Our folk have always been wed here," said Garanwyn's grandfather. "Long before Castell Maelduin with its grand chapels was ever built."

As far as Garanwyn could see, the church and the castle were approximately contemporary, so he wondered if the old man was exaggerating for the sake of a good story, or whether this blue-green valley had been the site of an earlier church, or even a pagan temple like the ancient chapel in the hill. Still, it was a lovely, peaceful spot, and he could understand why the Princess Eisiwed had chosen to be married there.

The ceremony, conducted by an earnest young friar, was brief, solemn, and simple. The bride was appropriately radiant in crimson and cloth of gold, and the groom, an undistinguished distant cousin, seemed properly dazzled by his good fortune. They exchanged rings and vows, drank from a single goblet. Then Eisiwed knelt, while her groom took a circlet of mayflowers wrought in gold and placed it on her brow.

Afterward, outside the church, a fierce-looking old cleric in the white habit and cowl of some religious order Garanwyn did not recognize, pronounced a final blessing over the bride and groom, and a little girl, also in white, presented them each with a sheaf of wheat bound with scarlet ribbons. Then most of the guests mounted up and followed the Princess and her husband back to Castell Maelduin for the wedding feast. But Garanwyn lingered by the church, looking for Fflergant and Tryffin, who had not departed with the others.

As they were nowhere in sight, he went back inside, expecting to find them there. Then he heard voices outside one of the windows. He found them behind the church, talking to the old man in white.

As Garanwyn watched, they knelt humbly before the holy man, beseeching him to bestow his blessing. For a moment, his wrinkled hands hovered over their two shining golden heads, then he touched them lightly and with evident affection. Fflergant and Tryffin rose gracefully to their feet, each taking one of the old man's hands and reverently kissing it. Garanwyn was as surprised as he was moved, for he had never before considered his cousins to be particularly pious young men.

Back at Castell Maelduin, the feast lasted for hours, and the dancing even longer. Garanwyn was ready to drop from exhaustion long before the entertainment ended. He could only retire to the sidelines with his grandfather and admire the energy of the others—particularly of Fflergant and Tryffin, who, shedding their weighty royal robes, not only participated in all the ancient dances but seemed bent on teaching *all* the dances they had learned at Cynwas's court to every young lady present.

• • •

In the morning, Garanwyn rose pale and heavy-eyed, to a beating of rain upon the windows and the howling of the wind around the tower. A wild storm raged over Castell Maelduin all that day and the next, and there could be no thought of departing as he had originally intended.

"We lose a day or two for rain—but you allowed for that at the beginning." Fflergant tried to cheer him up on the evening of the second day. "Chances are it will be clear by morning. These storms that come up so suddenly seldom last long. And we can make up any lost time down in the lowlands."

The balefire was burning low, scarcely more than glowing embers by now, and the girl sank to the ground exhausted, while the frenzy that had animated her earlier dissipated. She tucked her bare feet under her skirt, shivered in the chill night air. It was over now, there was nothing she could do but wait until the powers she had tried to summon chose to manifest themselves.

From far in the distance came a thunder of hooves, the baying of hounds. It was May Eve and the night of the full moon all in one, and the Wild Hunt was out—perhaps coming her way! She sprang to her feet, elated and terrified at the same time. Only one mortal dared to ride abroad with the Old Powers between the hours of sunset and dawn, only one man so careless of his life and his immortal soul. . . .

The Hunt was upon her almost before she knew it, the red-eared fairy hounds swarming all around her, panting and whimpering and tumbling over each other in their excitement. And he was there as well: Manogan fab Menai on his chestnut stallion, exhilarated by the wild ride, having finally outrun his anger, but still feeling reckless, still ready for anything.

He silenced the hounds with a single command and with a nod of his head banished those other, darker, figures who had followed behind him. He took in the whole scene at a glance: the barefoot girl with the charms and fetishes hanging around her neck, the remains of her fire, and the charred bones lying among the ashes.

"An odd place and an odd time and an odd circumstance to encounter the King's step-daughter," he laughed.

"But not to meet a prince of Tir Gwyngelli," she countered breathlessly, determined to put a bold face on the whole thing. But then a note of pleading crept into her voice. "You'll tell no one what you've seen here?"

Manogan did not reply at once. He looked her over from top to toe, and she was uncomfortably aware of her dirty feet and

*the sweat-soaked gown clinging to her body, and her auburn hair
tumbling down around her shoulders, damp with sweat, too, and
curling in little tendrils.*

*"I'll hold my tongue," he said (only half in jest), "for a
price."*

*And Diaspad, understanding him very well—for all that she
was only fifteen years old and still a virgin—lowered her eyes
to hide her sudden fierce elation, and replied softly, "That, my
Lord, I would give you for the asking."*

8.

All Hallows Eve

In her secret room above the kitchens, the Princess Diaspad
sharpened her knife in preparation for the Samhain sacrifice. It
was a beautiful piece of work, that knife: an ornate golden hilt
and a wicked ten-inch blade of the very finest steel. As Diaspad
vigorously applied the whetstone, tiny sparks ignited and flew
in all directions.

On the other side of that sable-draped chamber, Calchas
perched on a high stool, watching his mother's preparations with
mounting misgivings. Finally, he could contain himself no
longer. "That's steel, isn't it? I thought you said it was forbidden
to enter a sacred circle bearing cold iron?"

"You misunderstood me," said Diaspad, testing the edge of
the blade with the ball of her thumb. "I only meant that it would
be dangerous on that particular occasion to enter the circle uninvited bearing objects of power. But iron is permitted and has
its proper uses during certain ceremonies."

She put the whetstone down and gestured toward a cabinet
against the wall, a cupboard embellished with leering gargoyles
and strange grimacing masks. "Would you fetch me those two
flasks, dear boy? The silver and the bronze, upon the top shelf."
Calchas hastened to obey her.

"Do you know?" said the Princess. "It seems to me that you
have been asking a good many questions just recently. Is something troubling you?"

"Well," Calchas admitted, "there is something. You keep
telling me that blood always demands payment in blood and that

the price of a prince is another prince. So it seems to me that this bargain you intend to strike . . . well, don't you think it possible that the Lady might be . . . a tiny bit offended?''

"My precious boy,'' crooned the Princess, removing the stopper from one of the flasks and sprinkling water upon the blade. "One does not *bargain* with the Mother Goddess. One offers, and one sues for favor. But if one *were* to strike a bargain . . . do you not realize that Forgoll's bull is a prince—nay, a very king among beasts? Also, I intend to offer you to the Goddess along with the bull.

"No, no, no—not the way you imagine,'' she went on, "I do wish you wouldn't jump about so. There is a way that I might give you to the Goddess and keep you for myself at the same time.

"Ordinarily, there are two parts to the ceremony. The second is the consecration. After the sacrifice, those who are about to be initiated into the mysteries are presented to the Lady and anointed in blood. In ancient times, chieftains used also to send their sons or nephews to be consecrated. But at the Great Sacrifice, the sacrifice of the twenty-seventh year, only the heir of a king or a ruling prince, or the Glas-tann's chosen successor, may take part in the consecration.

"Cynwas has yet to name his heir, but you, my sweet Calchas, shall play that role tonight. That will benefit you (if she accepts you) and at the same time will offer something to the Goddess in return for the lives of Maelgwyn's sons. Such a precious little consort for the lady you shall make. . . . And surely, Calchas, surely you agree that you are worth *both* of Maelgwyn's sons.''

"Yes . . .'' Calchas agreed. "In a general way, yes. Is that holy water you are using?''

"It wasn't blessed by any sort of priest, if that is what you mean, but it did come from a sacred well,'' said the Princess, reaching for the second flask. She removed the stopper and poured a few drops of oil of bitumen upon the blade.

"The thing is . . .'' Calchas began.

"Yes?'' said his mother.

"The thing is . . . supposing she doesn't agree? Supposing she doesn't accept me? I mean, she's hardly likely to give us a polite 'No, I thank you' and leave it at that. Offending one of the Old Powers can be a chancy business, I should imagine, and from what you tell me, she can be terrible in her wrath.''

He began to pace restlessly around the chamber. "I can't help thinking about those people we saw at Midsummer . . . all those cripples and lepers and that dreadful old woman with the two twisted crones attending her. And the Goddess—you taught me that she brings forth life as the blessed Lady Celedon, and takes it back again as Donwy, the Dark Mother. But Celedon brings forth not only the strong and healthy but the sickly, the lame, and the deformed as well. And it is the Dark Mother, in her mercy, who grants them respite in death, offers rest to the old and weary. . . . That's right, isn't it?"

"Yes," admitted his mother, still rubbing oil into the knife blade. "She can be cruel as well as kind in all her guises."

She turned toward the tiny brazier containing charcoal and incense which was filling the room with a sweet, heavy fragrance. Three times she passed the blade through the smoke, subjecting it to a mixture of fire and air, just as she had previously primed the blade with earth and water.

"Well," concluded Calchas, "I wouldn't like to be struck down in my youth, that's all. I wouldn't like to fall victim to some loathsome disease."

"But why should you?" said his mother soothingly. "A bonny boy like you?"

"But you said, in the twenty-seventh year only a prince or the heir of a prince may be offered. And we're not exactly certain, when you come right down to it, that I'm any sort of a prince at all."

"Of course we are certain," said Diaspad, laying down her knife, taking his cold, clammy hand and drawing him near. "You are my precious son, and I am a princess of Celydonn."

"Yes, but there you are," protested Calchas. "Cynwas granted you that title as a courtesy only, and that's more than Anwas, our supposed father, ever did during his lifetime."

"We have been through this before, have we not?" said Diaspad. " 'As the child can never be unquestioningly accepted as mine, let her be Erim's and legitimate.' That is what he told my mother, and being a man of somewhat tiresome principles, he abided by that decision all the days of his life."

"So Morfudd says," Calchas persisted. "But what if she lies? She treated you like the dust beneath her feet in her days of power, and only promoted this other story when your star had risen and she needed a friend at court. You didn't trust her entirely then, when you were young and presumably more gullible—why should you trust her now that you've grown so much wiser?

"I admit that it has always been convenient to believe her up until now," concluded Calchas. "But with so much at stake, dare we take the old bitch's word for it?"

Diaspad did not answer immediately. She smothered the burning incense, returned the flasks to their cabinet, busied herself tidying up the clutter of candlestubs, ashes, and bloody entrails which her previous activities had left scattered around the room. Calchas eyed her warily, retreated back into his corner.

"Well, Calchas," she said at last, "there's a little something about *your* father that I've been meaning to tell you. No, not Corfil of Mochdreff, as you've always supposed. Another man, a man who gives you a very good claim by blood, if not legitimate descent, to the throne of Celydonn."

Calchas sat down upon his stool. "If you're about to tell me that Cynwas . . . I think I shall be sick, I really think I shall."

"Nonsense," snapped his mother. "You'll do nothing of the sort. And of course Cynwas is not your father—who puts such nasty ideas into your head? *Think* about it, Calchas, give the matter a little rational thought."

Her uncharacteristic spate of industry came to an abrupt halt. "Think the matter over, my bonny dark-eyed boy, and you should have no difficulty guessing the name of your father."

That same morning found Tryffin, Fflergant, and Garanwyn entering the gates of Dyffynog, a prosperous little town in southern Walgan, known for its fine craftsmen, canny merchants, and hospitable inns. Indeed, the first thought in the minds of Fflergant and Tryffin that morning was to seek out one of those inns and stop for a second breakfast. But Garanwyn, impatient to reach home, only consented to enter the town in quest of provisions, which were running low. Accordingly, the three boys headed for that part of the town where bakers and butchers, grocers and costermongers might be found.

Yet it was Garanwyn, as they threaded their way through the crooked little cobblestone streets of the town, who unexpectedly called a halt. He stopped in front of a tiny shop which boasted a newly thatched roof, freshly painted shutters, and (incongruously) a worn and faded black boot suspended from the roof-beam out over the street. "Gwenlliant's shoes!"

Fflergant and Tryffin stared blankly at the boot. "Gwenlliant's shoes," said Garanwyn again. "I promised her a new pair of shoes. All the time we were in Tir Gwyngelli, the thought never crossed my mind. Selfish, that's what I am!"

"This does appear to be a cobbler's shop," agreed Fflergant. "And I do believe that shoes can be bought already made up, but anything fine enough for Gwenlliant to wear . . . ?"

"He might have something that will serve," said Garanwyn, tossing him the reins. "Something gaudy if not well-made, to amuse her until I can buy something better."

He dismounted and opened the door of the shop. Inside, it was bright, cheerful, and uncluttered. Sunshine poured in through both windows, the floorboards had been swept and scrubbed until they were almost white, and the shelves were surprisingly bare. Garanwyn hesitated on the threshold. The shop was too new, too clean, and too empty—he did not think he would find what he was looking for here.

Then he spotted the shoes. Twelve pairs of shoes lined up on a shelf beneath a window, such shoes as Garanwyn had never seen before. Wonderful shoes of embossed leather in rich colors, stitched with thread of silver and gold. He closed the door behind him, crossed the room, and picked up a pair of little blue shoes.

Shoes as blue as a summer sky, with pointed toes and diamond buckles—and who in a little town like Dyffynog could buy such shoes as these?

"I crave your pardon, young man," said a voice behind him—a voice with a hint of Draighenach accent—"but those shoes are already spoken for."

With a guilty start, Garanwyn dropped the shoes and whirled round to see who had spoken. A red-haired man in a leather apron was standing just inside the back door of the shop.

"I beg your pardon," said Garanwyn breathlessly. "Are you . . . well, I mean to say, are you the cobbler?" For there was something in the man's bearing that was unlike any maker or mender of shoes the boy had ever seen before.

"The shoemaker . . . aye. And you'll be wanting a pair of shoes, no doubt." He bent and picked up the shoes which Garanwyn had dropped. "Shoes for a child, perhaps?"

"My little sister," said Garanwyn, and told the man exactly what he wanted.

"You're in luck, young man," said the shoemaker, ushering the boy into the little room at the back of the shop. "For see here: I've the very thing you are looking for."

There on his workbench lay exactly the pair Garanwyn had promised his sister: scarlet leather with soft grey miniver to line them, and a pair of tiny golden buckles. One shoe was nearly finished, the other cut out and waiting to be stitched. "But surely," said Garanwyn, "surely these shoes are spoken for as well."

"Well, yes, in a manner of speaking," said the shoemaker, fingering the scarlet leather. "They were meant for the Mayor's little daughter, a gift from the son of a certain wealthy merchant. There was a match in the making, you understand, most desirable for both families. But the fathers have quarreled, and so the merchant's son must look elsewhere for his bride. And there is little chance, I am thinking, he'll find another young lady with feet so dainty. The shoes are yours, young man, if you think they will suit your sister." And he named a price so low that Garanwyn was astonished.

The boy looked wistfully at the shoes. "I am expected home, you see. I really can't stay in Dyffynog, for even a day."

"The shoes can be finished before I sit down to my dinner," said the shoemaker, and Garanwyn, brightening, reached into his purse for the price of the shoes.

Outside in the street, he found Fflergant and Tryffin patiently awaiting him. "Well, that's fine," said Tryffin, when Garanwyn told him about the shoes. "A pity to disappoint the little dear with the shoes so nearly finished. But since we are to wait . . we passed what looked to be a good inn along the way. Tha second breakfast we were thinking of earlier—no reason that can see not to stop for it now. Tripe and sausage sounds goo to me."

Garanwyn laughed and agreed. "Very well, why not? Com to think of it, I'm hungry myself."

The inn, which had attracted Tryffin with an atmosphere good ale and roasting meat, provided them with a cozy priva parlor, a roaring fire, and an excellent meal of tripe and sausag eggs and ale.

Between mouthfuls, Garanwyn told his cousins about t

shoemaker, so mysteriously above his present station, and his amazing shoes. "Blue-azure, that's what they call the dye. I thought it was something of a lost art," said Tryffin.

"Perhaps they've rediscovered it," replied Garanwyn. "Your father's swordsmith told me that many craft secrets were lost, during the bad years before Anwas was crowned even in Tir Gwyngelli where most things remained unchanged. And he also told me that most of the lost arts came to light again after the coming of the High King."

Tryffin and Fflergant both smiled to hear him speak the title which only the Gwyngellach still used. "Well, anyway," Garanwyn finished sheepishly, "during the reigns of Anwas and Cynwas."

Tryffin served himself another portion of sausage and boiled eggs. "I wonder," he said soberly, "how much knowledge will be lost all over again, if Cynwas does nothing to halt our present decline?"

"Oh, but that's all over now," said Garanwyn. "Ever since the King and Queen patched up their quarrel, everything has gone back to the way it should be."

"Life at court is simpler and pleasanter," agreed Fflergant. "But elsewhere? This is a charming little town, but even here I noticed that too many of the shops were boarded up. And as for some of the roads we've traveled—not precisely what they should be, are they? Things aren't right in a number of places, and they'll be far worse if Cynwas doesn't wake up and take notice."

"You sound like . . . no, I won't say it," said Garanwyn, pushing away his plate. "You would hardly be flattered by the comparison."

"Ceilyn mac Cuel," said Fflergant, with obvious disgust. "We always seem to come back to Ceilyn—and I hoped we could enjoy our little holiday without him. But it happens in the present instance that we agree with him entirely.

"And not just because *he* says so, mind you! Our father and our uncle are of exactly the same opinion."

When the time came for Garanwyn to return to the shoemaker's shop, dinner was on the table and there was no budging either of his cousins. "Pease porridge, bacon, roast goose, and eels—I'd not forgo a meal like that to meet the most gifted man in Celydonn," said Fflergant.

"Oh, very well," said Garanwyn, and left by himself.

He did not return for over an hour, by which time the others had finished their meal and, taking their mugs of ale with them, settled down in comfortable armchairs by the fire. Garanwyn came in flourishing the shoes and offered them to Fflergant for inspection.

"Very neat," said Fflergant, passing the slippers over for Tryffin to examine. "You can hardly see the stitches, they're so tiny.

"A pity he took so long about it," he added with a yawn. "It will be dark in a few more hours. There is little point in going any farther today. But this is an excellent inn, and I propose that we spend the night right here."

But Garanwyn was more eager than ever to press on toward Caer Cadwy. "And lose another day? I promised Gwenlliant we would be home by the fourth at the latest. You said we could make up lost time in the lowlands, but we never did. It is my fault, I know, that we wasted most of today—but the horses have rested and so have we—why not travel part of the night?"

This daring suggestion, which might have appealed to Fflergant's sense of adventure another time, found no favor now. "You must be mad. Have you forgotten? Tonight is All Hallows Eve, and who but a fool would venture out after dark?"

"I hadn't thought of that. Still, if we carried lanterns, and charms and crosses . . ." Garanwyn suggested half-heartedly.

Surprisingly, Tryffin took a more optimistic view. "I don't know that we would be in any great danger. If we were anyplace else: the Rhianeddi Highlands, for instance, or the Coblynau Hills—even parts of Gwyngelli—I'd think twice, even three times, about traveling after dark. But this is staid, respectable Walgan, after all, and nothing extraordinary ever happens here, not even on Hallowe'en."

Fflergant was still reluctant to leave his cozy seat by the fire, but Garanwyn was so pressingly eager to be on the way and Tryffin so confident that there was nothing to fear, that at last he allowed them to persuade him.

"For Gwenlliant's sake, to avoid causing her any unnecessary worry—very well," he said, rising from his safe, comfortable chair. "But if we run into witches and hobgoblins all along the way, if things that don't even have names dog our trail the whole night long—you can't say that I didn't warn you!"

Then the maiden came back into the room with four and twenty damsels attending her, all clad in yellow silk with flowers in their hair, as though they were attired for a wedding.

"Now," said the magician, "you must tell me which one is my daughter, or your life will be forfeit." In his heart, the father was certain that Garanhir Bach could never perform this task; then the magician would not have to give him any of the things he had promised.

And Garanhir Bach was bewildered and knew not how to choose between them, for each maiden was so like to all the rest in face and in form that it was impossible to tell one from the other.

— From The Black Book of Tregalen

9.

Disguises and Deceptions

A long mirror in a gilded frame hung in the corridor outside the Queen's bedchamber. Ceilyn looked into that mirror and he did not like what he saw: the wavy reflection of a scowling young man in fancy dress, a young man unaccustomed to (and therefore embarrassed by) such light-minded fripperies.

He slipped a green half mask over his face, and secured the ribbons behind his head. Then he frowned at his reflection again. Some odd impulse had originally prompted Ceilyn to adopt the guise of a grey wolf for the Hallowe'en revels, but out of regard for the Earl Marshall he had soon abandoned that idea, choosing, instead, the green tunic, scarlet cape, and golden bells of a conjurer.

Ceilyn continued to study his own image. As a disguise, the half mask accomplished little; except from a distance he would be instantly identifiable: the cheeks so smooth, the posture so rigid, the curling brown hair that would *not* lie flat. But confusion rather than disguise was his real purpose and that would be served well enough if everyone recognized him the instant he entered the Hall.

Ceilyn believed that the Princess Diaspad would be leaving the Hallowe'en revels sometime that evening, in order to carry out some dark, secret design. Just precisely the nature of the mischief Diaspad planned, Ceilyn had only the dimmest notion; certainly Teleri had said nothing to enlighten him since the day they discovered the barrow down in the meadow. He had said far too much on that occasion and Teleri had retaliated by saying very little ever since. But whatever scheme Diaspad was hatching, Ceilyn intended to be on hand and prevent her if he could.

With this in mind, he had taken steps to conceal his own departure by providing his squire, young Gofan—whose height, build, and coloring closely resembled Ceilyn's own—with a nearly identical costume. He had not deemed it necessary to take the boy into his confidence. (*"If I am to make a bloody fool of myself,"* Ceilyn had growled, tossing the second costume down on Gofan's bed, *"there's no reason why you shouldn't do so as well!"*) but he hoped that a second conjurer, by his very presence, might serve to deceive and confuse anyone who made it his or her business to observe the comings and goings of Ceilyn mac Cuel.

Ceilyn's reverie came to a sudden end when someone threw open the door and the Queen and her attendants filed into the corridor. Not that it was possible, at a glance, for Ceilyn to guess which lady was the Queen and which others the young women who attended her, for all were masked and some had concealed their hair under fanciful headdresses, and (he suspected) there had been an exchange of gowns as well. Only Gwenlliant, a charming little gargoyle in grey satin and a full face mask, her cobweb-colored hair flying loose around her, was instantly recognizable.

No one said a word but all waited expectantly for Ceilyn to make the first move, from which he understood that they were testing him, challenging him to pick out Sidonwy for himself.

A plump young woman in a red gown and mask stifled a giggle and Ceilyn had no difficulty in identifying her as Megwen from Perfudd. Two other girls he also quickly eliminated: the one too thin, the other too short. But to distinguish between Fand, Finola, and the Queen was a formidable task.

Ceilyn hesitated, looking from one lady to the next. The woman on the left, wearing silk flowers in her dark hair and a gown and a mask the color of ripe wheat, with a self-satisfied smile hovering at the corner of her mouth, must be Finola, who disliked him most cordially and would undoubtedly be pleased to see him fail. But the other two—one in black and silver, the other in a gown of sea-green silk embroidered with pearls, a crown fashioned of seashells encircling her brow—were perfectly poised and expressionless, giving nothing away.

He was about to confess himself baffled, when the lady in the sea-colored gown moved, and Ceilyn, without really knowing what in that tiny flicker of movement had betrayed her, knew Sidonwy beyond all doubting. He stepped forward confidently, executed his most graceful bow, and kissed the Queen's hand.

The young ladies murmured their approval, the Queen laughed delightedly, and Gwenlliant clapped her hands together, exclaiming, "I *told* you he could do it!"

Ceilyn smiled in spite of himself, understanding that the jest had not been intended to humiliate him after all. He offered his arm to Sidonwy; she took it, and allowed him to lead her down the winding stairs.

In the Hall, preparations for the revel were still in progress. Brawny serving men were hauling in great wooden tubs and filling them with water, and the little pages followed after them wearing sacks full of apples and pears. Over by the fireplace, Gofan and another youth emptied a keg of wine into an enormous copper pot.

Ceilyn escorted the Queen to the dais and saw to it that she was comfortably seated, then he turned to survey the Hall. What he saw, he did not like. The drapes had already been drawn and the torches lit, but the servants were still bringing in branched candlesticks and filling them with red and orange tapers. Scented candles, he thought, and felt his stomach give a sickening lurch. Already, the air was as thick and sweet as honey.

The shrouded windows, the strange candles, the sinister masks worn by some of the servants, all created a disquieting effect. "Before God," he said, under his breath, "this place looks better suited to a Black Mass than to any Christian entertainment!"

He stalked across the room, poured a goblet of wine and tasted it, then brought it back to the Queen, his eyes, all the while, searching every corner and shadow in the Hall for Teleri. He could not find her. But perhaps she had stationed herself outside the Princess Diaspad's rooms, and would not appear in the hall until Diaspad did.

The Princess arrived late, in a feathered gown and a golden mask and headdress fashioned in imitation of some great bird of prey, which covered her face and hair almost completely and might have succeeded in disguising her entirely, were it not for those grotesque gilded fingernails which she had tried, unsuccessfully, to bring into fashion. By that time, the Hall had filled with revelers, and Ceilyn found it difficult to stay near the Princess.

She was surrounded by a protective circle of dwarfs and wildmen, whose physical eccentricities no costume could hide, and she was surprisingly active, drinking and dancing with unaccustomed abandon, in ceaseless motion from one part of the room to another.

The evening wore on, and still there was no sign of Teleri, no hint of her presence. Everyone was growing muddled and giddy from too much wine and dancing. Ceilyn felt a little light-headed himself, with the heat and the press of so many bodies, the cloying perfume of the candles. He headed for the door, where he stumbled into Gwenlliant and Finola.

"Time for bed, Cousin?" he asked, as he righted himself and the child. She removed her mask and held up her face for a good night kiss—a sadly drawn little face, heavy-eyed and listless. "Haven't you been sleeping well?" he asked, trying to remember if she had looked so, earlier in the day.

The little girl sighed. "I sleep. But I have bad dreams."

"Nonsense," said Finola impatiently. "You know that can be so! No one has nightmares at Caer Cadwy."

But Ceilyn, remembering what Teleri had said about prophetic dreams, felt a chill of apprehension, there in that overheated room. "Bad dreams? About what . . . about whom?"

"She worries about her brother, though he's not expected home for days," said Finola. "Of course everyone tells her there is nothing to fear. Garanwyn is with Fflergant and Tryffin. How could he be safer?"

How indeed? thought Ceilyn, dropping a kiss on Gwenlliant's cold cheek. "Sleep well and dream sweetly," he said aloud, as watching her leave the Hall he formed a silent prayer that it might be so.

Someone sneezed violently behind him, and Ceilyn spun around to find that he was face to face and at close quarters with the Princess Diaspad for the first time that evening. An uncharacteristically disheveled Diaspad, he realized. She was just tucking a loose strand of hair back under her headdress—dark brown hair, not auburn—with a hand all smudged with some bright substance. Possibly face paint, for the too-red mouth under the vicious golden beak was grotesquely smeared.

Ceilyn cursed himself for a fool. Mask or no mask, he ought to have seen through this deception long before, ought to have been on the lookout for some substitution from the very beginning. And where, now that he came to think of it, were Calchas, Derry, and Morc? Though they might be anywhere among the masked revelers, they were certainly not in attendance on the supposed Princess.

As for Teleri . . . the full extent of his folly was finally revealed to him. Teleri was not here and had never intended to be.

He pushed his way through the crush of revelers to the dais. On a stand between the thrones stood Lord Dyffryn's curious gift to the King. A glance at the timepiece told Ceilyn that more than an hour remained before midnight—not too late, then, for him to overtake events before they left him hopelessly behind.

The courtyard was cool and dark, the air blessedly pure after the heat and the cloying scents in the Hall. He headed first for his own room, where he discarded his mask and baldric of bells, girded on his swordbelt, and reversed the gaudy scarlet cape so that the darker lining was outermost. Then he ran downstairs and hurried toward the Wizard's Tower.

When he knocked at Teleri's door a few minutes later, he was relieved to hear a bolt sliding aside and watch the door inch cautiously open.

"Oh . . . Ceilyn," said Teleri blankly. "I didn't . . . I didn't expect to see you."

"No," he replied, folding his arms. "I don't suppose that you did. You thought I would be out of the way, all evening, watching Prescelli masquerade as the Princess. But *you* guessed exactly what she would do, and never said a word to me."

As he had wedged his foot between the door and the frame, she had little choice but to step back and let him enter. "It seemed the obvious thing for her to do—especially as the masked ball was her own idea. But it was only a guess. I couldn't be certain.''

"And yet," he said, closing the door and leaning back against it with his arms folded across his chest, "your guesses are always remarkably good—as I have reason to know—and you might have given me the benefit of this one. But perhaps you can tell me where the Princess Diaspad is right now?''

"Well, not just at the moment. But I think I know where she will be at midnight.''

Ceilyn frowned. Ideas were beginning to form in his mind, ideas he did not like at all. "Down by the burial mound performing some heathen ritual. And you were planning to go down there without me. Why?''

"You had made other plans. . . . How was I to know that your plans were not better than mine?''

It occurred to Ceilyn that this air of vague bewilderment, though undoubtedly a habit by now, was also a damned convenient way to fend off embarrassing questions. No doubt it worked very well with those who thought her simple or addle-witted, but he had come to know her better than that.

"And how," he asked, "were you planning to get out of the castle? Or did you imagine they would pass you at the Main Gate, tonight of all nights, without asking some awkward questions?''

Teleri shook her head. "No, of course not. I did think about the steps on the seaward side—the way the Princess will take most likely—but after the incident of the letter and the ring, don't suppose she will leave the postern unguarded behind her.'

"And that leaves . . . what, as an alternative? I *will* be accompanying you, by the way!''

"I explored the ruins on the northern side this morning," she said, picking up her cloak and fastening it on. "There is a place where the earthworks stand no more than ten feet high and the slope of the hill on the other side is not steep. We can climb over the ramparts there, and then down to the path below. And there are no guards to spot us, up on the northern wall.''

In fact, the walkway atop that wall had been rendered inaccessible years ago, as a courtesy to Glastyn, who liked privacy in his garden.

"No guards to catch sight of us from the northern wall. But what about down at the Main Gate?" said Ceilyn.

"The guards at the gate are there to watch the road," said Teleri. "They rarely even look in the direction of the ruins."

Ceilyn thought that over. "But there is one thing you have forgotten. We have to pass right by the gatehouse in order to enter the ruins on that side. The guards *do* take some heed of activities down in the outer courtyard."

"Yes, but there is another way to enter the ruins," said Teleri. She pushed aside the clothes chest at the foot of her bed, revealing a wooden door set into the floor.

"God's life!" exclaimed Ceilyn. "A secret passage, and I never guessed."

"Not really a secret passage," said Teleri, pushing the bolt aside and lifting the door. "Only a staircase leading down to the ruins below. There are similar steps beneath the Scriptorium, though I don't suppose the monks ever have cause to use them." She picked up a candle to light her way down the stairs. "There are many passages and rooms and stairways at Caer Cadwy which no one ever uses—but few of them were meant to be secret."

"And you are familiar with them all, I'll wager," said Ceilyn. "No wonder you are able to move about so swiftly, and usually unseen. And if I had been a few minutes later," he muttered, as she disappeared into the hole in the floor, "I would have missed you altogether." The thought that she might still contrive to slip away from him sent Ceilyn hastily down the narrow staircase after her.

Already, the curve of the stairwell hid her from view, but when he reached the bottom, he found Teleri waiting for him. She had placed her candle on a ledge above the door and was struggling to open it.

"Locked?" he said.

"I've unlocked it," she said. "It must be stuck; it's so damp down here." She stepped aside and allowed Ceilyn to try the door.

A few tugs and the door yielded. The rusted hinges creaked and the door swung open. A blast of air, colder but drier, rushed in to meet them.

Ceilyn stepped across the threshold, looked warily around him. Desolation spread in all directions: shattered towers, fragmented walls leaning at crazy angles, the smoke-blackened shells of lesser buildings.

Teleri spoke behind him. "You've never been down here before?"

"Only on the western side. Of course, I've seen some of this from above, but I never imagined the extent . . ."

"Yes," she said softly. "Down here the battle seems very real. Gandwy with his magical engines, and Siawn and his men with only their swords and their courage to arm them. It was somewhere near here that Siawn died."

They stood for a moment, thinking of Siawn fab Sarannon, last of Cynwal Mawr's royal line—if you did not count Dechtire's unborn baby—who had rallied the tattered remnants of his cousin's army and taken them back to Caer Cadwy for a last, desperate stand. Though already weakened by a dozen grievous wounds, Siawn had continued to resist when resistance was useless, and died, at the age of eighteen, unaware that he had been King of Celydonn for seven days.

His friends had later recovered Siawn's body and buried him with honor, and bards still sang of his heroic deeds against the army of the Warlock Lord, but most of the men who fought beside him had not fared so well. Their bones still lay scattered in the wreckage, unshriven, unnamed, and all but forgotten.

Thinking of that, Ceilyn felt his skin crawl. Had he been a wolf at that moment, his hackles would have risen. No ghosts walked at Caer Cadwy, thanks to the magic of Glastyn and the Clach Ghealach, but Ceilyn thought that the unhallowed dead slept lightly here in the moonlit ruins, that they lay restless and malicious beneath the broken stones.

"You need not fear them," said Teleri, guessing his thoughts. "No one who died here has any reason to resent us."

"Reason enough," said Ceilyn. "We're alive and they are dead. Reason enough."

Standing beside him, half in moonlight, half in shadow, shivering a little in the chill night air, Teleri seemed no more substantial than a ghost herself. "It is a lie, I think, that the dead hate the living. We are their children, after all."

"Perhaps," said Ceilyn. He looked around him. "Where do we go now?"

Teleri extended an arm, pointing the way. "There is a door in that wall over there—can you see it?—and steps leading down to the next level. If we head north from there, we'll come to a section of the outer ramparts which has never been repaired.''

"And if we are spotted, just by chance, scaling those ramparts?'' asked Ceilyn. "We'll be well within bowshot if anyone at the gatehouse decides to shoot.''

"We will have to hope that we are not spotted. Or, if we are, that the guards won't waste their arrows on anyone climbing *out* of the castle.''

"And coming back?'' Ceilyn asked, but Teleri did not answer.

Cautiously, they descended the broken staircase, crawled over the wreckage and through the tangled weeds, and reached the outer ramparts without incident. Ceilyn studied the earthworks, searching for hand- and footholds, testing the old woody vines to see if they could bear his weight.

"Well enough,'' he said, removing his cape. "But I will go first. And if anything goes wrong, you just forget about me and save yourself. It would take a damn good shot to kill *me*, so just remember that and look to your own safety.'' He gestured toward the gatehouse, not forty yards away.

Teleri removed her own cloak and Ceilyn wrapped it into a bundle with the other and tossed them over the wall. Then he climbed up to the top of the ramparts and reached a hand down to Teleri, to aid her climb and spare her from some of the vicious briars which had pierced his own hands. She had lost none of her childhood agility gained climbing the cliffs below Castell Aderyn, but her long full skirts hampered her and caught on the thorny branches.

For what seemed a long time, she dangled there, helpless to climb either up or down, in full view of the gate tower, and completely exposed to arrow fire should anyone spot her. Then, with a rending of cloth, she managed to kick her way free, and Ceilyn hauled her up to the top beside him.

"Next time,'' he whispered furiously, "have the sense to borrow some of my clothes!''

He dropped down on the other side, landed safely in the bushes below. A moment later, Teleri landed lightly beside him. They spent a few moments searching for their cloaks, then, slipping and sliding and grabbing at the bushes to keep from falling, they scrambled down the slope until they reached the footpath at the bottom.

Ceilyn donned his cape. He gazed uneasily toward the sea, thinking not so much of the Princess as of all the other things that might come up the path to meet them. Outside the walls of Caer Cadwy, beyond the protective ambience of the great sidhe-stone in Cynwas's crown, there was no telling what they might encounter. He heard ominous rustlings in the bushes, and he sensed something old, and cold, and venomous not far away.

He reached for Teleri. "I don't like this," he hissed in her ear. "The night things are out and abroad in great numbers tonight."

But Teleri looked in the other direction. She wriggled out of his grasp, and Ceilyn followed the direction of her gaze across the moonlit fields.

Something was missing: the campfire that provided the guards down in the meadow with light, warmth, and protection from the creatures who roamed the night, whose ruddy glow had been visible from the castle walls every night for a ten-night. "Someone has extinguished the fire—but why?"

"Not intentionally, I think," said Teleri, starting down the path. "More likely, something has happened to the men, and they have allowed the fire to burn itself out."

She broke into a run and Ceilyn followed at her heels.

Down by the fence which surrounded the pasture, four men lay sprawled in the dirt: the two guards who kept watch there each night, and two of their fellows who had volunteered to double the guard this All Hallows Eve. The coals of their campfire still glowed faintly and the remains of a late meal lay scattered on the ground.

Teleri picked up a leather wineskin and sniffed the contents, then bent down to examine one of the men.

"Is he dead?" Ceilyn asked.

"Only sleeping. She's used the same thing as before, I think, though she's made some attempt to disguise it."

Through the wooden bars of the fence they could see the bull, horns turned to silver in the moonlight, huge head hanging down, absolutely motionless—if the creature so much as breathed, Ceilyn could not detect it from this distance.

When Teleri slipped through the bars of the fence, Ceilyn uttered an inarticulate protest.

"I'll not wake him," she said, drifting across the field. "She'll have drugged him, too.'' She put a hand on one white flank, felt the beat of life beneath the skin.

Ceilyn watched them, amazed, sensing some mysterious kinship beneath the pale slender girl and the massive beast beside her: creatures of seafoam and saltspray both of them. "I wish," said Teleri wistfully, "that I dared to save him."

"Listen," said Ceilyn, hoisting himself up and over the fence. "Someone is coming."

Now Teleri could hear them, too: a thin voice raised high, as if in protest, and a lower voice answering impatiently. Ceilyn joined her and they cast about, searching for a hiding place. A cluster of leafless bushes offered the only cover, and scarcely enough of that for two people.

"No," Ceilyn protested, as she started toward the bushes. "We're certain to be discovered."

"There is no place else," she said, wrapping her cloak around her, sitting down among the tangle of bare branches. "We'll have to take a chance."

Ceilyn dived into the bushes beside her. "Think," Teleri breathed in his ear. "You were born and raised in the forest. Try to think like a shrub. . . . Imagine yourself part of a thicket somewhere in Gorwynnion."

Within moments there was no one to be seen in the middle of the field—nothing but the bull, the grassy mound, and a particularly dense and shadowy patch of bushes.

Manogan laughed. "Come then," he said, sweeping her up into the saddle before him. Then off they rode across the moonlit countryside at such a pace it seemed to Diaspad that he must be intent on killing them both.

Rocks, trees, and fences flew past them. The hounds could not keep pace and fell behind, one by one. The wind of their passage made speech impossible, and the girl hid her face against the stallion's neck, resigning herself to certain destruction.

Yet they came unharmed to a place they both knew, and there Manogan suddenly reined in and dismounted. He pulled her out of the saddle and into his arms and carried her to the little hollow, soft with new grasses. His lovemaking, as she had expected, was wild and angry.

But afterward he was gentle with her. "I would never have guessed you were still a virgin," he said, tenderly wiping away her tears, helping her to right her dress. "Why did you not tell me?"

"I have loved you since the first moment I saw you," said Diaspad. "That is why I was still a virgin—and why I did not tell you."

Manogan looked down on her with a mixture of pity and amusement. "You are such a child. What do you know of love?"

"What I did not know before you have taught me tonight," said Diaspad with a sniff. "But perhaps there are some things I might teach you. I'm not like her—not like your little goat-girl back in Gwyngelli, or any of the other women you might have loved. I am not fickle. Where I love, I love for all time, and where I hate, I never forgive."

Manogan sighed. "Better for both of us if this ends tonight. You are a wicked unhappy child, and I—I am a madman. What could we ever teach each other but misery and grief?"

10.

The Lady of the Castle of the Silver Wheel

Diaspad moved so swiftly that Derry could scarcely keep up with her. "It's all very well for you . . . the King's sister, after all," he protested. The rising wind tore everything he said into fragments and tossed half of it back to him. "Anyone suspects you of taking part . . . be sure they'll keep quiet. But Morc and I . . . not so fortunately placed. If anyone finds out that we were even here . . ."

"Derry," said the Princess, coming to an abrupt halt and hissing in his ear. "No one will find out that any of us were here tonight, if you and Morc do your job properly."

She set off again at the same brisk pace and Derry, Calchas, and Morc followed silently in her wake.

The guards had set up camp in the lea of the hill, sheltered from the battering wind. Diaspad arrived first at the campsite.

"The fools!" she declared, kicking at the cold ashes of their fire. "You wouldn't think they would be so sparing of their wood on a night like this. We must light the fire at once, before someone takes it into his head to come down and investigate."

Derry spoke up again. "Someone will be on the way down already. I say we go back and forget the whole—"

"Derry," said the Princess, showing her teeth. "Derry, you really are putting an enormous strain on my patience. Put that extra wood on at once or I may use *you* to kindle it."

Still protesting, Derry obeyed her, while Calchas and Morc moved about the campsite. Calchas picked up the wineskin and allowed the last few drops to trickle out. Morc's left arm was still immobilized in a sling, but he bent down, picked up an applecore and a greasy slice of bread with his right hand, and flung them into the firepit. Then he and Calchas searched the area inch by inch, making certain they had overlooked nothing. Finally, they joined the Princess and Derry beside the rekindled fire.

"Very good," said Diaspad briskly. "Now be off, the pair of

you, and keep your eyes and ears open. Let no one approach the meadow—we want no surprise this time! You have nothing to fear, Derry," she added contemptuously. "The charms I have given you and your own steel ought to ward you from any supernatural dangers. As for the natural ones, if any there be . . . just deal with them as you did at Michaelmas, when, by your own account, you acquitted yourself very well."

Derry flushed. "The man is dead. I did kill him, no matter what you pretend to think."

"So shall all who oppose us perish," Diaspad declared grandly. "Tonight it begins. If you feel your nerve fail, only think what we have come here to accomplish. Now about your business while I attend to mine. With every minute that passes after midnight, power will shift from the Dark Mother to the Maiden—a part which I am ill-equipped to play."

As Derry and Morc disappeared into the darkness, Diaspad threw off her cloak and tossed it to the ground. Then she took off all her rings and bracelets and dropped them on the cloak. She wore a simple gown of brown silk tonight and had scrubbed her face clean of all paint. Perhaps it was only the rosy glow of the firelight, perhaps the excitement heightening her already vivid coloring, but to Calchas she looked more beautiful in that plain gown than ever he remembered her. She pulled the jeweled hairpins and the ribbons out of her hair and the auburn tresses tumbled down her back and over her shoulders, as dark as blood in the firelight.

Then she began to dance around the campfire, an intricate little dance that wove a wayward path throughout the camp. She sang something under her breath, a love song or a lullaby, Calchas thought at first, but then the tempo increased and a harsh edge came into her voice, though still he made no sense of her words.

Her dance became wilder, more abandoned. Her velvet slippers flew off and sailed away in different directions; the brown satin, damp with sweat, clung to her body; her voice grew hoarse and her breathing irregular, but still Diaspad danced on, apparently tireless. And Calchas watched, atonished, to see his languid mother move so nimbly.

By the time she finally stopped, breathless and curiously triumphant, she no longer looked much like anyone's mother. She had declared herself ill-equipped to play the Maiden, and it was true that there was nothing *virginal* about her now, but a hectic flush lent her the appearance of youth, and she exuded a musky sensuality so raw, so elemental, that it might almost be innocent.

"Come," she said, and Calchas, shocked back to self-awareness, realized that he was soaked in sweat and weak in the knees.

Diaspad slipped through the bars of the fence, cautiously approached the bull. More cautiously still, Calchas followed her.

Diaspad put an arm around the bull's muscular neck; she breathed something into one white ear. Stepping back again, she reached inside her dress and pulled a black satin bag from between her pointed breasts. The contents of this bag she poured into one hand, which she held, palm up, right under the bull's nose. The beast inhaled the grey powder, twitched one white ear and then the other, lifted his head, and stared glassily at the Princess.

"Here," she said to Calchas, unknotting the girdle of braided silk which encircled her slender waist. "Wind this three times around his neck, and he will follow where we lead, as gentle as any lamb."

Wordlessly, Calchas passed the silken cord around the bull's throat and shoulders, while Diaspad emptied the last of the powder into her hand and allowed the bull to take another sniff. "Come," she crooned, "come with me, my prince of beasts."

She began to move backward toward the burial mound, and the bull lurched after her. "That is right," murmured the Princess, when they reached the top of the hillock. "This is the place and the appointed hour. Remove my girdle, Calchas, and give it back to me."

Calchas obeyed, and Diaspad knotted the plaited and tassled cord around her hips. "Now," she said, "hand me the knife."

Calchas reached inside his shirt and drew out something swathed in silk. "Look," he whispered, glancing nervously at the bull. "He's coming out of it. Kill him *now*."

"And send him to Donwy still dreaming?" said the Princess, uncovering the knife and eagerly stroking the blade. "But the Prince must see his death coming and accept the necessity, even as the blow falls. That is the custom.

"Now step out of my way until I call you, lest you hamper my movements."

Again she danced, clutching the long knife in one white hand, this time weaving a circle around the base of the hill, though with every pass the circle narrowed, bringing her a little closer to her victim. Meanwhile, the bull slowly regained consciousness, shaking his mighty horned head from side to side, and lashing his great tufted tail.

> *"I am a storm in summertime* (Diaspad sang)
> *I am the White Flood*
> *I am the sea rising*
> *I am the Lady of the Castle of the Silver Wheel*
>
> *I am the sow who devours her own farrow*
>   *The carrion crow, feasting after the carnage*
> *I am she who waits by the ford*
> *I am the fairy-mistress, the vampyre*
>   *Men have loved me*
>   *Poets and Warriors*
> *I am their inspiration, their strength in battle*
>   *Brief, brilliant lives I grant them*
>
> *I am the nightmare, I am madness*
> *I am all things to all men*
>   *Let them beware me*
> *I am passion, pain, betrayal, despair*
>   *And my touch is death."*

Her song held Calchas enthralled. But more terrible still was her face, for there was something so extravagant, so voluptuous about her beauty now, that she seemed quite literally capable of anything. He could not even imagine any excess so great, any enormity so tremendous, that it was beyond her now.

Diaspad faced the bull, poised to strike. "Now," she whispered. "Now!"

With a bellow that seemed to rock the earth, the bull lowered his head as if to charge. Instead, as Diaspad leapt forward, the beast shied violently away. But Diaspad was too quick for him. She managed to grab one curved horn and sink her knife deep into the bull's throat. With a mighty bellow, ending in a choked gurgle as blood filled his throat, the great beast toppled and fell at the Princess's feet.

> *"Blood is my price*
> *A life for a life*
> *Let the bargain be made*
> *For the sons of Maelgwyn*
> *Darkness and rest*
> *The peace of the grave*
> *The womb of the earth*
> *Beginning and ending*
> *Death is my gift."*

She called to Calchas, and he came to her with trembling limbs and dragging feet. "Kneel," she commanded him.

Calchas looked: at the knife gleaming wet in her hand, at her beautiful terrible face. "No," he said weakly.

"Kneel," she insisted, "or for your impudence I shall cut your throat, there where you stand."

Totally unnerved, Calchas fell to his knees. Diaspad hovered over him, knife held high, and he was certain, absolutely certain at that moment, that she would plunge the blade into his heart. As she knelt beside him, he quailed, but then . . . she dipped one white hand into the blood which pooled on the trampled grass, and she anointed Calchas on his hands and forehead.

> *"Thus I mark you for my own:*
> *You are my first born*
>   *flesh of my flesh*
>   *child of my own body*
> *Beloved above all others.*
>
> *You are my brother*
>   *my friend and companion*
>   *whose right arm defends me*
> *Loyal unto death.*
>
> *You are my lover, my consort*
>   *crowned by my favor*
>   *ruler of my lands and my people*
> *Mighty and glorious . . ."*

But Calchas heard nothing of this. At her touch, a rank, smothering sweetness overwhelmed him. And when she released him, he fell forward on his hands, retching so violently that it seemed he might cast up his very insides.

Diaspad watched all this dispassionately. But when the spasm had passed, she put her arms around him, cradling his head against her breast. "Are you well, my darling? She hasn't harmed you, has she?"

"You didn't tell me that would happen," he muttered, pulling out of her embrace, wiping his mouth on his sleeve.

"It is not an easy thing to bear, the touch of Donwy. But you have done well," she said, smoothing his damp dark hair. "And as you are unscathed, we can assume she was pleased to accept you." Suddenly in an ecstasy of delight, she clasped him to her again, and there amidst the blood and the matted grass and the regurgitated contents of Calchas's stomach, there with the bull lying in a huge ungainly heap beside her, she began to laugh triumphantly.

"We have done it, Calchas, and not a hand was raised to stop us. And no one, no one in all Celydonn will have the strength to hinder us now!"

Now it came to pass that the Moon heard tales of evil influences at work down in the fens, tales of hags and black warlocks casting their spells, stories of fantasms and banshees and the creeping horrors, which made of the marshlands no fit place for man or beast   venture. She decided it was time to go down to the fens and investigate.

She covered herself with a black cloak and went down to the marshes to see what was afoot. But the dampness weighed down her garments and the weeds caught at the hem of her cloak and she sank down into the bog beneath the dark waters.

The hags and the black men heard of this. They came to the pool where the poor Moon lay drowned beneath the water, and they set up a great stone to mark the spot.

— *A nursemaids' tale, told in Camboglanna and throughout the south*

11.

A Cry in the Night

Several hours earlier and a hundred miles distant, Fflergant, Gryffin, and Garanwyn had paused on the road, halfway between Fyffynog and the river Arfondwy.

"Look," said Fflergant, indicating with a wide sweep of his arm the low grasslands spreading before them. "It's all perfectly flat and easy, and we can save hours of travel if we leave the road here and cut across the meadows."

Garanwyn shifted uneasily in his saddle. There was something about the prospect before him and Fflergant's proposed shortcut which he did not quite like. "But if, as you say, this is the best way, why doesn't the road cut across here as well? And we haven't passed a farm or a cottage for miles. Why doesn't anyone live down there?"

Fflergant shrugged. "Land that lies so low and near the river is liable to flood during the spring thaw."

"People build dykes in other places," Garanwyn pointed out. "Then they don't have to worry if the river floods."

The sun was a huge crimson ball hovering just above the tops of the high grasses, and night would overtake them before very long. "And won't we pass awfully close to the marsh? I'd not care to be anywhere in the vicinity of Teirwaedd Morfa after the sun sets."

"We'll not come within miles of the marsh." Fflergant airily dismissed Teirwaedd Morfa and all the terrible tales associated with it. "And you were the one, may I remind you, who was determined to ride to the river tonight."

Still Garanwyn had his misgivings. He looked to Tryffin, hoping that his practical cousin would offer support, but Tryffin, having sided against his brother once today, merely shook his head and remained silent. Garanwyn gave in. "Very well, if you are certain it will save time."

Fflergant gathered up the reins and urged his big roan gelding down the shallow embankment and into the deep grass. Tryffin and Garanwyn and their mounts followed him. For the next two or three hours they rode through a land virtually devoid of landmarks, a vast, empty country where sky and grass surrounded them on all sides. The sun disappeared beneath the waving grass and a golden harvest moon rose up behind them.

As the light faded, Garanwyn watched Fflergant's scarlet cloak dim first to crimson, then to purple, and finally to grey. A sharp-edged breeze swept in from the sea, rattling the long dry grass like swords clattering in their sheaths.

Wrapped in his warm wool cloak, riding at a steady pace through that changeless country, watching the light of Fflergant's lantern bobbing about in the darkness ahead of him, Garanwyn grew drowsy. He yawned and shook himself, determined not to do anything so childish as fall asleep in the saddle.

For all that, he must have drifted off, coming back to consciousness with a jolt, minutes or hours later. A harsh, shrill singing filled the night on all sides of him, and the wind was blowing full in his face.

Ahead of him, Fflergant and Tryffin both reined in. "Those are *frogs*," Garanwyn declared accusingly, as he drew abreast of the others.

"Yes," Fflergant agreed sheepishly. "I know they are. At first I thought there might be a stream running along here, but now it occurs to me we've strayed from our course and onto marshy ground."

Garanwyn frowned. "But how could you? We wanted to go due west, and the moon . . ." He looked around him. But while he dozed, clouds had covered the sky, blotting out the moon and all the stars. "Where *is* the moon?"

"She hid behind a cloud an hour or two ago," said Tryffin. By the glow of their lanterns, his face was the same burnished gold as his hair, and his eyes were dark and mysterious. "But she'll be directly overhead by this time—no use to us now, even if we could see her."

"I thought I could keep us straight by keeping the wind on our left," Fflergant explained. "But either the wind has shifted or I've turned us around in spite of it." He inhaled deeply. "I think we are heading south. Can you smell the sea?"

"Well," sighed Garanwyn. "If that way is south, then west will be—"

"If that way is south . . . but to tell the truth, it's a chancy thing, plotting your course by the wind," said Fflergant. "I can't imagine what possessed me to try such a thing. I hate to be the one to suggest this, but perhaps we had best set up our camp right here and wait until the moon shows herself or morning comes. If we go on now, we could wander around, completely lost, all night long."

"Set up camp . . . on the edge of the bog?" Garanwyn asked incredulously.

"Well, we could go back the way we came for a mile or two—just to be safe—and stop there for the night," Tryffin suggested.

It seemed the best plan. Fflergant passed his lantern over to Garanwyn. "You can lead the way, if you like. Though we've cut such a clear track behind us, I doubt even I could lose our way again."

A trail of bent and broken grass plainly marked their path, so Garanwyn accepted the lantern, turned his horse around, and confidently led the way. Yet they had not been riding in this new direction long when he pulled up again. He lifted his lantern high, staring ahead with a puzzled frown. "I can't believe it. It seems that I have lost our track. It just—just disappeared."

"Impossible," said Fflergant, taking Tryffin's lantern. He bent down to examine the grass more closely, certain that he would detect some sign of their previous passage. "It can't end here. Three great horses couldn't possibly blunder through here without a trace. We'll just have veered a mite off course again. If we fan out a bit, we're bound to find our trail somewhere around here."

Fflergant and his brother each started off in a new direction, while Garanwyn continued on as before. As the minutes passed, the boy became more and more convinced that he was heading in the wrong direction entirely. The grass grew higher and tougher, the singing of frogs became louder. Somewhere off to his left, he heard water splashing, and Tryffin shouting—whether a warning or a cry of distress he could not tell. Though Garanwyn feared the worst, he waited for Fflergant to catch up to him. Then, together, they headed in the direction of Tryffin's voice.

The grass thinned out a bit and they came to the edge of a vast expanse of dark water. Tryffin and his horse were just scrambling back up the grassy embankment.

Except where the water had been disturbed, the mere was utterly dark and still, the water so murky that the lantern cast only a feeble glow upon the surface. Lift his lantern and strain his eyes as he might, Garanwyn could not determine the extent of the pool, only that it stretched for a considerable distance on either side of them.

"This," he said indignantly, "was not anywhere along the way that we came."

"No," Tryffin agreed, patting his shivering gelding on the flank. "I wasn't expecting this at all. We walked right into it and it was only luck that saved poor old Roch from a broken leg."

Fflergant and Garanwyn dismounted also. "This isn't grass," said Garanwyn, examining the thick, triangular stalks. "These are *reeds*." He took a step and mud sucked at his feet, water welled up and soaked through his boots.

Tryffin nodded grimly. "I don't think there can be any doubt about it. We have strayed into the marsh."

"But how did we get here?" Garanwyn heard his voice rise high in panic, despite his best efforts to keep it calm. "This has to be the way that we came. It has to be—but it isn't!"

"They do say that Teirwaedd Morfa has a way of reaching out

and drawing travelers in, whether they would or not," Fflergant offered.

Garawyn glanced uneasily over his shoulder, expecting to see hostile, inhuman eyes staring at him out of the rustling grasses. He knew many disturbing stories about the marsh: tales of ghosts and restless spirits, of water-witches and mossfolk, and of worse things lurking beneath the murky waters, just waiting to reach out with their long, strong, sinewy green arms and pull the unwary traveler down to a muddy death. He glared reproachfully at Tryffin.

"And you said we had nothing to fear in decent, respectable Walgan."

"Well," said Tryffin. "I didn't think of the marsh. The marsh isn't in Walgan, properly speaking. Teirwaedd Morfa is just . . . Teirwaedd Morfa."

"Just Teirwaedd Morfa," Garanwyn echoed bleakly. "And what do we do, now that Teirwaedd Morfa has invited us in for a visit?"

Tryffin squeezed water out of his cloak. "I suggest we go back the way we just came—back where the land is a little higher and drier—and set up camp and a fire for the night. Whatever hazards Teirwaedd Morfa may present, they are best faced in the morning."

But several hours later they were still looking for that higher, drier campsite. By that time, they were on foot, not only to spare the horses but also because they still hoped to stumble across their own trail and follow it out of the marsh. Instead, every step they took drew them deeper and deeper into the fens.

The reek of stagnant water and rotting vegetation was pervasive, and the damp soaked through their boots and their woolen hose until their feet grew numb and leaden. Garanwyn, younger and smaller than either of his cousins, was already reeling with exhaustion.

He stumbled into a pool of dark water and ropey weeds, lost his footing in the sticky mud, and was obliged to wait there until Tryffin fished him out. "Why don't you ride for a bit?" Tryffin suggested. "Take Roch. He's so used to my weight, he would hardly notice yours."

Garanwyn shook his head. As tired and discouraged as he

was, he was keenly ashamed of his own weakness and determined not to show it. "I can go on. For a while, anyway."

"What I can't understand," said Fflergant, as they staggered on, "is what we've *done*." He and his brother had reckoned up all their geasa, examined all their words and actions for months past, and could not come up with a single transgression between them. "We made a mistake somewhere though I can't for the life of me remember what it was."

Suddenly he stopped. "Hark to that!" They all listened. Somewhere in the darkness ahead of them, they could all hear the distant rush and gurgle of running water.

"The river?" said Garanwyn. "No, that can't be it. That doesn't sound like Arfondwy. The river is broader and quieter the farther south you go."

"Well, then," said Fflergant. "If not Arfondwy, then one of the streams that feed it. Running water means a river, no matter how far south you go. And if it is Arfondwy, we can follow it out of the marsh."

Garanwyn fingered the chain of the silver cross he always wore beneath his shirt. "But is it safe to follow the river? I've always been told that the Arfondwy is the very heart of the danger in Teirwaedd Morfa."

"It's the same river here that it is up north," scoffed Fflergant. "The same river we forded a few weeks ago, the same river little children play in, in all the villages to the north. 'Gentle Arfondwy' they call her." He was impatient to press on, now that he believed his sense of direction had been restored to him. "As for the danger—you've seen for yourself, it's all a pack of nonsense. We've been wandering here for hours and on All Hallows Eve, too, but aside from getting lost and tired and a good deal wetter than we like to be, nothing has happened to us. Nor have we seen anything to frighten us: not a single corpse-candle, or water-wraith, or creeping horror the whole blessed night. The country around Caer Cadwy is more dangerous than this!"

Without looking to see if the others followed after him, Fflergant continued to push on through the high grass. After a brief moment of hesitation, Tryffin followed, and Garanwyn, rather than be left behind, trailed along, too. But a muffled wailing issued from the darkness behind him, causing the boy to whirl about and look in all directions. "Who's there?"

"Who is where?" Fflergant asked wearily.

"That sound. Surely you heard it? Like a little girl crying."

Fflergant and Tryffin both stopped to listen. "I don't hear a thing," said Fflergant, at last. "Whatever it was that you heard, it's stopped now."

Garanwyn continued to listen for a moment longer. The night was still, save for the distant sound of the river. "You're right," he admitted, feeling rather foolish. "It's stopped now."

They squelched on toward the sound of running water, Garanwyn bringing up the rear. But a minute later he cried out again. "There it is. Surely you heard it this time?"

Fflergant was growing exasperated. "No, I did not. You have a vivid imagination, laddie, but this is not the time—"

"No, I heard it, too," Tryffin volunteered, surprising the others. "A marsh bird, maybe, or—"

"There it is again," Garanwyn insisted, as the heart-rending sobs tore through the night again. "It isn't a bird at all. I swear to God, it sounds just like Gwenlliant, and she keeps saying, *'Go back, Garanwyn, go back!'* "

"Oh, for the love of . . . Now, what in God's name would your little sister—or any little girl—be doing here? A bird, maybe, but—"

"No." Tryffin's tone was apologetic. "It did sound like Gwenlliant, that second time I heard it. Not so clearly as Garanwyn . . . but it was like her voice."

Fflergant groaned. "I take it all back. Teirwaedd Morfa is more dangerous than I thought, if the marsh air breeds delusions in *your* rock-hard head."

"I'm going back," said Garanwyn. "No, you can't stop me. Whatever . . . whoever it was, I have to find out."

As neither of the others made any move either to stop or accompany him, he struck out on his own, back the way they had just come.

"Madness," Fflergant declared, shaking his head. "Even if he did hear something, who's to say it's not a trap of some sort?"

"A trap baited with Gwenlliant's voice?" Up to his ankles in mud, confused, weary, and thoroughly chilled, Tryffin still contrived to sound utterly reasonable, perfectly willing to stand there and discuss the matter at length if necessary. "We've heard of such things, of course: a cry in the night, the voice of a loved one, and the thing with the voice is never anything you'd care to meet. But if that's what it was, why didn't you hear something, too?''

"Yes, but you can't really believe—''

"Why not?'' asked Tryffin. ''We know Gwenlliant is gifted, we know she is capable—well, we don't know what she is capable of doing. I say we heed her warning, if that is what it was, and go back the way that we came.''

"But we don't know which way we came,'' insisted Fflergant. ''And the river offers us our only sure guide out of this wretched place.''

"Maybe so,'' said Tryffin, beginning to sound a little impatient. ''But when all is said and done, we can't really allow Garanwyn to go wandering off all on his own. If he is determined to go, then we—''

"He'll come to his senses,'' Fflergant broke in. ''If we don't humor him. If we go slowly, he will see our light and catch up with us as soon as reason returns to him.''

Tryffin shook his head. ''He won't, you know. About some things, Garanwyn can be just as stubborn as you.'' He led his horse around and set out in the direction of Garanwyn's light.

Utterly flabbergasted by this unexpected defection, Fflergant hesitated, then obstinately pushed on in quest of the river.

The song of the river grew louder, and Fflergant thought that he could smell the water, a fresher scent on the night air. Ahead of him, the rushes bent their heads low, as if flattened by the river's current. He felt a surge of relief and his natural good-humor returned. He would just wait on the riverbank for the others to come to their senses and catch up with him, and then they would all find their way out of the marsh together.

Then his horse balked and refused to take another step.

"Oh, for the . . . Not you, too!'' exclaimed Fflergant, tugging at the reins.

After much coaxing and pulling, he was able to urge the gelding a few steps forward. The gurgling water sounded tantalizingly near now, and Fflergant's eagerness to reach the river was so great that he did not stop to think why his usually dependable steed had suddenly turned recalcitrant.

Another reluctant step, and the roan balked again, absolutely refusing to move another inch. Fflergant threw down the reins. ''Very well, then. Stay there if you like.''

He pushed through the grass and the reeds and found himself

standing on the verge of another vast pool of water, the surface unmarred by even the tiniest ripple of movement. The gurgling river song which had lured him there suddenly stopped.

A thrill of horror snaked down Fflergant's spine. What had he said to Tryffin, only minutes before, about traps?

Whether he slipped on the slick trampled grass, or whether the ground crumbled beneath him, or something reached out of the mere to trip him up, Fflergant was not afterward certain. He landed in the water with a loud splash, dropping his lantern.

The pool was shallow but the mud at the bottom was soft and deep. And when he tried to scramble to his feet, the clinging ooze refused to release him. The harder he struggled, the deeper he sank into the bog. His exasperated curses changed to hoarse cries for help.

A faint voice answered, assuring him that help was on the way. Then he heard the high-pitched screams of the horses as all three caught wind of something which terrified them. Under the water, something icy cold clamped itself around Fflergant's leg.

Tryffin appeared on the shore, bearing a lantern. Fflergant shouted out a warning. "Be careful. There's quicksand here. Watch out or you'll be in here with me!"

And there between the hills was a broad, grey land with a dark stream flowing through. Nothing grew in that land, neither trees nor grass nor any living thing, and that was the Valley of Lamentation.

The boy rode down into the valley. He was seven days crossing the plain. On the seventh day he came to a mean dwelling. He entered the hovel with great misgivings and sat down by the fire that was burning on the hearth.

There were some large bones lying about on the floor and a great black pot was cooking on the fire. The cauldron began to boil, and the lad lifted the lid to see what was inside. Then a great fear came over him, for the pot was filled with the blood of men.

—From The Black Book of Tregalen

12.

Blood to Call Forth Blood

As soon as the Princess and Calchas left the meadow, Teleri emerged from the bushes. Ceilyn did not follow her immediately. He was experiencing a profound disorientation, much as he always did when entering into or leaving the shape of the wolf, and he was uncertain whether he had just spent the last hour creating an illusion, or had actually turned himself, fantastic as it seemed, into a bush of the holly for which he had been named.

Rising unsteadily, he felt for the iron bracelet, found it there on his wrist, and released a sigh of relief. Of course he and Teleri had only created some kind of illusion between them! Even without the bracelet, the other was impossible.

Teleri knelt down beside the carcass. She reached out and touched the terrible gash at the throat. Her hand came away red and sticky, and she examined the stain wonderingly, as though she had never seen anything like it before. "So much blood," she said softly. "It seems there is always bloodshed . . . and I am powerless to stop it."

"It was a dreadful deed we witnessed here," Ceilyn agreed, coming up close behind her. "But there was nothing we could reasonably have done to stop her. The only thing for us to do now is to decide whether or not we dare take such a bizarre story to the King."

She scarcely seemed to hear him. He bent down, took her by the hand, and tried to help her to her feet. She resisted—not with the shrinking resistance, the passive denial she had always offered when he touched her before, but exerting a strength he would not have suspected she possessed. "Can you feel it?" she asked.

"I feel the lines here, as I always do, if that is what you mean."

Teleri shook her head. "No, I don't think that is it. It's more like . . ." Her gaze flickered toward the sea and back again. "She brought it here. Not with her, but it came . . . yes, it came at her summoning." She looked down at the bull and her eyes filled with hot tears. "I wanted to save him, you know."

"Yes," said Ceilyn gently. "I know that you did. Poor dumb beast. The butcher's knife would have offered him a cleaner death. But he is far beyond hurting or helping now."

She looked up at him. "You really don't know what has happened here, do you? You don't understand any of it. I don't understand all of it, but . . . Ceilyn, I could make things right here. I could do it."

"Best not to meddle with it," he said. "These are dark things, terrible things. These things have nothing to do with you or me."

"You think not?" she said. "But I—I have a feeling that they have a great deal to do with me."

A sick feeling was growing at the pit of his stomach. "But you told me . . . not a witch or a pagan, you said. You said you were raised in the same faith as me. You said—"

"But I was also trained as a wizard," she said. "And I was taught that certain . . . ancient powers exist in the world. Whether they walked abroad of old in form and manner like to men and women—as pagan gods and goddesses, you would say—

or whether those who worshipped them lent them form, investing them with personalities they could recognize and understand, I do not know. But they have names, they can be . . . invoked . . . and they can appear in a variety of guises.

"That power which Diaspad brought here . . . I *know* it, I recognize it in some way I can't explain. And I could call it here, shape it to a fairer form, enlist its aid, reverse what the Princess has done. I could do that, Ceilyn."

"But you don't want to," he insisted. "You can't possibly want any part of the kind of power that . . . thing . . . whatever it was . . . could offer you."

"Yes," she whispered. "Yes . . . I think that I do."

She gathered resolution, squared her shoulders, and lifted her chin. "I understand, of course, that you want no part of this. So be it. If you lack the courage or the conviction for this task, then I must find enough for two. And you can go back to Caer Cadwy without me."

Absently, she wiped her bloody hand on the grass, and ignoring his offer of assistance she stood up. "Yes . . . go," she said. "And leave me to do what has to be done."

Ceilyn frowned. "Surely you don't believe that I would abandon you here? Or that I would just walk away and allow you to do this thing you propose to do?"

"If you try to prevent me," she said breathlessly, "if you interfere in any way . . . I will never forgive you. No, and I doubt you will ever forgive yourself, if Diaspad has her way, if everything she has labored to accomplish should ever come to pass."

She sounded so certain that he did not know how to reply.

"Do what you think you must do," he decided at last. "I don't—I can't approve, but you are right . . . I don't really understand. I won't leave this spot without you, but neither will interfere."

"I am afraid that is not enough," said Teleri. "I daren't risk any tales of Black Magic carried back to Caer Cadwy. But what you don't actually see, *that* I know you cannot tell."

"You know I would never betray you," Ceilyn protested.

"Truly," she said, "I do not know what you would do. If later on, you thought of all you had seen and heard here and concluded that your silence in some way made you guilty . .

you might feel obligated to speak. Especially as you would have nothing to lose by it.''

"Nothing to lose?" he said. "Have you forgotten that I love you and I want—I want to protect you?''

He watched her eyes grow wide in amazement. "But you had to know. Between me and God! We've discussed the matter any number of—well, not in so many words, perhaps, but what did you think we were talking about, that night I almost died?''

"About friendship," she said. "Friendship and loyalty and . . . and sharing. I don't remember that anyone said anything about love.''

"That day down by the sea, then, when you said you might never be able to feel the same way I did?''

"I thought . . . I thought we were talking about . . . the other thing.''

"You thought I was trying to *seduce* you? That all I cared about was taking you to bed with me? And you so innocent . . . What kind of man do you take me for?''

Teleri shook her head. "I thought you were already in love with somebody else. I thought you loved the Queen.''

Ceilyn sighed. "That was something I outgrew. A boy's passion, no more. But I love *you* . . . and I've never said those words to any other woman.''

"Yes," she said. "If you say so, it must be true. But I—you know that I have no experience in these matters. You say that you love me, and I must believe you. But I don't really know exactly what that means.

"You must offer me something I can understand. Either you stay here and help me to do what has to be done—implicate yourself along with me—or you go away and remain ignorant as well as innocent.''

"I have been trying for a long time now to help you understand," he said bitterly. "But every time that I do, you just look the other way.''

"Yes," she said faintly. "I suppose that I do." She did not look away now. She stared at him for a long time, at his flushed face, the way he gazed back at her with such a mixture of resentment, humiliation, and naked need, and for the first time she began to understand something of that other power—a woman's power over the man who wants her—and to recognize the nature of the influence she exerted on him.

A hunger for power had been awakened in her tonight, and the temptation to test this one, to see what she could make him do, was irresistible.

"Ceilyn," she said softly. "Do this for me. Show me . . . how much you love me. I have such a difficult and frightening task before me. I can do it myself if you refuse me, but it would be so much easier if you would help. And it grows late and I am so tired . . . I have only so much courage and resolution, only enough for what I have to do, and none to spare for arguing or for trying to convince you. But whatever it is you want . . . if you will do what I ask, I will grant anything you might ask in return."

Horrified, he placed his hand over her mouth. "Don't say that," he whispered, wounded to the quick. "Don't even think it. You will cheapen everything I ever felt for you." Pain rapidly turned to anger. "As though it were something that could be purchased that way! As though it were something you could give me, even if you wanted to. No . . . you just don't have it in you to give me what I really want, and it's dishonest for you to even offer."

She sat down on the ground, defeated and humiliated. "We don't know that," she said weakly. "I've never been indifferent to you, Ceilyn, though God knows I often tried to be. Perhaps I could learn. . . . Perhaps I do love you already, only I've been afraid to admit the truth, even to myself."

Anger departed as swiftly as it had come. Suddenly drained of all emotion, he sat down beside her and the horrible bloody thing that had been the bull, and he took her hand in both his own. She shivered at that contact but did not pull away from it. "Is this really necessary . . . something that must be done?"

"I have said so," she replied tremulously.

"And you know that what you propose here goes against everything I was ever taught to believe . . . that we may both burn in *Hell* for this night's work?"

"I know it," she said. "I also know what is at stake here."

"Oh God," he said, closing his eyes. "May God have mercy on my soul. Tell me what you want me to do, and I will do it."

All this time, there had been a part of her that resisted, hating herself for what she was doing to him. But now, in his yielding, she yielded, too. As he opened his eyes, she turned away from him, lest he recognize the sudden fierce elation that surged through her.

"I will need your sword," she said.

Ceilyn dropped her hand. "My sword?"

"I left my little knife behind."

Ceilyn reached for his dagger. "Use mine, then, if you must."

"It would hardly be suitable," she said. "You have put it to too many profane uses. Besides, swords are inherently magical. And yours was made in Tir Gwyngelli and all the old ceremonies attended its making."

"But that is why . . ." Ceilyn began to feel that sick feeling again. The very thought of defiling his sword—the gift of the eccentric stranger who was his grandfather, consecrated in the church the day that he was knighted, then girded on by the Queen herself—horrified him. "I'm sorry, I can't lend it to you. I am sorry."

"I suppose," she said, "I suppose it would accord better with your precious honor if we were to use the sword of one of the guards—and he unaware of the use to which we put it?"

Ceilyn winced. And after all, what did it matter? He was in so deep now, would be in deeper before the night was over, what difference would a little thing like dishonoring and defiling his sword make?

Without further protest, he got to his feet, pulled the blade from his scabbard. (And somewhere at the back of his mind, Sidonwy's voice echoed, *"Wear this in token of your valor—and be you a good knight!"*)

Teleri stood, too, unclasped her cloak and allowed it to slip off her shoulders and down to the ground. "You're not—not going to dance, are you?" Ceilyn asked apprehensively, watching her step out of her shoes, thinking that he could not bear it if Teleri started to do obscene dances around the carcass.

"It is long past midnight. And after all, I am better suited to the role of the Maiden. My dance will be different from Diasrad's, I think."

Ceilyn scowled darkly down at the bull. "I don't know what you think you are going to do. The poor beast has been dead for some time now. I doubt you will be able to draw much blood."

"He will bleed," she said, taking the sword from him, a chilling certainty in her voice. "Give me your hand."

Startled, Ceilyn put both his hands behind him, like a child caught in some misdeed. "I don't understand. I don't—don't remember this part."

"It is as you said. The bull has been dead too long. Blood will be needed to call forth a sufficient quantity of blood."

As he still hesitated, she sighed and said, "Very well. If I were to cut the palm of your hand the pain would not last long, there would be no scar afterward. But my blood will serve just as well, if you are afraid."

Ashamed to appear a coward in her eyes, he offered her his hand. She put her own hand over his, clasped them around the blade, and drew his palm quickly and ruthlessly along the cutting edge. The blade was dull, the sword a weapon meant to hack through steel and leather, not unprotected flesh. Ceilyn gasped, set his teeth, and tried not to flinch.

She turned the palm up and examined the shallow, ugly wound. Then, apparently satisfied, she turned it over again and allowed the bright blood to run down the blade.

She released his hand and stepped back, leaving Ceilyn to stand alone over the body of the bull. Then she began to dance. In the beginning, Teleri's dance bore little resemblance to Diaspad's. This was only a sedate circling of the bull, with now and then a turn or a pause. Ceilyn could see that she was not quite certain what she was doing. He allowed himself to relax a little. He did not know what he had been expecting, but this was not it.

> *"I am the rain in time of drought* (Teleri chanted)
> *I am a spring of sweet water*
> *I am spring after winter*
> *I am heather on the hillside*
> > *The seed in the furrow*
> > *The blossom on the bough*
> *I am the new moon*
> *I am the crest of the wave*
> *I am she who sits among the stars of the*
> > *Northern Crown*
>
> *I am a draft of cool air*
> > *A pool of bright water*
> *I am a note of music*
> > *The voice of the river*
> > *And of the lapwing*

> *I am the roe-deer in the thicket*
>   *Not easily won*
> *I am the eyas in the nest*
> *I am all things to all men*
>   *Sister, lover, playfellow, friend*
>   *But they love me at their peril."*

Three times Teleri circled the bull, and every time the circle was completed more swiftly and the steps she executed became more complex. Her bare feet beat an erratic but compelling rhythm into the earth. Intent, at first, on the dance, uncertain of the steps, she gradually gained confidence. And when she finally met Ceilyn's eyes she flashed him such a smile as he had never seen on her face before. Ceilyn began to feel uncomfortable again—he did not like this at all.

A stamp of her foot, a half turn, and she came so close that her skirts brushed against him as she passed. A strong sweet perfume washed over him: Prescelli's musk and orris root. (And Prescelli's voice said in his ear, *"Don't you ever long to do something utterly, outrageously wicked?"*)

Almost he answered her (*"Constantly, that's why I never, never can"*) but caught himself just in time.

The dance was taking Teleri around to the other side of the hill; a series of intricate steps brought her to face him across the carcass of the bull. But now he saw Sidonwy gazing across at him, a gently regretful Sidonwy. (*"It makes no sense, Ceilyn. I am trying to understand, but I really cannot."*)

Too late, Ceilyn understood what he was in for. He might have run, but something held him rooted to the spot.

Stamp, circle, sway, and turn. (His mother's eyes filled with pitying tears. *"Please, Cuel, don't be so hard on the boy. I'm sure he didn't mean to do wrong."*

(*"Oh yes,"* snapped Prescelli, *"a few words and all is mended, so long as it's only a woman you've insulted!"*)

As if in a dream, he watched Teleri lift the sword high, watched the sudden swift descent.

(*"The Prince must see his death coming and accept the necessity, even as the blow falls."*)

Another slash appeared across the bull's throat, just above the wide cut Diaspad had made there. Amazingly, the wound bled—not just a trickle, but a dark crimson stream.

Teleri knelt and dipped one hand in the blood. What she said, Ceilyn was too far gone to comprehend, but he had a dim impression that Teleri had shaken off her doubts and gained not only confidence but a sure knowledge of what she was doing. He wondered, numbly, just what it was she was always studying in those dusty old books of Glastyn's.

(*"I've seen those signs before,"* said Prescelli. *"They're magic, aren't they?"*

(And Teleri said: *"I was raised in the same faith as you, though not so strictly, I will admit."*)

He knelt in the grass beside her and she painted his hands and forehead with blood. Ceilyn braced himself, determined not to behave as Calchas had done earlier, but something sweet and terrifying and insistent beat down the last of his resistance, and all the memories of all the emotions he had suppressed for so long, overwhelmed him.

"Ceilyn, can you hear me?" said Teleri. She wore her own face now, very white and frightened. "Ceilyn?"

"Yes," he said faintly. "I can hear you."

"I was afraid—but she treated you very gently, didn't she? It was easier for you than it was for Calchas. That is—that must be a good sign," she whispered.

"Gently?" Ceilyn found that he was drenched in cold sweat and trembling in every limb. "My God . . . *gently?*"

A long time later, after he had wiped his hands and his sword on the dry grass, after he had scrubbed at the blood on his face with his sleeve, and helped Teleri to gather up her shoes and her cloak, he followed her back up the path to the castle. Neither of them spoke, not even when he offered her his hand, climbing the wall.

The moon had disappeared behind a cloud and Teleri's face was hidden from him. But he thought, from the irregular sound of her breathing, that she might be crying.

"Beware," said the wizard Glastyn, "the calling forth of Powers. Like the sword of legend which must drink blood before it be sheathed again, so power, improperly summoned, may demand a terrible payment before it depart again."

13.

A Struggle in the Dark

"And so it is done," announced the Princess Diaspad, allowing her cloak to slip from her shoulders and fall to the floor behind her.

"And without any surprises or interference this time," added Derry, stepping over the pile of velvet and fur as he, Morc, and Calchas followed her into her bedchamber.

The room was lit by dozens of the red and orange tapers that Ceilyn had taken exception to down in the Hall, and an aromatic fire of cedar and sandalwood crackled on the hearth. Derry lounged across the room and arranged himself in a high-backed chair by the window, Morc slumped down on an elaborately carved stool by the door, and Calchas walked over to warm himself by the fire.

But the Princess remained just inside the door, staring dreamily at her own reflection in the long mirror at the other end of the room, reliving the events of the evening. Little remained of the terrible beauty which had been hers but a short time ago, and the image within the ebony frame with its carved gargoyles and gilded scrollwork was not an attractive one. Her eyes were dark and bruised-looking, and her tangled auburn hair, hastily braided and pinned into place after the ritual, had escaped again to hang down her back in a frizzled and knotted mass. Yet her lips curved in a smile.

"I wonder how she will take them?" she mused, absently

removing some of the jeweled hairpins. "I fear it may be long before we hear of it. If an accident befalls them on the road, word may go first to Castell Maelduin. Or perhaps . . . perhaps no word will come at all. Perhaps no one will ever hear of Maelgwyn's sons again."

"Yes, but I would like to hear it," said Calchas, turning his back to the fire. "I want to know. We can't spend the rest of our lives looking over our shoulders, wondering if they will turn up again when we least expect to see them. I don't care for that notion at all."

Diaspad shrugged. "I imagine we will hear something, by and by. It is unlikely that they will simply disappear. But how amusing it would be," she went on, playing with a long strand of her brilliant hair, "to be at Castell Maelduin when *they* hear of it! Imagine, if you can, the consternation, the grief . . . the simple folk mourning, in their simple way, for their poor lost princes . . . the tearful young women . . . the bereaved parents—"

"—and here at Caer Cadwy, the grief-stricken uncle?" Calchas finished for her.

Diaspad looked faintly annoyed. "Manogan fab Menai? I told you once before: I don't concern myself with Manogan, his joys or his sorrows. That cold man who walks these halls is a stranger to me, and the fiery youth I knew and loved is dead. I should know, for I killed him. We all three played a part in destroying Manogan: Madawc's daughter, with her bare feet and her goats, stupid little Gwdolwen, dazzled at finding herself with *two* princes at her feet—but it was I who struck the killing blow, I who loved him."

She wandered over to the fire, instinctively held out her hands as if to warm them, took a deep breath of the scented smoke, but her mind was very far away. "That handsome, passionate youth . . . so wild and yet so tender. He had a head of dark curls like a gypsy and eyes like—the Devil take you, Daire Ruadh mac Forgoll," she interrupted herself. "What do you mean by sneaking up behind me that way?"

Derry jerked back the hand he had placed on the back of her neck. "I was only . . . I thought you liked me to do that."

"Well, I don't," snapped the Princess. "And when I want you to touch me, I will tell you so. And why in Celydonn," she added with a shudder, "have you taken to painting yourself in that hideous fashion? Do you imagine it is becoming?"

She flung herself down on the silver chair, and her glance chanced to alight on Prescelli, curled up on the tygerskin rug, completely unnoticed until just this moment. "Do get up, you lazy girl, and try to make yourself useful. You can comb my hair."

Prescelli dragged herself to her feet. She had already discarded the feathered costume and the heavy golden mask, and she looked pale and plainer than ever in one of her old shabby gowns and a threadbare cloak. She was tired and dispirited, a headache was beginning to press at the back of her eyes, and all this talk of death depressed her even further.

"Don't sulk, Derry," Diaspad advised, as Prescelli pulled an ivory comb through the tangled auburn mass. "It's so very unbecoming. Pour me a cup of wine and one for yourself, and we will have a drink together before you go off to bed."

Derry frowned. "I'm not staying here tonight? But you promised . . ."

"I am too tired for any of that. And you are so amazingly loathsome tonight," said Diaspad, "that I don't think I could bear to have you near me."

"I thought we were going to celebrate," Derry pouted. "And I don't see why you are so cross with me. I haven't—"

"*I* don't see that you have anything to celebrate," Prescelli put in unexpectedly. "You all talk as though Fflergant and his brother were as good as dead, but as far as I can see, there's no reason to suppose that they won't come riding through the front gate, as hale as ever, before the week is out. Yes, and I will tell you something else as well: I will be glad when word comes that they have!"

"Would you believe it?" said Derry, affecting surprise. "Our Prescelli has conceived a passion for one or both of our fine young princes—a hopeless passion, or do I need to tell you?" He took two wine goblets down from a shelf: a plain silver goblet for himself and one much larger, elaborately decorated with a latticework of gold and glittering jewels, for the Princess.

Prescelli sniffed. "Your mind does run on the one thing, Derry. And you're absolutely wrong. You think that everyone is exactly like you, but they aren't—thank God! I remember how you go on: You tease a girl and you coax her, you tell her pretty lies . . . and all the time you're only trying to get her into your bed, so you can treat her like a whore and discard her."

"And you imagine," Derry said indulgently, as he poured wine into the two cups, "that our young heroes are different? I say imagine, because I know very well that neither of them has ever given you a second glance."

"That's just it," said Prescelli, unknotting a tangle. "That's just exactly it. They aren't interested in me that way at all—I don't suppose they even like me. But you would never know that from the way that they speak to me. Fflergant and Tryffin are always polite and considerate and they don't want *any*thing in return."

"Hardly to be wondered at," smirked Derry, placing the heavy goblet in Diaspad's hands, "since much more attractive women are theirs for the asking."

"Very likely they are. But they don't boast of their conquests, like some men do, or make filthy jokes about women. And they don't maul the serving girls, like Morc does, and they just seem to have a natural respect for people, whether they happen to be females or not—so I'd much rather see them alive than dead, that's all," she finished breathlessly.

"But if they are dead . . . why, then, you are just as much to blame as the rest of us," Derry pointed out cruelly.

"That's not true," protested Prescelli. "I didn't do anythin really. Just dressed up in a silly costume and—"

"But you knew," Derry goaded her. "You knew, and neve made any attempt to—"

"By all the powers!" exclaimed Diaspad, as Prescelli, in he agitation, yanked the comb through her hair. "What do yo think you are doing? You *are* a clumsy girl!"

"I can't help it," said Prescelli sullenly. "There's a fearf knot back here."

"Well, then, leave it be. Leave it for someone else," sa Diaspad impatiently. "You're not good for much, after all! Pic up my cloak and put it away, and then fetch Brangwengwen f me."

Prescelli threw down the comb, stooped to pick up the di carded cloak. Behind her, Diaspad was saying, "Calchas, whe did you put my knife?"

"Your knife?" said Calchas. "I did nothing with your kni Why do you ask me? You had it last."

"Don't be absurd. You carried it down to the meadow, a naturally I expected you to bring it back."

Prescelli folded the velvet cloak neatly, carried it over to the painted chest at the foot of the bed.

"It must be somewhere about. Don't stand there staring at me," demanded Diaspad. "Search the room, all of you. I want you to find it at once!"

Derry groaned and put down his wine goblet, Calchas sighed, but stayed where he was, and Morc actually stood up and began to search the room. But Prescelli, defiantly, continued on with the task originally assigned to her. She opened the chest, was about to lay the cloak down inside with the other gaudy silks and velvets . . . when something heavy within the folds of cloth attracted her attention.

She put her hand between the layers and discovered a concealed pocket in the lining. Her probing fingers touched something cold and metallic. Prescelli opened her mouth to speak, then closed it again.

She looked over her shoulder to see what the others were doing. Diaspad was still staring, frowning, into the fire. The others were conducting a half-hearted search on the other side of the room. Prescelli turned back to the clothes chest and drew out the knife.

The silk wrappings around the blade shimmered in the firelight, the intricately worked hilt gleamed golden. It was beautiful, that knife, and obviously valuable, and Prescelli—who never could resist anything that was precious and not her own was gripped by an overwhelming desire to possess it.

"If it isn't here," Diaspad said behind her, "you must have dropped it down in the meadow or the ruins. How could you be so careless? If anyone finds it there tomorrow . . ."

"There is no reason for anyone to guess that it belongs to you," Calchas pointed out. "A pity to lose it, but—"

"I don't intend to lose it," retorted his mother. "You are very quiet, Prescelli," she added suspiciously. "Have you seen my knife anywhere?"

"No," said Prescelli, thrusting the knife into her belt, under the shabby cloak where it could not be seen. "I haven't seen your horrid knife." And she was surprised at how calmly and convincingly she said it. She closed the lid of the clothes chest. "Do you want me to help them look for it or do you still want me to find Brangwengwen?"

"Fetch me Brangwengwen," said Diaspad irritably. "And mind you don't go to bed until you find her!"

Prescelli walked to the door with a wildly beating heart. Once she was outside the room she ran down the drafty corridor until she came to the little bedchamber she shared with the hunchback, Brangwengwen. And it was then, and only then, that Prescelli finally took time to consider: Just what in the world was she planning to do with the Princess Diaspad's knife?

Back in that other, grander, bedchamber, Diaspad was saying, "Well, Derry, it seems that you and Morc will have to retrace our steps and see if you can find the knife."

"Morc and I?" Derry exclaimed, knocking over a half-dozen orange candles in his consternation. "Why not Calchas? He was the one who left the knife behind. Why should we go down?"

"Because I tell you to," snapped the Princess. Then, surprisingly, she changed her tone entirely.

"Derry, my dear, I wouldn't ask you to go if there were any threat to your safety," she said, caressing his arm. "The guards won't wake yet—not until the others come to relieve them at dawn. You have plenty of time to conduct a search. *Do* be a good boy and run down there, just to oblige me?"

Derry appeared to consider. "Well, maybe I will. If you are certain that it's safe. Oh, very well. Come along, Morc."

Morc shuffled after his brother, closing the door with a crash behind him.

"But you can't be so gullible," Calchas protested. "You don't really believe that Derry will go all the way down there at this hour, just to be obliging? If you ask me, he will just go straight to his room, crawl into bed, and tell you in the morning that he looked—he looked just everywhere—but couldn't find your knife."

"I don't doubt that you have guessed Derry's intentions," purred the Princess. "Nevertheless, I expect he will soon undergo a sudden change of heart."

"What makes you say so? How can you be so sure?"

"Because," said Diaspad sweetly, "I took the liberty of relieving Derry of this." And she held up a long, narrow dagger with a polished brass hilt, the dagger which Derry habitually wore up his left sleeve, which Ceilyn mac Cuel or Fergos fa Neol—or any of a dozen others who had shared quarters with Derry over the years—could instantly identify.

"I do think," said Diaspad smugly, "that Derry will trace our steps with great care and search the meadow most minutely, if he suspects that his own blade is down there with mine."

"Try to be still," Tryffin advised his brother. "They say if you just float there, you won't sink so fast." Fflergant shivered in the chilly grip of the mud and water but he forced himself to relax. Tryffin nodded approvingly.

"That's the way; don't move a muscle. I'll be right back to haul you out of here."

He pushed the reeds aside and went back to the spot where Garanwyn was holding the horses. "He stumbled into quicksand. For God's sake, we have to be calm and use our heads! Have we any rope? No . . . then it will have to be the reins," said Tryffin, handing the lantern over to Garanwyn and pulling out his dagger.

"We can use the horses," Garanwyn began, then thought better of it. The horses were still sweating and shivering, terrified by something they could scent but the boys could not.

"Too dangerous, the state they're in," Tryffin said, cutting off the second pair of reins. "And I don't know that the ground near the pool will support their weight. A great hysterical horse wallowing around in the mud with him—that would finish Fflergant for certain. But we can pull him out by ourselves, the two of us."

A minute later, they stood at the edge of the pool offering words of encouragement to Fflergant, relieved to see that he had waited calmly and was not sinking any deeper into the mud. "Did you slip?" Tryffin asked, testing the footing at the edge of the pool.

"I think so. The grass—" But Tryffin was already uprooting the slippery trampled grass. Then, working swiftly and deftly, he knotted the three lengths of leather into a long rope with a noose at one end, and tossed that end to his brother.

Fflergant slipped the harness over his head and shoulders, tightened it around his chest. "We pull together," Tryffin told Garanwyn, as they both took hold of the reins. "On my word—now!"

Together they heaved with all their might, but the only result was that Tryffin lost his footing and they both ended up in a heap, half in and half out of the water.

"God of Heaven!" Tryffin panted, scrambling to his feet. "What is holding you?"

"I don't know," said Fflergant. "I can't feel a thing below my waist."

By the light of their remaining lantern, Tryffin looked pale but determined, and his quiet confidence steadied the others. "We try again," he said.

But after an eternity of straining and pulling, they were forced to stop again, in order to catch their breath and ease their aching arms. Though Fflergant's head still remained well above the water, they had not succeeded in pulling him any closer. And they could not continue this terrible stalemate forever—the chill and the exposure would eventually claim him, even if the quicksand did not.

Apparently, that same thought had occurred to Fflergant. "It seems," he said bleakly, "that the marsh is determined to take me. And she'll have you, too, if you don't take care."

Tryffin ground his teeth audibly. His monumental composure was beginning to crack. "This filthy foreign mudhole is taking no one!" he spat.

They braced themselves for another struggle, and pulled with all their might. But the harness creaked ominously under the strain. The wet leather was stretching perilously thin. Soon, it would snap, leaving them with no means to pull Fflergant out.

And the embankment was crumbling away beneath their feet, their footing growing increasingly treacherous. One misstep, thought Garanwyn, just one misstep and, just as Fflergant had predicted, he and Tryffin would slide into the bog with him.

Crouching atop the earthworks, Ceilyn fractured the sullen silence. "Listen!"

Expecting to hear some alarm issuing from the gatehouse, Teleri looked that way first. Then the wind brought her a fragment of the conversation which had alerted Ceilyn.

"A fool's errand, no doubt," Derry was complaining, as he and his brother came up the path from the beach. "Like as not she took it herself to give me a scare. But just in case . . ."

Morc answered in a low rumble, perhaps warning him that they were about to pass below the gatehouse, because they were both silent after that. Ceilyn allowed them time enough to pass then inched over to the edge of the rampart, preparing to lower himself into the bushes.

"Ceilyn . . . where are you going?"

"I don't know what further mischief Morc and Derry are plotting," he whispered, "but those men down there are in no condition to defend themselves."

He landed lightly in the bushes and slid down the hill again. Teleri, uninvited, followed after him. The moon remained hidden, but they moved down the path cautiously, treading warily lest the snap of a twig or the skittering of a stone betray their presence to those they followed.

They skirted the guard's camp, keeping their distance from the fire. Ceilyn slipped through the bars of the fence, automatically reached out to help Teleri. They could hear Derry cursing in the darkness ahead of them, and Ceilyn was able to just make out his shadowy figure moving across the meadow. They moved in that direction.

"Damn it! About as black as pitch out here. How am I to find anything? I'll go back to the fire and fetch—Morc!" Derry interrupted himself sharply. "Is that you, over by the fence?" And Ceilyn realized with a sinking heart that he and Teleri had inadvertently placed themselves between Derry and the campfire.

Morc growled a reply, somewhere off to their left, and his words were followed by the soft sound of a sword deserting the scabbard. It was at that precise moment that the moon chose to unveil herself.

Ceilyn stared grimly across the moonlit meadow. Morc and Derry, with their swords drawn, were both moving cautiously but resolutely his way. "Damn!" he said, drawing his own sword, with a frustrated sense that he had been here before. Over his shoulder, he said to Teleri, "How fast can you run?"

Teleri answered him, her voice unsteady, but nevertheless determined. "I'm not going to run, Ceilyn."

Garanwyn and Tryffin were growing dangerously tired. Though neither wanted to admit it, they both knew they were losing their struggle with the bog. Fflergant knew it, too. The water came nearly up to his chin, he was chilled and numb from the shoulders down, and he was certain that he was going to die.

He felt inside his shirt, clumsily seeking the little leather bag which dangled from a thong around his neck. Just above his heart, where Garanwyn wore his silver cross, Fflergant carried a handful of earth, soil from the valley of the little church back in Tir Gwyngelli. Tryffin wore a similar token: It was a custom dating from time immemorial, a precaution in case either of them should die and be buried in foreign soil—to the Gwyngellach, the most tragic fate of all. Finding the leather bag, clasping his nearly lifeless fingers around it, Fflergant took comfort from its presence. He would die, but a little bit of Gwyngelli would remain there with him.

"Why don't you put an end to it?" he asked wearily. "I'm finished anyway. There is no use killing yourselves along with me."

Tryffin set his teeth, dug in his heels, and pulled harder. "No one is going . . . to die here," he panted. "I told you . . . this place is taking . . . no one!" Something stirred inside him, like a dragon uncoiling, filling him with a rage so vast, so tremendous, that it nearly crushed the breath out of him.

"Get out of my way. . . . You're only in my way!" he snarled at Garanwyn, with a face so terrible that the boy instantly released his hold on the reins and retreated to a safe distance.

Tryffin wrapped the slack around his hands until the leather cut deep into his flesh, dug in his heels for one last effort, and pulled—pulled until the blood roared in his ears and every muscle shook with the strain.

He was exhausted. Every bone in his body ached. And Fflergant, weighed down by his heavy clothing and whatever it was that anchored him, was a dead weight at the other end of the harness. But pain and weariness both disappeared in one surge of overpowering fury.

"Give him back, Teirwaedd Morfa," he hissed through his teeth. *"You old bitch, give him BACK!!"*

"Sweet Jesus and all the saints!" breathed Garanwyn. "He's actually doing it!"

Inch by painful inch, Tryffin moved back and away from the dark pool, hauling his brother along with him. Once, Tryffin started to slide, but regained his footing with difficulty and continued his agonizingly slow progress. The water began to bubble and hiss.

The leather creaked and finally snapped, sending Tryffin sprawling helplessly backward. But Fflergant was just within reach now, and Garanwyn stretched out to give him a hand.

Then Tryffin scrambled to his feet, and between them he and Garanwyn dragged Fflergant out of the pool and into the high grass on the verge. Then they all three collapsed in a heap.

Something long, strong, and slippery detached itself from Fflergant's leg and slithered back into the bog.

And when they all caught their breath again, words seemed inadequate to express their triumphant relief. Garanwyn sat up and stared at Tryffin, who, practical as ever, was already trying to rub some life back into his brother's waterlogged limbs. Garanwyn had been more impressed by the sight of his usually tranquil cousin in a towering passion than he had been by Tryffin's feat of strength, but now he was beginning to realize that he had just witnessed something truly amazing.

"How did you do that?" he asked wonderingly. "We couldn't do it together, as hard as we pulled. . . . How did you find the strength to do it alone?"

Tryffin shook his head. Now that he had descended from the heights of his rage, he was embarrassed by his lack of control, ashamed to think that he had not succeeded by good sense and determination alone. "I don't know. Didn't anyone ever tell you that I have the Devil of a temper?"

Garanwyn began to laugh helplessly. He leaned back on his elbows and howled until his sides ached as much as the rest of him did. "I guess you must! Before God, I guess you must!"

"Look," Fflergant broke in, raising a feeble arm and pointing. All around them, the marsh was suddenly alive with little twinkling lights.

Garanwyn swallowed the last of his laughter. "Fireflies . . . at this time of year?"

"Not fireflies—torches," said Tryffin. "Torches and boats . . . Can you hear the oars? But that's not possible. Nobody *lives* in Teirwaedd Morfa—nobody human."

Ceilyn stared disbelievingly down at the bodies of the two men he had dispatched with so little effort. "That was much too easy."

Teleri, who knelt on the ground at his feet, did not reply immediately—she was too busy examining all that remained of Morc and Derry. "They are dead," she finally pronounced in a hollow voice.

"Dead?" said Ceilyn. "Of course they are dead. You don't

have to be a physician to see that. But what I want to know is: Did *you* kill them, or did *I*?"

"I?" she protested. "How could I do such a thing? I have no spells to kill a man. That's not what I was trained for."

"Yes, and that is another question I've been meaning to ask," he said. "Just what *were* you trained for?"

"Not for this," Teleri replied faintly. "Not for this." Very gently, she closed Derry's clouded blue eyes. She had watched men die before, but never violently, and the experience had shaken her. "But Ceilyn . . . I don't understand. Didn't you strike to kill?"

Considering the battered state of Morc's head and the fact that Derry had been practically disemboweled, the question was ludicrous. Ceilyn did not laugh. "Of course I . . . but it was too easy. It happened too quickly. Morc . . . Morc just stood there with his sword upraised and a startled look on his face, and Derry didn't even *try* to turn my blade."

He jerked her suddenly and sharply to her feet. "Well, then," he said roughly. "It's done, however it chanced to happen. There is nothing you can do for either of them, supposing you wanted to. We had best be on our way, just in case whatever it was you started down here isn't quite finished yet."

"Yes," Teleri agreed bleakly, rubbing her wrist. "We had better be on our way."

"The woman is a witch!" said Teilo. "She it is who robs the nests, who snatches the infant from the cradle. Cast her out, I charge you, cast her out. Is it not written in the Scriptures: Thou shalt not suffer a witch to live?"

A great fear came over Rhonwen then, and she threw herself at the feet of the saint. "Mercy," she cried. "Have mercy on me, for I repent all the evil that I did."

Teilo gazed down upon the woman, and his heart inclined toward mercy. Yet he was resolved to put Rhonwen's penitence to the test. He sent a boy to the church for holy water, and the lad carried it back to him in a little clay cup.

The saint sprinkled the water upon the witch, and she cried out as if in pain. The woman disappeared in a clap of thunder, leaving a foul reek upon the air.

—From a fragmentary account of The Life of St. Teilo

14.

Wormwood and Gall

In the darkness at the foot of the stairs, Ceilyn caught Teleri suddenly in his arms. Her hands instinctively went up to ward him off, but he imprisoned her wrists and held her pinned against the rough earth wall. "You said," he breathed in her ear, "you said any payment I might care to name. I've a mind to collect that debt right now."

She made a tiny sound, more of surprise than protest, but he felt her tremble in his grasp. The damp musty air of the tunnel mingled with the sweet scent of her fear, and he found that her helplessness pleased and excited him.

"You're angry," she whispered. "You want to punish me. . . . Perhaps you have reason."

"Perhaps?" he said. "You think I might have reason? I was

as ignorant of what was in store for me as that poor dead beast down in the meadow. And you led me into it like . . .'' His fingers tightened around her wrists for a moment. "You had a very good idea of what would happen from the very beginning, but you never spoke a word of warning. And you used me, played shamelessly on my feelings for you, involved me in Black Magic and murder—''

"You insisted on being there," she protested. "I never asked you to accompany me—I tried to send you away. And I didn't know what the Princess was planning, though I had my suspicions. But it was your idea to follow Morc and Derry, never mine.''

He continued to press her up against the wall with the weight of his body. "I don't know why you should call it murder," she protested. "They attacked *you*. And why should you even care? You are a fighting man, you have killed men before. That is what *you* were trained for.''

The violent mood passed, leaving only a kind of weariness, a vast disgust. "I've *never* killed a man before. Not for all my training. And it wasn't at all the way that I thought it would be. These were men I knew. And God knows I never liked Morc and I *despised* Derry, and if I had killed them cleanly in a fair fight . . . But to kill men who couldn't move a hand against me, to kill by sorcery . . . !''

"They didn't die by sorcery," said Teleri. "Not by any magic of mine. But why should it matter? They are both dead. By your sword or my sorcery, it makes no difference to Morc or Derry now.''

"My sword," he said bitterly, as he released her wrists. He stepped back and glared at her reproachfully. "Yes . . . my sword that you have defiled with your filthy heathen rites. I am glad that you reminded me of that.''

"I am sorry about that," she whispered. "I really don't know what made me insist.''

"You don't know. It seems to me there is a great deal you don't know, and that you've done a good deal of meddling to night, for one who knows so very little.''

He turned away and began to climb the winding stairs. Teleri followed him without a word. Upstairs, the room was dark and cold, and Teleri knelt on her little hearth to rekindle the fire.

"Would it make you feel any better to know that by slayin

Derry and Morc you've probably saved the lives of your kins-men, Fflergant and Tryffin?'' she ventured at last.

Ceilyn, reaching for the handle of the secret door, looked up. ''I beg your pardon. I did what?''

''I was forgetting,'' she said, ''that you understood very little of the ceremony. The Princess asked her Goddess for the lives of Maelgwyn's sons.''

''Maelgwyn's sons?'' The trap-door fell into place with a crash. ''But surely it's Cadifor and Llochafor she wants to destroy?''

''Apparently, she has changed her mind.'' Teleri moved to the table by her bed, poured water from the earthenware pitcher into a bowl. ''Maybe she knows something that we don't.''

Ceilyn watched her wash the blood from her hands. ''You did say something before. . . . If Maelgwyn fab Menai ever chose to do a thing, it would be difficult to stop him. But you don't believe that he and his sons cherish *ambitions*, do you? God knows, Tryffin and Fflergant were just about everywhere during the time the bones were here, and especially the night that they disappeared. But still . . .''

''That would certainly be enough to arouse Diaspad's suspicions, and her enmity,'' said Teleri, drying her hands on her cloak.

''True,'' said Ceilyn, taking his turn at the wash basin. ''She wouldn't require much convincing, would be willing to kill them both, just on the chance. . . . But what has this to do with Morc and Derry?''

''Well,'' said Teleri, ''the Princess did ask for the lives of two young men. And two other young men, of about the same age, are dead instead. And you don't believe they put up a proper resistance. It seems more than coincidence.''

Ceilyn dried his hands, sat down on the edge of her bed, upon the scarlet blanket. ''Before God!'' he said, in a voice trembling somewhere between laughter and horror. ''Derry and Morc for Fflergant and Tryffin—there's a dreadful irony in that!

''Still,'' he added gloomily, ''we don't really know that we have saved them, do we? Or even if we ought to have interfered. Because dreadful as it sounds: Supposing she is right and they do have ambitions? Supposing they are actually at the center of some plot against the King?''

Teleri sat down on the three-legged stool by the fire. ''I don't think we ought to worry about that. When you save a man's life, you don't trouble yourself wondering whether he might commit some misdeed, perhaps years in the future.''

"*I* do," said Ceilyn. "*I* trouble myself worrying about things like that." He had already wiped his sword clean on the grass in the meadow, but he took it out now and examined it curiously. Somehow, he had expected that the blade would be all tarnished and black, but it still gleamed as brightly as ever. "And the rest of the ceremony . . . the part where Diaspad painted Calchas in blood? What was that all about?"

"I think . . ." Teleri hesitated for a long time. "I think that the Princess, acting the part of the Goddess, named Calchas as heir to the throne of Celydonn."

Ceilyn groaned, sliding his sword back into its leather scabbard. "And you set me up as a rival claimant? That's lovely. Yes, that was all that was wanting. Black Magic, murder, and now High Treason."

"No, no," she protested. "What the Princess did and what I did . . . I was playing another role entirely. And that which Diaspad bestowed on Calchas: In ancient times, that was always the gift of the Mother."

"I see," said Ceilyn wearily. "Well, I don't see, but let us pretend that I do. And just what gift was it that you bestowed on me?"

Teleri flinched. "I don't know."

"You don't know. Another convenient lapse of memory, I take it?"

"Ceilyn," she said pitifully. "I don't enjoy being stupid at times like this. I really don't."

"But you weren't stupid—as you are pleased to call it—down in the meadow," he pointed out. "You seemed to know exactly what you were doing and why."

"Yes," she said. "For once in my life, I was completely sure of myself. It was intoxicating. Though thinking back on it now, it frightens me."

In the gatehouse down below, a single bell tolled, a deep hollow sound. "The guard will be changing now," said Ceilyn. "It won't be long before someone goes down to the camp below and discovers the carcass—if the men down there haven't done so already. Then someone will find the bodies of Derry and Morc."

He stood up, began pacing restlessly from one part of the room to another. "That all this should happen on All Hallows Eve—so much blood spilt and no other explanation—there is going to be talk of witchcraft, you know! Naturally, you will be the first person that most folk think of—and not altogether unfairly, as it turns out. That is going to be rather embarrassing for me, isn't it?" he asked coldly.

"Not if you repudiate me," she said faintly. "If you behave as though you suspect me, too, if you refuse to have anything more to do with me."

Ceilyn scowled horribly. "Naturally I would do that—after all my protestations of devotion down in the meadow, naturally I would turn my back on you just when you need my friendship and all the protection I can offer you!

"The best that can happen is that I am going to look a besotted fool, and the worst . . . the worst doesn't bear thinking about. Someone might actually accuse you of something, and I would be forced to fight him. And how would I live with myself if I killed him?" Then, softening, at the thought of her very real peril: "What would become of you, if I didn't?"

Almost, he could hear the crackling of the flames, smell the reek of burning flesh. He had watched men and women burn, all those years ago back at Caer Celcynnon, but he would never stand by and allow that to happen to Teleri.

"We won't permit it to reach the point of accusations," he said firmly. "We will put a stop to all speculation at the very beginning. You will have to prove your so-called innocence for everyone to see."

"How?" Teleri asked apprehensively. "How could I possibly do that?"

"As you offered to prove yourself to me, not long ago. You can go to church this morning and take the bread and wine. Not just for me to see, but before everyone. This is a holy day, the Feast of All Saints, and nearly everyone will attend Mass this morning. Yes," he added wryly, "there should be quite a turnout this particular morning, and people will be noticing who is and who isn't there. If you are there, too, taking Communion, all Caer Cadwy will take notice." Then, struck by an unpleasant thought, he asked, "You can do it, after last night, can't you?"

"Yes, I think so. But Ceilyn—"

"That ought to be enough for most people. They have a touching faith in that sort of proof," he sighed, thinking of a time when it would have been proof enough for him.

"But Ceilyn," she protested, wringing her hands. "I would much rather not. Not while so many people look on. If you like, I'll do it another time, privately, but this morning—"

"There is still the matter of a debt between us," he reminded her. "Anything I cared to ask for, you said. And this is not an unreasonable request. I might ask—I could still ask—a great deal more.

"And you are not to play any of your old tricks," he added sternly. "No fading away so that nobody sees you but me. Just make certain that you are seen!"

He turned on his heel, started for the door, but paused on the threshold. "And no convenient forgetting, either. Because if you forget to come," he said ominously, "if you do that, I will be forced to come back here and drag you there bodily. And you will take Communion this morning—if the bread turns to ashes and the wine to gall in your mouth—you will do it. Is that perfectly understood?"

"Yes," she said softly. "I understand you. I have—I have no choice but to be there."

"No," said Ceilyn, just before the door slammed behind him, "you have no choice in the matter at all!"

The Princess Diaspad broke her fast, that morning, about an hour later than was her custom. Even at that advanced hour she felt abnormally listless, her usually voracious appetite blunted by exhaustion. She poked experimentally at the joint of beef which the dwarf, Brangwengwen, had placed before her, closed her eyes, and shuddered violently.

"I don't think that I can do this justice," she said faintly, lying back against the satin pillows and the rumpled sleeping furs and pushing the silver tray away. She was pale and unpainted this morning and the bruised look around her eyes had not yet faded. "Take this away, Calchas, and give it to the cats."

Calchas obediently removed the offending piece of meat, and carried it over to the spot by the fireplace where the leopards customarily took their meals. The big cats rumbled and rubbed themselves against his legs in anticipation of the promised treat.

It was then that Prescelli, very full of news, burst into the room. "They are dead . . . horribly dead. Both of them dead."

Diaspad sat up, brightening visibly. "So soon? Word has come of Maelgwyn's sons so soon?"

Prescelli pushed back the purple brocade bed curtains so that colored light from one of the stained-glass windows fell across Diaspad in her nest. "Not Fflergant and Tryffin." She paused, apparently giving some thought to her position as the bearer of unwelcome tidings, took a deep breath, and continued, "It's Morc and Derry. Down in the place where the bull was kept. Though what they were doing—"

"Derry and Morc are dead?" The plate which Calchas had been carrying hit the floor with a crash and both leopards pounced at once. It took two dwarfs and both of the woodwoses to restrain the cats and rescue Calchas from the midst of the fight.

"I hope, for your sake, that this isn't your idea of a joke," said Calchas, nursing a bleeding shin.

"It isn't a joke," said Prescelli.

"A mistake, then?" suggested the Princess, sinking back against the pillows.

"Nor a mistake. I saw the men bring in their bodies," said Prescelli, shuddering at the memory. "Morc is missing part of his head and there is a fearful gap where most of Derry's insides ought to be . . . and they are both quite, *quite* stiff!"

"But who . . . the guards, of course." Diaspad answered her own question. "But I was certain they would sleep until dawn."

"Not the guards," said Prescelli. "They say they know nothing about it. And it was all quite awful and terribly mysterious: The grass around the bodies was scarcely bent, and Morc's and Derry's swords not even bloodied. An ambush in the dark, maybe—but what was Derry doing down there?"

No one bothered to answer her question. "What does all this mean for me?" Calchas asked his mother. His face had acquired an unbecoming greenish tinge. "Did she refuse your offering or just claim more? Is she still offended, or will Morc and Derry be enough to satisfy her? And what is going to happen to *me*?"

"Now, now," said the Princess soothingly, though she, too, had experienced a shock. "There is no reason to panic . . . not just yet. She may have taken exactly what she wanted and be satisfied. Or it may be just a dreadful coincidence. Down by the burial mound in the early morning hours, Derry and Morc might have met with anything. Best to wait and see. When Maelgwyn's sons ride in through the front gate . . . that will be our time to worry.''

"Oh yes," said Calchas, limping across the room, "that will be our time to worry. If some horrid fate doesn't overtake me in the meantime."

"Calchas," the Princess reminded him matter-of-factly, "if Donwy, the Dark Mother, wanted you dead, you would *be* dead. But you have been spared . . . for better things, one hopes."

"For better things—or for worse?" Calchas countered.

But Diaspad was not yet ready to admit that her beautiful plan had gone so far astray. "We won't think about that now," she said. "Time enough to worry later."

By mid-morning, the shocking news of the bull and the mysterious deaths of Morc and Derry mac Forgoll had spread throughout the castle. The result, as Ceilyn had predicted, was unprecedented attendance at Mass in the grand painted chapel dedicated to St. March. Everyone made a point of demonstrating his or her own piety; all were eager to observe their neighbors at prayer.

There was considerable curiosity, too, about how the Princess Diaspad was taking the murder (under circumstances strongly suggestive of witchcraft) of her two young kinsmen. She arrived late, supported by Calchas, very pale and to all appearances grief-stricken, seemingly oblivious to the excited whispering and craning of necks that greeted her arrival in the gilded gallery.

But in all that restless curious crowd, among all the habitual shirkers who attended today merely for show or for morbid curiosity, who ought to have felt themselves out of place in church that morning—not one of them felt so uncomfortable, so miserably certain that he had no right to be there, as Ceilyn. He knelt in his usual place in the gallery, behind the Queen, trying desperately to compose his mind for prayer and failing utterly.

He had arrived at the Mermaid Tower earlier, intending to escort the Queen and her ladies to the chapel, only to find that the first rumors had preceded him. Though Sidonwy had whisked him aside, stifling the first spate of questions with a furious glance, he could not ignore the silent speculation that had followed him everywhere since. Even now, he felt certain that everyone in the chapel watched him covertly. Even the great winged lion painted in green and gold behind and above the altar seemed to glare at him in frozen disapproval, and the martyrs, apostles, and evangelists chasing each other around the domed ceiling appeared to pause in flight and stare down at him in horrified disapprobation.

To make matters worse, the very atmosphere of the chapel—the music and incense, the candlelight reflecting off the jeweled vessels upon the altar, the sight of Sidonwy's rapt face as she recited the prayers, even a glimpse of innocent little Gwenlliant bent studiously over her illuminated missal—all this only increased his guilty sense of trespass. Never since he could remember had Ceilyn been able to walk into a church without the firm conviction that God merely tolerated his defiling presence in his house, and that that toleration was wearing thin. And now he had added witchcraft to his other sins, participated in bloody and unspeakable rites, made a mockery of the sacred vows of knighthood by defiling his sword, and *now*, now he was compounding his guilt, not lessening it, by daring to appear in church with all his sins unconfessed and unabsolved.

Had he been there by himself, Ceilyn would have prostrated himself on the cold stone floor before the altar, wept for the state of his soul, heaped abuse both mental and physical on himself. As he was not alone, such excesses of penitence were denied him. He could only clasp his hands together so tightly that the knuckles ached, and pretend to pray.

By the time Teleri finally arrived, Ceilyn had worked himself into a perfectly wretched state. His place in the gallery commanded an excellent view of the floor below, and he spotted Teleri the moment she slipped in through the door, long before anyone else recognized her. She wore her customary coarse grey, but covered her face and her hair with a light veil of some cobwebby material.

Under the veil, her face was as still and contained as ever he had seen it. If she felt any apprehension at entering the crowded chapel, she concealed it well. As she stepped into a pool of clear light, spilling down from one of the high, narrow windows, she appeared to be clothed entirely in radiant white, and the limpid serenity of her whole aspect made Ceilyn ache with rage and love.

Because she had cheated him again. She was there physically for all to see, but it was obvious to him if not to anyone else that her mind was elsewhere—and not, as would have been proper, contemplating higher things. She was playing another one of her games of make-believe—the Princess Goewin, perhaps, that was one of her favorites, or maybe St. Niamh, conveniently blind and therefore oblivious to her surroundings.

Ceilyn was the first, but by no means the only one to recognize her. As she searched the floor for a vacant spot on which to kneel, a murmur passed through the crowd. And as she found a place among the upper servants and dropped to her knees, there was a rustle of movement as everyone shifted uneasily away from her.

Ceilyn was blushingly aware that every eye in the gallery was on him now. But he was determined to stand his ground. After all, he was in his own appointed place behind the Queen, while Teleri . . .

"Witch!"

Ceilyn had no way of knowing who, in all that vast echoing chamber, had said the word, or even if it was directed at Teleri. But he knew that she had heard it also. All in an instant, she was no longer remote, serene, and untouchable, but small, frightened, and surrounded by hostile faces.

Ceilyn ground his teeth. She was every bit as guilty—in act if not intent—as everyone imagined her to be. She deserved to face them all alone; it was time she learned to face up to the unpleasant things in life.

But if she was guilty, he admitted miserably, then so was he. And she, at least, had only done what she believed to be right and necessary, while he, in yielding to her pleas, had done what he knew to be wrong. He sighed and rose to his feet, whispered his excuses in the Queen's ear and received her leave to go, made a sketchy obeisance to the King, and descended the stairs to the floor of the chapel.

Conscious of a hundred pairs of eyes burning at his back, Ceilyn forced himself to walk down the aisle. As he knelt beside Teleri, he stole one curious, sidelong glance, and was gratified to see that she looked every bit as miserable as he felt. Almost he felt a momentary softening.

But he was still too angry to relent, so he hardened his resolve and his heart, and fastened his attention on the Lion of St. Marc painted above the altar, rather than risk meeting her eyes.

A half hour later, when the monks came around with the bread and the golden chalice, Ceilyn realized the full awkwardness his position. Having placed himself in the public eye, having courted notoriety by aligning himself with Teleri, he was obliged to take Communion, too—unconfessed, unshriven, in no proper state of mind, and for all the wrong reasons—or excite just the sort of comment he must particularly avoid.

Teleri accepted the sacrament without incident—if the bread was dry or the wine bitter, she gave no indication—and Ceilyn had no choice but to follow her example. He had difficulty swallowing, but somehow succeeded and he felt both a guilty relief and a firm conviction that he was the greatest hypocrite ever born. He buried his face in his hands and fervently wished that he were dead.

Up in the gallery, the Princess Diaspad dismissed the priest with a curt shake of her head, refusing both the plate and the chalice. But Ceilyn, weighed down by his sense of sin and inadequacy, remained with his head bowed, and so did not notice the stir that she caused.

Nor was he aware, at the end of the service, when Teleri stood up and slipped out of the chapel, without a word or a glance his way.

Then Finarfon mounted the white steed and took the maiden up before him. At her signal, they started out at a great pace, nor did they halt even when they came to the sea but plunged on even more furiously than before. And Finarfon beheld cities and palaces from afar, and foreign lands where strange beasts roamed, and all manner of curious and wonderful things that he would not afterward remember.

At last he saw, at a great distance, rising up out of the waves, a fair green island, and upon it a great house more splendid than any he had ever seen, shining with many colors in the sunlight. And the white horse brought them to shore, and many fair youths and maidens came out to meet them.

"We are come," said Finarfon's maiden, "to the Land of the Ever Young."

—From The Book of the White Cockerel

15.

In the House of the Horned Moon

The sky went from black, to rose, to palest blue, and the boatmen extinguished their rushlights one by one. The first rays of sunlight painted the high grasses a brilliant living gold and the birds in their nests among the cattails and bulrushes began to stir and twitter.

But Garanwyn huddled at the bottom of the first canoe, cold and damp and utterly miserable. Like most Rhianeddi, he harbored a deep distrust of boats, and this little craft constructed entirely of bundled reeds seemed particularly flimsy. Nor did he know what to make of the boatmen, the swarthy little men who had arrived so unexpectedly with their torches and their strange craft, to take him and his kinsmen . . . where? Nothing had been said of their destination as yet, but every stroke of the double-bladed paddles took them deeper and deeper into the fenlands, farther and farther from the place where they had lost the horses.

It was all water in this part of the marsh, not a bit of dry land anywhere to be seen. Perhaps they had finally reached the river; the water was clear and smelled clean; there was a current flowing south. Or maybe that had something to do with the retreating tide, as they headed toward the sea.

Wreaths of grey mist rose up from the marsh, pale tendrils of fog hanging on the damp air. Garanwyn craned his neck, trying to catch a glimpse of Fflergant or Tryffin, but a veil of mist obscured the other boats and the nearest was only a shadowy silhouette. It was impossible to make out the passengers. He shivered and pulled a cloak of dyed skins more closely around him. The garment had been lent to him by one of the boatmen, the old fellow who sat facing him now, propelling the canoe with light, even strokes. The cloak had an odd, smoky scent to it, not precisely unpleasant but decidedly foreign, as outlandish as the man who owned it.

Garanwyn studied the boatman. There was a great economy in all his movements, every action light, quick, and somehow predatory. For all his tiny size, Garanwyn thought he might make a formidable opponent if it came to a fight.

"Is your home near here?" Garanwyn's voice came out in a croak. "Do you live . . . here in the marsh?"

The old man nodded his head. Garanwyn cleared his throat. "I was always told that nobody lived here. That everyone gave Teirwaedd Morfa a wide berth."

For the first time, the marsh man smiled, revealing white, even teeth. And when he spoke, his accent was certainly strange but his speech was that of an educated man. "The farmers and the herdsmen who live closest to the marsh know we are here, but prefer not to admit to it. It is better than being invisible, to have neighbors so willfully blind."

Garanwyn did not like the sound of that at all. He had lived long enough in Camboglanna to know what kinds of things southerners preferred to ignore. Being of northern stock himself, he was bound to ask: "But why should your neighbors pretend not to see you?"

The marsh man shrugged. "Who would admit to an encounter with the Sidhe—the Fairy Folk? His friends would think him mad—or intoxicated."

Garanwyn shifted uncomfortably, by no means certain that the fellow was jesting. "And are you . . . Fairy Folk?"

The old man smiled again. "What do you think?"

Garanwyn looked him over carefully, taking in his strange bright attire, the feathers woven into his hair, the belt decorated with the brittle little beaks and skeletons of tiny birds. In contrast to these primitive ornaments was a heavy silver bracelet of exquisite workmanship encircling the old man's wrist. Garanwyn was more or less certain that the Sidhe could not bear direct contact with anything made of silver.

He shook his head. 'I think . . . I think I would like to reserve judgment on that question."

The marsh man nodded. "A very good answer," he declared approvingly.

The houses of the marshfolk stood on stilts. Erected on a cluster of tiny, muddy islands, they were long windowless structures of wattle and daub, thatched with bulrushes or willow bark, standing on stout wooden legs like so many fabulous birds or beasts. The house to which Garanwyn and his cousins came was the House of the Clan of the Horned Moon, which perched on six thick legs carved to resemble the legs and feet of some monstrous feline. There was a set of branching antlers tacked up over the door, and a long rope ladder hanging from the doorsill.

It took four men to hoist Fflergant up the ladder and into the house. When Garanwyn tried to follow, he found that his own limbs were weak and shaky, unwilling to obey him. But a small brown hand reached down and pulled him up onto the doorsill, then guided him past the goatskin that served for a door.

Inside, there was a fire and warm drinks, and tiny dark-haired women in long saffron-colored gowns waiting to help him out of his boots and outer clothing. Tryffin and several of the men from the boats set to work on Fflergant over by the fire. Garanwyn simply did as he was told, followed where he was led. He was too exhausted to protest, too dazed and dizzy after the ordeals of the night, the surprising events of the morning, to ask any more questions.

The old man from the canoe took up a rushlight and led Garanwyn up a flight of narrow ladderlike stairs at the back of the house. The loft, like the room below, was low-ceilinged and windowless; the rafters were hung with hammocks and fishnets, bundled herbs, and roots and vegetables done up in long chains or suspended in bags of woven hemp. Along one wall stood a dozen or more covered wicker baskets, and a pile of sacks that might contain grain were arranged in one corner. A round hole cut in the middle of the floor allowed smoke to rise up from the floor below and from the loft out another, smaller, hole in the roof.

Someone had made up two beds on the floor, and had set a light, a little earthen bowl of burning oil, on a low stool between them. "You will sleep here," said Garanwyn's guide.

Glad to obey, the boy shed the rest of his clothing, climbed in between the pile of blankets and neatly stitched goatskins and the feather mattresses, and fell almost instantly asleep.

For days, Fflergant lay cold and pale and listless in bed, in a little alcove off the main room. There could be no question of continuing their journey, no question of refusing the generous, unexpected hospitality of the marshfolk. Fflergant could only lie on his back warmed by the hot stones his hosts tucked in with him, drinking quantities of willow or coltsfoot tea (to fight off the chill in his lungs, his nurses informed him), or lulled to sleep by the songs and chants and stories that his brother and the women patiently recited to him. Fflergant, who had never been sick a day in his life before, might have enjoyed all the attention had he not felt so wretched.

Garanwyn was soon up and out of bed, but not much better off. He sat most of each day wrapped in blankets by the clay hearth in the center of the long lower chamber, where he subsisted on bowls of broth or broiled grain sweetened with honey and milk, and listened to the stories of Arfondwy, the daughter of the house.

Arfondwy had a pleasant voice and she was, like all the other men and women who lived in the house on stilts, a skillful storyteller. Her range was amazing: She had a store of tales appropriate to every theme, season, and occasion, and when she grew weary of the old tales she created new ones.

When her voice grew tired, she played for Garanwyn upon the harp or crwth. When he wanted to talk, she was an attentive and responsive listener. As the days passed, his interest in her grew. Wherever she went, whatever she was doing, he loved to watch her. Her wide sea-colored eyes changed with every mood, and she had a vast quantity of light brown hair so fine that a breath, a sigh, might lift it. Even to see her going about her daily tasks delighted him, for her figure was neat and graceful, her movements deft yet somehow expressive. In her hands, a spindle, a shuttle, even the old heather broom that she used to sweep the floor acquired some of that grace, a quality of movement. . . . Garanwyn knew that he was in danger, and not from a chill in his lungs. What he did not know was what he was going to do about it.

Mornings and evenings, Arfondwy swept the hearth, brought in fresh water, and then knelt down to pray before the little carven altar set up in one corner of the room. There was no cross or crucifix, no holy vessel that Garanwyn could recognize, only tiny decorated baskets, bits of shell and bone, and dried flowers that the children of the house placed there. At the beginning of every meal, Arfondwy took a bowl of grain or a platter of meat or honeycakes and put it on the altar. After the meal, she poured the contents of the dish into the fire. Garanwyn had a very good idea of what she was doing, but earnestly attempted to convince himself otherwise.

When Tryffin was not in attendance on his brother, he cheerfully insisted on sharing the work of the household, whether it was peeling vegetables like a kitchen-boy, helping the women card their wool, or the men to mend their fishnets and fletch their arrows.

"But must you take on all the dirtiest and most demeaning tasks?" Garanwyn asked indignantly, momentarily roused out of the lethargy that weighed down his arms and legs and sometimes muddled his thinking.

He eyed the pile of turnips at Tryffin's feet. "I'm sure it courteous to offer to help, and I know that you have always found amusement in some of the oddest places, but . . ."

"Where I was raised," Tryffin began, "nobody sees any—"

"I know what people think, where you were raised," said Garanwyn, exasperated. "If a prince of Tir Gwyngelli does something, it must be all right. Excuse me for forgetting that

"That's not precisely the way of it," said the imperturbable Tryffin, "but close enough. What I was going to say was: Nobody in Tir Gwyngelli sees anything inherently demeaning any form of honest labor.

"Something which *I* have never been able to understand,"

went on amiably, "is why it should be perfectly natural, in most places, for a noble youth such as you or I to serve at meals, to clean another man's boots, polish his armor, curry his horse, even dress and spit and cook game for him so long as it's done out of doors, while other tasks, like skinning and boiling turnips, apparently no more dirty or degrading, are considered strictly beneath us."

Garanwyn sighed. They had had this conversation before, or one very like it.

The truth was, Garanwyn soon decided, that Tryffin was in his element: asking questions and making his own observations, learning new skills, and fascinated by the lives and customs of the marshdwellers. He always had been insatiably curious about people in other walks of life—a trait that had, up until now, both amused and scandalized Garanwyn. But Garanwyn was curious, too, as soon as he began to feel better, and eager to hear what Tryffin had concluded.

"Distant kin to the Mochdreffi and the Hillfolk . . . they must be," said Tryffin. "You've only to look at them. They call themselves the 'Korred' and claim to be the original inhabitants of Camboglanna and most of the south. I'm inclined to believe that: most of their songs and chants, though not precisely familiar, have a certain sort of *sound* to them that strikes me as somehow similar to something I've heard before."

Garanwyn nodded. "I've noticed that myself. But what I want to know is this: Where do they get all the fine things they own—the harps and the other musical instruments, the books and the silver brooches? And even the ordinary things, like wheat and oats and the wool the women are everlastingly spinning—you can't raise grain or sheep in country like this."

"They trade for them," said Tryffin. "Yes, I know. Their neighbors like to pretend that nobody lives here. But it's this pretense about fairies—very reminiscent of my own folk, that convenient little fiction. The farmers leave out their own goods: their wool, or flax, or seasoned wood, and the marshfolk come after nightfall to take what they want and leave their linen and wicker baskets, their medicinal roots and dyes in their place."

Garanwyn coughed feebly into his hand. "I don't see the point."

Tryffin lowered his voice. "The point is . . . these people are pagans in case you didn't guess, and your little friend, unless I am mistaken, is their virgin priestess. I see that you have guessed, but preferred not to believe it. We'll make a proper southerner of you yet. But you can sympathize with their nearest neighbors: If anyone took official notice of their presence here, sooner or later someone would feel obliged to root them out. And that would be a pity—for you can see for yourself that they are fine people.''

They *were* fine people—even Garanwyn, with all his northern prejudices, had to admit to that. If the people of the Clan of the Horned Moon were any example, the pagans of Teirwaedd Morfa were warm-hearted, hospitable, and cultured folk. It was unfortunate that they were not Christians as well.

"They might be converted," Garanwyn pointed out.

Tryffin gave him a pitying look. "You don't imagine that nobody's ever tried that before? With more convincing arguments than you or I would ever care to employ. We wondered, the other night, why nobody lives near the marsh, what it was that frightened them away. But now I reckon we had it backward. The people didn't run *from* the marsh; they came *into* the marsh and hid themselves, a long time ago, fleeing persecution. They lived here, apart from other men, because that allows them to practice their own faith unmolested . . . and unconverted.''

Garanwyn sighed. Tryffin would naturally look at things that way—the Gwyngelli Hills, by all accounts, were alive with pagans, and Maelgwyn fab Menai never lifted a hand either to punish or convert them. Which reminded Garanwyn of another question. "But those other things . . . the books and the silver jewelry, for instance . . . they didn't gain those by trading with Camboglannach farmers.''

Tryffin shook his head, moved a little closer to the fire. "The books, I don't know, unless perchance they've scribes among them, which would not surprise me at all. But the brooches and the arm rings come from Tir Gwyngelli, I am certain of that. Not much chance I would mistake the workmanship of our own craftsmen. I think there must be some connection, some manner of direct trade between the Korred and the pagan Hillfolk. That would explain the hospitality we have received here.''

Garanwyn was shocked. "You mean that some of your own people maintain secret dealings with the marshdwellers? I can scarcely believe that. Surely your father—''

Tryffin shook his head again. "As to secret . . . yes and no. There are a good many things going on in the Gwyngelli Hills that outsiders know nothing about. God knows, there are any number of things going on there *I* never hear about. But there is nothing, no matter how trivial or how important, happening anywhere in Tir Gwyngelli, the hills or the lowlands, that my father doesn't come to hear of it. Whether he encourages a secret trade with these people or merely tolerates it, suffice to say he'll have his reasons, and I'm not the one to question them."

The inhabitants of the house were many, and Garanwyn never succeeded in sorting them all out or in determining the relationship of each to all the others, for there was a strong resemblance among them that added to his confusion. Among the tiny, warm-skinned marshdwellers, Garanwyn felt odd and out of place, strangely pale and attenuated by comparison. The only three who stood out clear in his mind were Arfondwy and her mother, Gonwenlyn—who were fairer and milder than the others, both in appearance and manner—and Anwe the Weaver, who would have stood out in a crowd of thousands.

The Weaver—apparently a title of some special significance— was a young woman of immense dignity and extraordinary beauty, with flashing dark eyes and a wealth of silky black hair. For all her tiny stature, for all the awkwardness of her late pregnancy, she presented an imposing figure in her scarlet wool gown, a checkered mantle of many colors draped over one shoulder and pinned in place with an enormous silver brooch. Her other ornaments, of which she wore quite a number, binding her hair or strung on leather thongs around her neck and wrists, were fashioned of bone and shell.

The truth was, Garanwyn was a little afraid of Anwe. He had seen the others move aside when she passed, the deference everyone paid her, and he believed there was more to it than the fact she was soon to be a mother. And according to Arfondwy, the Weaver possessed strange powers. It had been she, for instance, who sent out the men to offer aid to Garanwyn and his cousins.

"It was a dream she had and she roused us all in the middle of the night," said Arfondwy. "There was bad luck on your kinsmen. Anwe saw it, like a black cloud hovering over them. And the fire of the red dragon was nearly extinguished."

"And was it your cousin who lifted that cloud?" Garanwyn

asked, fully convinced that the beautiful Anwe was capable of that—if favorably disposed—and of more terrible things—if not.

But Arfondwy shook her head. "That was the favor of the Lady. Is not the dragon her beloved, first among her consorts? It was the Lady who rekindled the dragon's flame, to lend him strength in his battle with the bog-creature. Yet after that struggle had been won, there was still the cold and the damp, which can be deadly, too. So Anwe insisted that the men go out in their boats to rescue you. As you can imagine," she added, with a hint of a smile, "when Anwe makes her desires known, even my father and her own father hasten to oblige her."

"But why? Not why should your father wish to oblige Anwe . . ." (Garanwyn did not believe that the man existed who was courageous enough to deny that formidable young woman anything) ". . . but why should your cousin care what happened to us? We were strangers, men of another faith. . . . Why should the Weaver, or anyone here, exert herself on our behalf?"

Arfondwy opened her eyes wide in surprise. "But you do not think that the Goddess bestows her gifts in order that we may ignore them—or use them only for our own selfish ends?" she protested. "If Anwe has dreams and visions, if knowledge of your plight came to her in the night, was it not a sign that we were meant to act on it?"

Garanwyn puzzled that one out. Though he trusted Arfondwy and most of the others, he was still inclined to distrust the Weaver and her motives. And Arfondwy's poetic story of the Lady and the dragon made no sense at all, unless it implied, as Tryffin had hinted, some secret alliance between her own folk and the pagans in the Hidden Country. Perhaps, after all, that was the explanation.

Or perhaps (Garanwyn told himself grimly), perhaps Anwe and her many-faced Goddess had some other, darker, design, of which Arfondwy and the others were entirely ignorant.

Weep you men and women of the isles, weep!
For Siawn the young, the valiant is no more
I saw him ride forth into battle, brave in silver and green
Siawn the fairest and wisest of all Cynwal's kin
Now he lies dead among the broken stones and only the cold
*   snow covers him*

Dead is Siawn—weep you women of Camboglanna!
Your sons were his guard of honor
Where are they now?
Where is Morn, the long-limbed, the golden-haired?
Where is Donnotaurus, the sweet-singer, the minstrel of the
*   birds?*
Where is Cefn? Where is Maelwys, beloved of maidens?
Gone, they are all gone
Black grief over the hills of Camboglanna!
Wailing on the plain of the tall stones!
    —Owain's Lament for Siawn and the Men of the South

16.

A Thoroughly Dreary Affair

The Princess Diaspad buried Morc and Derry quickly, quietly, and inexpensively in the little graveyard below Brynn Caer Cadwy. The Draighenach custom of a wake on the night before the funeral had been dispensed with altogether (*"Who would come?"* Calchas had asked, purely rhetorically) and the funeral itself was a hasty and shabby affair, poorly attended.

Twelve dwarfs wearing death-masks carried the flimsy coffins out of the castle. Pergrin the giant sang a dirge in his high, unpleasant voice, the woodwoses beat a dreary accompaniment with their staves, and the Princess, Calchas, and the rest of her odd household straggled behind. It was, if not precisely a mournful procession, at least a thoroughly dismal one.

Down in the graveyard, a stormy-eyed youth and a pale little girl were waiting—though these two could scarcely be counted among the mourners. They watched the ceremony from the low stone wall which surrounded the cemetery, and kept themselves aloof from the bereaved household.

(*"But I need to go,"* Gwenlliant had pleaded earlier. *"I want to be certain that Derry and Morc are really dead."*

(*"What an idea!"* Fand exclaimed. *"Where do you get these morbid fancies? The funeral would only make you worse, and haven't you troubled us enough with your dreams and your cries in the night?*

(*"Besides,"* she had added, *"you can't properly go alone, and Finola and I absolutely refuse to be seen at a Leth Scathach funeral!"*

(Much to everyone's surprise, the child had found an unlikely supporter in Ceilyn, who offered to escort her to the graveyard.)

"Bloody hypocrites, both of them," said Calchas to Prescelli, eyeing these uninvited observers with open hostility. "What were Derry and Morc to either of them, I would like to know?"

"Ceilyn mac Cuel cherishes a great concern for all lost souls," Prescelli replied sarcastically, though her voice lacked its accustomed edge.

"As though Derry ever *had* a soul to be prayed for," smirked Calchas. "But you are taking all this rather hard, I must say." Ever since Prescelli had discovered what errand took Derry and his brother down to the meadow, she had been surprisingly downcast. "I thought you hated Derry—and this touching display of grief can hardly be for Morc's sake."

"I was fond of Derry . . . once. That was my first mistake," said Prescelli bitterly.

Her most recent error had been stealing Diaspad's knife. While she could not summon up much genuine regret that Morc and Derry were no more, she did not like the thought that she was indirectly responsible. And this was not the first time that an ill-considered act of hers had ended in bloodshed and death. Prescelli supposed that there might be a grisly satisfaction in killing maliciously and intentionally, but to kill by sheer *stupidity* . .

To make matters worse, she had not yet disposed of the knife. Its continued presence in her clothes chest caused her consierable uneasiness; the consequences, should the Princess discover the whereabouts of her blade, did not bear thinking about.

The dwarfs lowered the coffins into shallow, stony graves, an unkempt and underfed traveling friar mumbled an incoherent prayer. A few clods of earth were ceremoniously tossed in.

The Princess, observing the absence of an appreciative audience, found that she was really too fatigued to indulge in any prolonged demonstration of grief, shrugged her shoulders, and left the graveyard without further ado. Calchas and all those others not directly concerned with filling in the graves made haste to follow her.

As soon as they were alone with the two newly covered graves, Ceilyn dropped from the wall, dusted off his dark green tunic, and reached up to help Gwenlliant down from her perch. "Are you satisfied, or would you care to inspect the graves?"

"Yes," she sighed. "I am satisfied." For all that, she presented an achingly forlorn picture in her darkest gown and drabbest cloak. A sensitive child, she had been shocked by this funeral, which struck her as a particularly heartless affair.

"I knew that someone was going to die. I dreamed about it again and again, and I was afraid—is it wrong, do you think, to be so glad it was only Morc and Derry?"

"I wouldn't let it trouble me, if I were you," he said kindly.

They left the graveyard and trudged up the hill to the castle. "You know," he said, looking down at the dusty little figure beside him. "I am terribly fond of you, Cousin. I know that you are accustomed to taking your problems to Garanwyn—which is as it should be," he went on diffidently. "But if you are ever disturbed by something . . . something you don't think that anyone would understand, I think that *I* might understand your problem better than anyone else might. Do you know what I am trying to tell you?"

"Yes," said the child. "I guess that I do. Only . . . I always thought that you would disapprove. Worse than Garanwyn even."

"No," said Ceilyn earnestly. "No, I would not. You needn't be afraid to tell me anything. Or if I'm not here . . ." (for he had been troubled, lately, by the idea that he might soon be forced to go) ". . . if I am not here, and you are particularly disturbed, go to Teleri ni Pendaren."

• • •

Had Gwenlliant and Ceilyn left the cemetery a little earlier, they might have passed through the Gamelyon Gate into the inner courtyard in time to witness the return of Diaspad's knife.

It was the dwarf, Bron, who slipped off his death-mask and pulled the silk-sheathed blade out of some pocket hidden beneath his cloak. "This was found earlier this morning, gracious Lady."

The Princess lifted her dark veil and regarded the proffered blade as though she doubted its authenticity. "But how is this? You told me that the meadow and the ruins were thoroughly searched yesterday. I was beginning to fear that someone had picked it up."

For a moment, the dwarf's gaze rested on Prescelli—poor Prescelli who had turned quite green and stood with her hand pressed against her mouth as though she was about to be sick. Then the old man bowed his head and said apologetically, "I can't think how it was, Lady, but we neglected to search the steps on the seaward side. As soon as I realized that, I went down to take a look. I beg your pardon, Lady, for causing you needless worry."

The Princess was willing to be generous. "I will overlook your neglect . . . this time," she said sweetly, handing the knife over to Calchas, who put it inside his doublet. "Since no harm was done. Indeed," she continued melodically, "everything falls most providentially to my advantage. The blade is safe, and Morc and Derry—who witnessed my presence down in the meadow—are dead. I could hardly have arranged things more neatly myself.

"Of course," she added airily, "I will miss Derry. He was a pretty boy and occasionally useful. But he was becoming insufferably tedious at times—and now I needn't be troubled on his account ever again." She smiled radiantly on Prescelli and the rest. "I hope that the rest of you, my dears, will remember that it never pays to outlive your usefulness."

She picked up her train and ambled off in the direction of the Keep and her own bedchamber, thinking of a nap before the afternoon meal. Calchas and most of the others followed after her, leaving the old dwarf and the stunned girl facing each other beside the wrought-iron gate.

"Why?" asked Prescelli. "You don't owe me any favors, that is certain. *Why* did you do that?"

The dark-eyed little man smiled into his beard. "I assure you young lady, that I've never in my life done anything to serve you.''

Up in the Queen's bedchamber, Sidonwy and the older girls were preparing to go out, donning their best cloaks and fur-lined slippers, pulling on their fur-trimmed gloves. The day was chilly, and they were all going down to Treledig.

At sight of Ceilyn and Gwenlliant just returning from the funeral, Sidonwy frowned disapprovingly. "But did you forget? We are going to the Lord Mayor's Pageant, Ceilyn. Surely you do not intend to put in an appearance wearing *that*,'' she exclaimed, viewing with disfavor the plain tunic and dark cloak which Ceilyn had considered appropriate for the graveyard.

"I had forgotten, I beg your pardon,'' Ceilyn replied remorsefully. "But I can change in a quarter of an hour, if you don't mind waiting so long.''

"And did you enjoy the funeral ceremonies?'' Fand asked Gwenlliant, as Ceilyn clattered back down the stairs. "I must say,'' she added, still a bit miffed, "that some people have a strange idea of entertainment.''

"And very odd that Ceilyn should take it into his head to attend with her,'' Finola agreed in a low voice. "But then, he's been behaving very oddly indeed—even for Ceilyn—these last few days. You would almost think he *knew* something about Morc's and Derry's lamentable demise. You would almost think . . .'' She trailed off, quelled by the Queen's reproving glare.

"What should anyone think, but that Derry mac Forgoll has finally fallen victim to one of his own wicked schemes?'' Sidonwy asked indignantly, pulling her glove on the wrong way so that she was forced to strip it off and begin again. "That boy was always too clever for his own good, and Morc, not being clever at all, was willing to follow wherever Derry led him. The matter seems plain enough to me: Derry had been dabbling in the Dark Arts, perhaps for some time now. He convinced his father to send the bull, used it in some wicked heathen ceremony, and succeeded in summoning up . . . well, what he may have summoned up does not bear thinking on. Suffice to say he could not master it, any more than he could master his own vicious tendencies, and so he and Morc met their ends. That is what I think and the King agrees with me. It is a wonder to me

that the Church allowed those two to be buried in hallowed
ground.

"Or have *you* any reason to suppose that either Derry or his
brother was above involving himself in witchcraft—or worse?"
she asked, looking from Fand to Finola and back again.

The young ladies exchanged a shame-faced glance. Certainly,
neither of them had anything to say in Derry's defense, or in
Morc's. "I thought not," said the Queen.

Yet she, too, had noticed an unwelcome change in Ceilyn,
and when he returned, very fine as to his clothes and very pale
as to his face, she took him aside. "You look positively haggard,
Cousin. Have you been fasting again?"

And when he reluctantly admitted it: "This will not do, Ceilyn, I will not have it. Whatever sins real or imaginary you have
on your conscience, I cannot allow you to make yourself ill in
this way."

Ceilyn sighed. "Yes, but—"

"Did you or did you not promise to obey me in all things?"
Sidonwy interrupted him.

"In all earthly matters, yes," Ceilyn replied wearily. "But in
all things spiritual, all matters of conscience, I have always insisted and you have always permitted—"

"But it is this *earthly* body of yours you are abusing," the
Queen exclaimed impatiently. "You walk though my rooms ex-
uding such an atmosphere of hairshirts and grisly penances that
you are scarcely a pleasant companion. But it is much worse
than that. Is your arm strong to defend me when you will not
eat or drink? Is your mind sharp to serve me if you lie awake
all night for lack of a pillow, a blanket, or a proper bed?

"Do you not see, Cousin," she added more gently, "that you
would be better use to me whole and healthy and happy, than
restless, ill, and tormented!"

Ceilyn shook his head. "Whole and healthy and happy," he
echoed hollowly. "No, I am not that now—nor do I remember
when I ever was."

"Well, then," said the Queen, "you had best take whatever
steps are necessary in order to become so."

Forty nights passed without any Moon to light the sky. And men marveled and wondered and they were mightily afraid. For in those days, you must know, the men who lived in these parts were pagans and they worshipped the Moon.

At last a band of the heartiest came together and they resolved to search the fenlands where the Moon was last seen. But first they went to a wise woman they knew of, to ask for her advice. "For," said the men of the south, "the marsh is a perilous place for anyone to venture, and if the Moon herself came to grief there, then how can we hope to walk there unscathed?"

The wise woman told them they must carry salt in their pockets and shoots of hazel in their hands, and they must turn all their clothes back to front and wear them that way. And above all, they must not speak a word to anyone. "Nay, not even a single word among yourselves," said she. "For if you do, you will place yourselves under the power of the creatures who live there."

And she told them they would know the spot where the Moon was lost by three signs: an old woman in a black gown, a coffin, and a crown of thorns.

—A nursemaids' tale, told in Camboglanna and throughout the south

17.

Queen of the Bees, Mother of Multitudes

On the fourth day of his stay in the house on stilts, Garanwyn felt much stronger. "It is time you went out for a breath of fresh air," said Arfondwy as she prepared his breakfast, mixing up a batter using ground nuts and seeds instead of flour, dried berries for sweetening, then baking the little cakes on the hearth.

Tryffin seemed perfectly content to remain behind entertaining his brother. So Garanwyn wrapped himself up in every stitch of clothing he had with him, and followed Arfondwy past the goatskin and down the ladder.

"Yes," he said, inhaling deeply, savoring the sharp clean bite of the air. "This is what I really needed."

"You have been breathing too much smoke," said the girl. "We burn herbs on the fire to sweeten the smoke, but still, fresh air is always best."

The horses were lodged in a temporary stable under the house. The men had brought them in only yesterday, so Garanwyn inspected all three carefully, discovering to his relief that none of them had suffered any ill effects running loose in the marsh for so many days.

Around behind the house was a smaller hut, this one on four unadorned legs with a long ladder attached diagonally like a staircase, wherein dwelt the family goats. Garanwyn laughed to see the intelligent little creatures swarming up and down the ladder, as agile and as comical in their antics as children.

"Everything we build, we raise up as high as we can," Arfondwy explained. "During the heavy rains, and especially during the spring floods, the water comes up almost to the top of the ladder, and over at the house we can moor our boats and climb into them directly from the doorsill."

"It must be like living in a boat," said Garanwyn, eyeing the ark-shaped building, trying hard to imagine it, "like a boat riding on the sea."

Every day after that, Garanwyn and Arfondwy went out, paddling around the marsh in her little canoe. The boy from Rhianedd was fast overcoming his fear of boats, and Arfondwy assured him that the water was not deep at this time of the year. "Barely enough to float a boat on, except on the river—that is why we build these boats so small and light," she said, skillfully maneuvering the canoe through a forest of cattails gone to seed. The spindle-shaped heads stood high above the green water.

"Of course," she added, "there are places where nobody cares to go: places where the willow trees uproot themselves and follow after a man, muttering ominously; places where the bog is bottomless, and creatures ancient and malicious dwell—like

the thing that tried to take your cousin. Such creatures have no
voice or shape of their own, and can only mimic: the voice of
the wind, the song of the river. But if the thing had taken Fflergant it would have assumed his shape, spoken with his voice.
Then it would have been more dangerous than before.''

"The marsh is always changing,'' she told him another time.
''Teirwaedd Morfa has many faces. But if you do not take her
for granted, if you treat her with respect, she can be kind, even
generous.''

Even now, with fall hastening toward winter, Garanwyn could
see that the marsh teemed with exuberant life: the silver gleam
of fish under the water, waterbugs skating on the surface, ducks
paddling and diving in the shallows, plovers and herons and
gulls. . . .

One place they did not visit, though they often passed that
way, was a solitary hut on a lonely island, a dwelling rendered
faintly ominous not only by its remote location but also by the
great flocks of crows and blackbirds that nested in the surrounding cattails. At all hours of the day, they could be seen in their
hundreds, feeding in the reeds or among the blackberry thickets
that covered the island, circling overhead, or perched on the
thatched roof of the hut. Garanwyn could not repress a shudder
whenever he drew near the island, for it was there, Arfondwy
told him, that her great-grandmother lived, and she was the
priestess of the Dark Mother, incarnation both of the marsh and
of the Goddess of the marshdwellers in her most fearsome aspect. The old woman lived alone, except for two ancient servants
who attended her; she received few visitors, and those only at
night. The reasons for this were appropriately mysterious.
''There are some things we do not speak of under the light of
the sun,'' said Arfondwy.

Yet the people of Teirwaedd Morfa kept few secrets from Garanwyn, welcoming him into their homes and inviting him to
participate in all the meaningful events of their lives. On all
occasions, their hospitality was lavish, and whenever two or more
families came together there was an exchange of gifts—for the
marshfolk reckoned wealth not by the things that a man hoarded
away, but by how much he could afford to give.

One afternoon, about ten days after his arrival in the marsh,
Arfondwy took Garanwyn to meet her friend Ceinach, who was
soon to become a bride.

On a piece of dry ground outside the House of the Clan of the Wild Goose, someone had kindled a fire. An old woman in a faded yellow dress was stirring something which bubbled and steamed in a huge black pot. Garanwyn caught a glimpse of the contents as he walked by, and could not repress a violent start.

"But she is only dyeing cloth—the linen for Ceinach's wedding gown." Arfondwy's laugh was a ripple of liquid merriment. "It does look like a cauldron of blood—do you know that old tale?"

Inside the house, the women were baking and brewing, the young girls making wreaths of dried flowers and brilliant feathers to adorn the wedding party. Arfondwy ceremoniously presented a basket of oats and wheat to the bride-to-be. "This is the grain for the bread you will bake for your wedding feast. It comes with the blessing of the Maiden and of the Mother."

"All praise to the Maiden and the Mother," the girl replied solemnly.

Outside again, behind the house, they discovered the young men of the clan hard at work, rough-shaping four great logs they had pulled out of the river. It was just possible to make out the huge legs and talons of some tremendous bird of prey emerging from the wood.

"In the late spring or early summer, the men will build a new house, and Ceinach and Efa and their husbands and their children will live in it," Arfondwy explained. "That will be a great occasion for all of us, for it is long since any clan has grown so numerous that it was necessary to divide the house."

And Arfondwy sang for him the Song of the Mother, the hymn the women would sing at Ceinach's wedding:

> "*I am an appletree laden with fruit*
> *The corn in milk*
> *I am the hawthorne*
> *The hazel tree*
> *The sloe and the bramble*
> *I am a rose*
> *I am the Queen of the Bees*
> *Mother of multitudes*
> *I am the Mistress of the Castle of the Four Winds*

> *I am the fertile sea*
> > *A lake on the plain*
> > *A well, with depths unplumbed*
> *I am the full moon*
> > *Golden and round*
> *I am the grey goose*
> > *Feathering her nest*
> > *The roe-deer with her fawn*
>
> *I am all things to all men*
> > *A fire on the hearth*
> > *Honey in the hive*
> > *Bread in the oven*
> > *Wool to the spindle*
> > *And children in the home*
> *I am generous, I give without stint*
> > *For I am the cauldron of plenty.''*

"Is there another song for you—for the Maiden, I mean?" asked Garanwyn.

"The Song of the Maiden is the song of the river," said Arfondwy solemnly. "I will sing that for you—but not today."

But Garanwyn did not ask if the people of Teirwaedd Morfa sang hymns to the Dark Mother, because that was one aspect of Arfondwy's life and religion which he wanted to know nothing about.

The next day, Fflergant announced that he would not spend another minute in bed. The women who had nursed him protested, but the young Prince insisted, until Gonwenlyn, the mother of Arfondwy, appealed to the Weaver, certain that she, if no one else, could convince him.

Anwe arrived in state, to stand at his bedside, her hands folded atop her magnificent belly, her dark eyes flashing. She regarded the invalid with ill-concealed contempt. "If he feels strong enough to attempt to stand, he should be permitted to do so," she said. Adding with a sniff: "And if, perchance, he should fall flat on that handsome face of his, it will only teach him to respect the opinions of those who are so much wiser."

Undiscouraged by this daunting pronouncement, Fflergant threw off the covers and managed to get to his feet. Only by a tremendous effort of will was he able to avoid the ignominious fate which Anwe had predicted, and one wobbly turn around the hall was sufficient to convince him that he was better off in bed.

Yet the next day he was up and remained so a little longer, and every day after that he felt better and stronger. His appetite returned and a little color crept into his cheeks.

Garanwyn watched Fflergant's progress with mixed feelings. His eagerness to return home had all deserted him, yet he knew that every day he spent in the House of the Horned Moon his feelings for Arfondwy grew stronger, and that he was moving dangerously close to declaring those feelings.

"Did you know that Ceinach and I were born in the same month?" Arfondwy asked him one evening. They were both sitting on the stairs at the back of the house: she with her little drop spindle spinning flax into a smooth, fine thread, Garanwyn mending one of the leather harnesses which Tryffin had destroyed in order to rescue Fflergant. "Now Ceinach is to be married and soon to be a mother. It makes me suddenly feel very old."

Garanwyn did not ask how she knew that her friend would soon be a mother—the fact was plain to see. Ceinach was nearly as far gone as Anwe. Nor did he answer her at once, not trusting himself to speak.

Arfondwy sighed. "Garanwyn," she said wistfully, "do you think us very wicked because our young women are not virgins when they wed?"

"Not at all," said Garanwyn, very busy with the leather. He knew there was nothing artful in her question. The marshdwellers spoke openly of all such matters—even the small children expressing their curiosity, if not their intimate knowledge of the subject, so frankly that the boy from Rhianedd was often embarrassed.

"At least," he added, trying hard, for her sake, to be broad minded, "not very much. It sometimes happens among my own folk that the betrothal and—and the bedding—precede the church wedding by months or even years. And in the old days, I believe people sometimes didn't marry at all until there was a baby on the way." He did not tell her that the practice was now condemned, held up as an example of the kind of iniquity which had weakened his ancestors morally and so brought them to accept the rule of the kings of the south.

Arfondwy nodded, deftly set her spindle twirling, and watched her thread grow. "Well, then, you will understand: Our numbers being so few we must be careful, as your ancestors were, to insure that no union is a barren one. Our women usually go to their weddings already with child or even suckling. That is sensible, don't you agree?"

Garanwyn nodded. His experience of the girls of the marsh was that they were entirely "sensible," and would have welcomed a similar attitude on his part. Fortunately (or unfortunately) he wanted none of them but Arfondwy—who, as Maiden Priestess, was forbidden him. This was a wonderful aid in fighting off temptation, but it kept him awake nights, lying in a cold sweat, and counting the hours until dawn.

He thought it was time to change the subject. "Everyone here has been so kind . . . and answered all my questions so openly. All except one."

Now it was Arfondwy's turn to blush and look uncomfortable. "It is not for me to answer that question, but for Anwe, as priestess of the Mother, to choose the proper time.

"Only believe me, Garanwyn," she added earnestly, "that no one here intends you any harm."

Nevertheless, he continued to wonder: When the day finally arrived that Fflergant was well enough to travel, would the marsh-dwellers really allow their visitors to leave the marsh and return to Caer Cadwy?

Garanwyn woke from a fitful doze to the sound of hurried footsteps in the room below. His first thought was that Fflergant had suffered a relapse. He crawled out of bed, reached for his shirt and hose—but then he heard the voices of the women, more excited than distressed, and he guessed what was happening. He crawled back into bed, pulled the goatskin coverlet over his head.

In the morning, everyone looked pleased and relieved, and the beautiful Anwe—no longer formidable, but as tired, proud, and happy as any other new mother—lay in her bed in an alcove off the main room, with a dark-haired baby at her breast, and received the congratulations of her delighted kinsmen.

Someone had suspended a pair of scissors over the bed. "Lest the mossfolk or the gro'ach steal the baby—he is vulnerable until he is named, and the water spirits, bearing few children of their own, are always covetous," Gonwenlyn explained, leaving Garanwyn to wonder what kind of changeling might be exchanged for a fairy child.

The child could not be named until the guests arrived and no guests could be admitted until the house was properly prepared for them. Privately, Garanwyn thought that the homes of the marshdwellers were the tidiest houses he had ever seen, but tidy was apparently not good enough for an occasion such as this: Arfondwy's family spent the rest of that day scrubbing, sweeping, rubbing down the floorboards with the bones of cuttle-fish, and scouring.

The next morning, everything was ready. The guests arrived laden with gifts, and Anwe herself, in her role as priestess of the Mother, rose from her couch to preside.

She anointed the infant with rainwater, with honey, and with milk. She sang over him, blessing him in the name of the Mother, the Maiden, and the Crone. Then she gave him his own name: "Be thou *Kederyn*, the strong, the mighty." Throughout the ceremony, the infant roared lustily, displaying a mighty set of lungs, thereby exciting the admiration of kinfolk and visitors alike.

The inevitable gift-giving came next. Even Fflergant and Tryffin, caught up in the mood of celebration, stripped off their heavy golden armrings and placed them at the infant's feet. Garanwyn was embarrassed. His obligations to these people were beginning to weigh on him, he would have liked to make some small return—yet there he stood, alone of all that company, with no gift to bestow.

He searched his mind for a suitable offering. He possessed nothing of value except the silver crucifix he wore on a fine chain around his neck—and that would never do. Then he thought of the little bone-handled knife he carried in his belt. Not a costly blade, to be sure, but perhaps here where iron was so rare . . . He took the knife and placed it among the other gifts, and the Weaver rewarded him with a dazzling smile.

The next afternoon, Arfondwy took Garanwyn aside. "You have seen how we prepare for a wedding and how we name our children. Now comes an opportunity for you to witness a darker side to our lives. Would you see how we greet death when it touches us?"

Garanwyn frowned; her invitation was hardly appealing, and

he certainly had no desire to attend one of their funerals, but he did not like to say so. "If no one would be offended by my presence . . ." he murmured doubtfully.

"It is entirely appropriate for you to attend," she assured him.

Among the marshdwellers, brown was the color of death: "The leaves and the grass die and turn brown, the earth is brown and barren in winter, which is the season of death." So Garanwyn borrowed a brown cloak from one of the young men, and accompanied Arfondwy down to the place where she moored her boat.

They climbed in, each one taking a paddle—Garanwyn was, by now, quite proficient—and pushed off. "Will she be there . . . your great-grandmother?" Garanwyn asked. He still dreaded a meeting with the old woman.

To his relief, Arfondwy shook her head. "The rites of the Dark Mother are always performed apart."

They paddled westward, in the direction of the river, and landed on a bare little island they had never visited together before.

"Look," said Arfondwy, pointing.

Though an hour or more remained before nightfall, a long broken line of torches could be seen moving across the river. As the boats came nearer, Garanwyn began to make them out: long and low with high wooden prows—very different from the little canoes made of reeds. They glided across the water smoothly and silently, apparently without the aid of oars. Watching them, Garanwyn felt a chill slide down his spine.

"How many boats?" he asked.

"Five," said Arfondwy. "There will be five barges."

For a time, the boats disappeared among the bulrushes, but when they reappeared Garanwyn could see the boatmen and the long wooden poles they used to propel their boats. On the prow of each barge were painted symbols: spirals and intricate knots; the sun, the moon, and stars.

As soon as the first boat landed, eight men climbed out onto the rocky beach. A second barge landed and disgorged a similar number. All the men who were not carrying torches began to unload the boats. Garanwyn caught a glimpse of their cargo and felt his stomach lurch.

Out of each barge came a crude litter, and on each bier lay a corpse in a bloody winding-sheet. And the boy did not like the look of the nearest body: The size was entirely wrong. Even allowing for the shroud, this was the body of a tall, powerfully built man. Had other strangers wandered into the marsh—only to meet death where Garanwyn and his cousins had met with friendship?

Other barges arrived, and one of them carried a crowd of women in long brown cloaks. They came ashore, gathered around the bodies, and immediately set up an eerie wailing. "Were they . . . men of importance?" Garanwyn asked.

"They were men of no importance," replied Arfondwy. "Here . . . or in the outside world. But they died violently, and so there is bad luck to be dispelled."

Meanwhile, the boatmen unloaded bundles of wood and dried rushes, and piled them around the biers. As one of the men approached the bodies, torch in hand, Garanwyn caught his breath. "They aren't going to *burn* them?"

"Your own people do not practice this?"

Garanwyn shook his head.

"Yet they do burn pagans and witches alive?" she asked innocently, and Garanwyn wished fervently that he had held his tongue.

"To save them from the fires of Hell . . . it is accounted merciful. But you don't—you don't think that I've ever been a party to anything like that?"

The wood and the rushes caught fire; smoke began to rise from the pyres. Arfondwy touched Garanwyn's hand. Her own was as cold as ice.

"I do not," she said softly. "Do you think we could be friends if I believed you capable of anything like that?"

Later, long after sunset, they paddled back toward the house on stilts. The night was clear and a thousand thousand stars burned in the sky, reflecting on the face of the water. All was still, but for the rippling of the starry water and the soft splash of the oars. To Garanwyn, the terrors of his first night in Tei waedd Morfa seemed distant in time and space, his life before that immeasurably remote.

"Garanwyn," said Arfondwy. "The time has come, now that you have seen all these things, for me to answer your questions.

"But perhaps," she added hopefully, "you have already

guessed why I was instructed to show you and teach you so much?''

"No," he replied. He thought that he might have an idea, but was not certain it was the right one. "It would be logical to assume that you would wish to keep your secrets from outsiders like myself."

"Even when, from the very beginning, you already knew our most dangerous secret—the fact of our very existence?" Arfondwy shook her head. "If you returned to Caer Cadwy carrying tales of the pagans who live in Teirwaedd Morfa, we would all have been in danger. Surely you must see that once you knew that much, it was necessary for us to make certain you would be silent."

Garanwyn frowned. The conversation was taking an ominous turn. "And you determined to do that . . . how? You told me once—more than once—that nobody here intended me any harm."

Arfondwy sighed. "By the time that I told you that, it was true—but it was not always true.

"Of course," she went on earnestly, "had we left you to die of exposure in the marsh, there would have been no problem. But I have already told you why we could not do that. And once we had taken you in we had only so many choices. We might kill you, or continue to keep you here against your will. Or Anwe might have clouded your mind until you remembered little or nothing of your time among us. You would have believed, then, that you had been taken in by fairies, and spun such a tale of your adventures afterward that no one would have believed you.

"But we did not want to do any of those things if we could avoid them. We hoped that it would be possible to teach you instead, to make you our friend. It is true that your Rhianeddi birth and breeding spoke against you there, but we believe that just as prejudice feeds on ignorance, so knowledge drives out fear. We hoped that when you really knew us you would return our friendship—and a man does not take risks with the lives of his friends. Naturally, we did not make that decision immediately. It took Anwe almost a day to examine your mind and your heart. But when she told us that you were one to be trusted, when she instructed me to begin your education, that was a great relief to everyone.

"And especially . . . especially that was a relief to me," Arfondwy concluded, "because I already knew that you and I were meant to be . . . the best of friends."

Garanwyn could not think what to say. Though her words only confirmed what he had already guessed, still it was shocking to learn for certain that she and her kinsmen had once contemplated his death.

At last he said: "I notice that you say nothing at all about Fflergant or Tryffin."

"There was never any question of harming or detaining the sons of Maelgwyn fab Menai," she admitted. "We know the Gwyngellach and trust in their friendship. And there are other reasons, compelling reasons, why the lives of your kinsmen should be precious to us. Yet we never believed it would be possible, without Anwe's arts, to gain their complicity in any scheme that was harmful to you."

That sounded rather better. "Then you never seriously considered . . . disposing of me?"

"It was our last, our most desperate choice," she said. "To harm a guest under our roof, to tamper with the minds of two Gwyngellach princes . . . yet to secure the safety of all our people, it was something we were forced to consider."

They continued on in silence for a time, skimming across the dark water in her lightweight canoe. Finally, Arfondwy said, "And do you hate us now, Garanwyn, now that you know these things? Do you hate . . . me?"

"I do not," he replied without hesitation. And he saw that Anwe had been wise in counseling Arfondwy to withhold the information; had he known all this at the beginning, he might have judged them more harshly.

But now he was unable to keep from speaking. "Arfondwy . . . there is something I must say to you."

"Tiffaine," she said. "Arfondwy is the Maiden Priestess, and the river. My real name is Tiffaine."

"Tiffaine, then. I am glad to learn that, because I wanted to say . . . Tiffaine, I could never hate you. The truth is . . . think that I love you."

He heard her sharp intake of breath, but for a long time she gave him no other answer. He silently castigated himself for stating it so baldly, for so impulsive and graceless a declaration. Then she said, "I hoped that might be so."

Garanwyn let out a long sigh of relief. Yet he wished that he might see her face better, to tell what she was really thinking. "Then . . . you are not offended?"

"Because you love me? I am very far from offended," she said with a breathless little laugh. "I am glad that you told me, and I shall treasure the memory after you are gone.

"I have loved you," she added, just above a whisper, "since the very first moment I saw you."

That was more, so very much more than he had dared to hope for, that he could not think what to say next. Instead, he leaned forward impulsively and kissed her—hard—on the mouth, nearly capsizing the boat in the process.

"But you are crying," he said, as they drew apart.

Arfondwy shook her head. "If I weep," she said, "I weep mainly for joy . . . but also for the sorrow that is to come."

And Garanwyn finally remembered why he should never have spoken at all. "Sweet Jesus," he whispered. "I was so . . . so amazingly happy that I actually forgot. What in the name of Heaven do we do *now*?"

"I do not know," she replied tearfully. "Let your God and my Goddess be my witnesses: I really do not know what we can do."

And morning and evening he went down to the shore, at the high and the low tides, and the little seals came out of the water to meet him, and gathered around him like so many faithful brown hounds. When he returned to the place where he and the Princess were lodged, he was sick and silent by reason of his great longing for the sea.

Goewin saw these things and a black foreboding came over her, but she knew not how to name the thing that she feared. She said, "My lord, it grieves me to see you so, and I would fain give you comfort. But how may that be? You converse with the wind and the waves, yet you say nothing at all to me."

And he spoke, finally, and said to her, "The wind and the waves are my cousins, the seals my younger brothers. But what can I say to you, who are neither my kith nor my clan?"

Then Goewin knew the thing that she feared, and the shadow of their parting fell between them.

—From Goewin and Ellwy: The Death of Goewin

18.

Shadows of Parting

Ceilyn paused outside the laboratory door, one hand raised to knock, cursing the necessity that brought him there, doubly angry at the weakness that made him glad for the excuse.

He had neither seen nor spoken with Teleri since the morning they had taken Communion together in the chapel, had been determined to keep his distance. She had used him so shamefully, that he was not minded to offer her the opportunity to do so ever again.

Yet here he was, still angry, resentful at finding himself there, trying to convince himself that it was hard necessity that brought him to the Wizard's Tower, and not any desire to see Teleri.

On second thought, he decided not to knock, uncertain what he might do if she refused him entry. And the door was not locked; he had only to turn the handle and push it open.

A strong odor of camphor, anise, and beeswax filled the tower room; red and yellow firelight danced on the walls. Teleri hovered over a pot of hot wax, dipping candles. She was so intent on the task that she spared him no more than a sidelong glance as he entered. Yet he did not think it was the heat of the room which brought about her sudden change of color.

Ceilyn opened a window to let in a little fresh air, and perched on the broad stone sill. "I don't suppose that I am particularly welcome here," he said stiffly. "If you wanted me, you would have sent for me—you know your power now, far too well."

"I wanted to see you," she said, just above a whisper. "But I hoped you would come here on your own."

Ceilyn folded his arms across his chest. "You mean you knew that I would find my way here eventually, as I always do. Or, if not, then you could always bring me here at your need. It's bad enough to be a fool," he said bitterly, "but a predictable fool at that!"

"Ceilyn," she said, looking at him at last, "this frightens me. *You* frighten me when you talk like that. Whatever influence I have over you, I admit that I used it poorly that night, but I don't want to *be* like that. I don't want to use or misuse that influence in any way ever again."

"You say that now, but you will use it—and me—readily enough, the very next time that you have need of a pawn or a tool. You are utterly heartless," he said. "You tried to tell me as much, long ago, but I didn't believe you. I know you rather better now."

"I am sorry," she said. "I can only plead ignorance. Whatever else I may have intended, I never meant to hurt you. I don't think that I ever properly understood that I could."

"Ignorance!" he exclaimed, rising indignantly to his feet, then gaining control of himself and sitting down again. "Ignorance! And you a Wizard—what right have you to be ignorant of the important things: loving and hurting and living and dying? Even a child like Gwenlliant knows more of these things than you do. And being who and what you are, it will be nearly impossible for you to reach for one kind of power without employing the other if you can. Besides, it's instinctive. You've been casting your little spells over me from the beginning. All those charming little games in the garden, the clinging vines and the rest, bringing me close—but not too close . . . !''

"I have no control over anything that happens in the garden," she insisted. She looked pale and fragile this morning, but he steeled himself against any stirrings of a protective instinct.

"You think not? But what did you say that night? That you recognized the power that the Princess had summoned, knew it in some way you couldn't explain. Well, I know it, too. I ought to, after what you put me through. And it's akin to that something which always passes between us in the garden."

"Perhaps you are right. You sound very certain, and I . . . I'm not certain of anything anymore," she admitted, abandoning her candlemaking for the moment. "No, I am not pretending to be stupid again. But whatever power it is that my presence and your presence in the garden may bring to life, I have no desire to use it. On you, or on anyone else."

"Nevertheless," he replied, "that power rests in your hands, whether you want it or not. And you, of all people, ought to know that power misunderstood is bound to be misused."

She was silent, gazing past him, staring at her own doubled shadow moving on the far wall. He grew impatient, waiting for her to answer.

"Why don't you tell me that I, of all people, have no right to reproach you? Why don't you just say—" Curiosity overcame his exasperation. "Don't you *ever* stand up for yourself?"

She shook her head. "No, I never do. I have very little courage—I thought you knew that."

"I know nothing of the sort," he said. "Well, perhaps where some things are concerned . . ." He slipped off his perch, joined her by the fireplace. "Anyway, it wasn't to discuss any of that that I came here today."

"Why . . . why did you come?" she asked, putting more wood on the fire, carefully avoiding his eyes.

"I have a problem and need some advice. The advice of a Wizard, in fact. Or have you decided that being a wizard frightens you as much as being a woman?" he asked, leaning up against the stone wall to the side of the fireplace and folding his arms again.

"No," she said, picking up a long-handled wooden spoon and stirring the contents of the iron pot. "But perhaps I should

After the other night—dabbling in mysteries I scarcely understood. That is the one thing that Glastyn told me never to do. And for all the good that it did. Fflergant and Tryffin and Garanwyn are not back, and no one has any idea what has delayed them. You as much as said it yourself—what right do I have to call myself a Wizard?''

"Well, you don't, as a matter of fact. Call yourself a Wizard, I mean," said Ceilyn. "I don't remember that I ever heard you put any sort of name to yourself, now that I come to think of it. And I always thought that wizards had a talent for naming things.''

With a sigh, he returned to the problem which had brought him there. "I have been suffering from bad dreams, almost every night. As I understand it, the warding powers of the Clach Ghealach protect us from nightmares and sendings, but presentiments—prophetic dreams, omens, portents, and the like—being potentially beneficial, it has no effect on them. Is that right?''

"That isn't exactly how it works," she said, testing the consistency of the wax. "But yes . . . essentially that is true."

"So if I have dreams that trouble me, dreams that seem to warn of dire possibilities ahead . . . then they must be true dreams, mustn't they?''

"No more than your pleasanter dreams," she said, stirring the wax. "It is difficult to say. The power of the sidhe-stone protects us from magical deceits, from malignant forces outside the castle, but it doesn't affect natural things like our own fears—or desires. And not everyone possesses a capacity for prophecy—though in your case, considering your other gifts, it is not unlikely. But even then, dreams don't always mean exactly what we think they mean.''

Ceilyn thought that over. "This one . . . this one seems rather obvious. And along with it comes such a sense of impending disaster . . .''

There was something in his tone that made her reluctant to question him, but she forced herself to ask: "What . . . what is your dream, Ceilyn?''

"I dream of a great grey wolf with a little seagull crushed between his jaws. The gull has grey wings. Do you remember the night that I almost died? Do you remember what I told you?''

Her face was partly turned away from him and mostly in shadow, so it was impossible for him to read her expression. "I remember what you said to me, yes," she replied softly. "Did you really come here for advice—or did you come to warn me?"

"I don't know. A bit of both, perhaps. Can you help me?"

"I'm sorry," she said. "But no, I am afraid that this is one dream you will have to interpret for yourself."

She began dipping candles again, a pair at a time, then hanging them over a rack away from the fire to cool. But Ceilyn remained by the fireplace and gave no sign that he was ready to leave. "Is there something else?"

He unfolded his arms. "Yes, but not anything that need trouble you. It's the iron bracelet. Several times, especially in the last few days, I've felt a temptation—almost a compulsion—to take it off. But I know what to do about that. I am going to ask a blacksmith to rivet the clasp shut."

She considered that, decided that she did not like the idea at all. "I don't think you ought to do that. It could be dangerous. If the need became too great, there is no telling what you might do to rid yourself of the iron."

"There is no telling what I might do if I discard the bracelet," he countered.

"Let me try to think of something," she insisted. "Before you do anything at all. There might be something I could do . . . more signs I might put on the bracelet, words I could say over it."

"Very well," he said wearily. It would be a relief to pass the burden of responsibility on, at least for a short time. "But I can't wait more than a few days. When winter comes, when the wolves begin to howl, I have to be certain the danger is past."

In the morning, Garanwyn was nowhere to be found. His cousins searched for him in all the little alcoves off the main room, upstairs and downstairs a half a dozen times, before they were satisfied he was not in the house. Then they climbed down the ladder and searched the entire island, beginning with the stable and proceeding to all the outbuildings around and behind the house.

Tryffin finally found him on a strip of shoreline where some of the boats were beached, sitting on a piece of rotting log which someone had pulled out of the water.

"If you stay out here in the cold and the damp much longer, you'll catch your death," said Tryffin, sitting down beside him.

"A fine thing that would be, for you to take ill just when Fflergant is nearly well enough to travel."

"I wish that I *was* dead," Garanwyn replied vehemently, kicking savagely at a sharp piece of rock sticking up out of the mud. "Miserable, worthless, ungrateful wretch that I am!"

Tryffin studied his boots, pretended not to notice that Garanwyn had been crying. "Perhaps you'll explain what you mean by that?"

Garanwyn laughed mirthlessly. "What would you call a man who, after wandering lost and ill in a hostile land, being taken in by strangers and nursed back to health, then treated with every possible kindness, was tempted to repay that kindness by violating their hospitality with an act of . . . unspeakable ingratitude?"

Typically, Tryffin considered his answer carefully before he replied. "Assuming as I do that the act of ingratitude—the violation, if you will—involved a certain young female . . . I would remind you that these people do not regard these things in the same way we do, and might not think the act so very wicked—might even, in fact, regard it as a perfectly natural expression of your affection for the girl."

Garanwyn shook his head mournfully. "If it were any of the other girls . . . but Arfondwy? She is the Maiden Priestess, dedicated to her Goddess and to perpetual chastity—"

"But there you might be mistaken," Tryffin interrupted him. "Oh yes, we both know that Arfondwy is the virgin priestess here, and as such holds high honor. But what we do *not* know is whether or not anyone expects her to continue in that role any longer than it feels natural and right. From what I know of the Korred, I would guess that they would regard anything in the nature of a vow of perpetual chastity as stupid and wrong and wasteful."

Garanwyn stared at him. As usual, everything Tryffin said made good sense. And now that he came to think of it, if Arfondwy's people had any interest in keeping her chaste, they had certainly gone the wrong way about it. If anything, the Korred had actually encouraged their intimacy.

But then he thought of all the other reasons why it would be wrong. "If it were only a matter of seducing the girl . . . an inclination toward pleasure for both of us . . . But she loves me, you know, and I love her. And that being so: Would it be honest, or decent, or right, for me to encourage her attachment in . . . in that particular way, knowing all along that there is no possible way we could be together in the future? I'll be leaving in another day or two, and I certainly can't take her with me. Can you imagine the reaction if I rode back to Caer Cadwy with her riding pillion behind me? They would accuse her of terrible things, say she had bewitched me with her wicked heathen magic . . . .

"And as for staying here with her—" He stopped, and looked at Tryffin with a sudden impossible hope in his eyes. "It *would* be impossible, wouldn't it?"

"If Fflergant were here he would undoubtedly declare you stark, staring, raving mad," said Tryffin flatly.

Garanwyn took a deep breath. "Yes, but what do *you* say? You've nothing to say against sleeping with the girl, but what do you say to staying here and marrying her?"

Tryffin shook his head, apparently rendered speechless. "You do understand," he said at last, "that you are proposing to spend the rest of your life among people who . . . who practice human sacrifice?"

"Yes," said Garanwyn. "I mean, no! Arfondwy told me that nothing like that has happened here since long before she was born."

Tryffin sighed. "Yes, but the point is: Whether they actually do it or even if they don't, they don't think it wrong—we do. And that is just one of many ways these people differ from you and me!"

Garanwyn glared at him. "This sounds very well, coming from you. You've spent your whole life living among pagans."

"Living among them—not living with them. There is a difference, though you might not see it now. And I admire and respect the Korred quite as much as you do: Their lives are, in many ways, exemplary. But will you continue to think so, back at Caer Cadwy where everyone thinks exactly the same way you used to do?

"Or would you then," he asked, "consider all that living here would actually mean: adopting a new way of life, turning your back . . . if not on God, at least on the consolations of the Church . . . and giving up everything you ever hoped for, wanted, or planned . . . all for a girl you've known for something less than a month?"

"I suppose you are right," Garanwyn sighed, beginning to feel miserable again. "I suppose I *will* feel different. I would be a fool to give it all up: knighthood and a place at court, and all the grand adventures we three planned together—to say nothing of my inheritance up north. . . .

"But maybe," he said wistfully, "I will not change my mind. Perhaps I will still feel the same. And all those things I just mentioned will seem exactly as they seem now: trivial and worldly, and more than a little selfish."

*The men did as the wise woman told them. They put on their
clothes back to front and they loaded their pockets with salt.
They took up hazel wands in their hands and they went silently
into the fenlands to search for the Moon.*

*After a time, they came to a place where an ancient crow with
ruffled feathers perched in the branches of a withered tree in the
midst of a blackberry thicket. And that was the old woman in
black and the crown of thorns. Beside the thicket there was a
pool of dark water and in the middle of the pool a great long
stone shaped like a coffin. And that was the place where the
poor dead Moon lay buried beneath the waters.*

*Without speaking a word, the men set to work to move the
stone. They took up dead branches and used them to shift the
stone aside, and the Moon, reborn, rose up out of the muddy
waters, bathing the marshlands in her pure, silvery light. She
blessed the men who came into the fens to save her and promised
ever afterward to watch over them as tenderly as any mother.*

*—A nursemaids' tale, told in Camboglanna and
throughout the south*

19.

A Visit to Spiral Castle

Garanwyn woke in darkness with the sound of her voice in his
ear. "Tiffaine . . ." he said groggily. "Surely it's not morning
yet?"

"Only a little after midnight," she said. "But there are things
we must speak of before you go. Rise and dress yourself and
meet me on the stairs."

She slipped quietly away. Garanwyn climbed out of his bed
and dressed in the dark, taking care not to wake either Fflergant

or Tryffin. Then he groped his way across the loft to the top of the stairs.

Arfondwy was waiting for him, sitting on the bottom step with a lantern at her feet. Like Garanwyn, she was fully dressed, in a long gown of creamy wool and a checkered mantle.

"You will be leaving in an hour or two," she said, as he sat down beside her. "The Elder Priestess just sent word: She will speak to you and your kinsmen before you leave the marsh. It is a great honor, Garanwyn, and you would be foolish to refuse her. She is very old and tremendously wise, and if she is favorably disposed she will prophesy for you, telling you many things that it would profit you to know. Unfortunately, this summons makes your time in this house that much shorter, and I have many things yet to tell you."

She reached under her mantle and brought out a tiny wooden box, exquisitely carved. "This was given to me by Anwe. It is for you, Garanwyn."

He was reluctant to accept it, having received so much from the people of the marsh already. And she had presented him with a personal parting gift only the day before: a cloak made of fabric she had spun and woven and stitched with her own hands, then dyed a deep rich blue to match his eyes.

"You must take it," she insisted. "It is the Weaver's gift to you and your kinsmen, but she has instructed me to entrust it particularly to you."

Garanwyn opened the box. Inside was a fragment of polished bone, about the size of his little finger, its shape suggesting a sewing needle or a weaver's shuttle. A hole had been drilled near the center, and a fine dark thread passed through. He took this curious device out of the box and examined it with great interest, marveling especially at the strength and lightness of the thread.

"You have seen something like this before?" Arfondwy asked him.

"I think so . . . perhaps," he replied. "I have seen Glastyn wear a similar device on a golden chain, only his was made of lodestone—magnetized iron, he called it. When he held it suspended in the air, the needle always pointed north."

Arfondwy nodded. "This works in much the same way, but always points in the direction of the island of the blackbirds—

whether that be north, south, east, or west of the place you happen to be standing.

"I told you, once, that Teirwaedd Morfa shows many faces," she went on. "And you have heard tales, no doubt, of the way she reaches out to draw unwary travelers in. Had you stayed with us longer, you would have seen that the fenlands are always changing: The river floods, the tide rises and ebbs, the weather is wet or dry . . . all these things alter the contours of the marsh. Men are surprised to wander onto marshy ground where days or weeks ago the land was dry. Then they lose their sense of direction and claim to be pixy-led or lured in by the marsh herself. It is all nonsense, of course," she declared, "but useful to us; it suits our purposes very well when our neighbors fear the marsh.

"But most of these changes, as sudden as they may seem to those who live outside the marsh, actually take days, weeks, sometimes a whole season to occur. We who live in the marsh watch them happen, and so we are never confused by them. But for you, Garanwyn, after leaving the marsh, you would grow hopelessly lost if you ever tried to return. For that reason, Anwe has prepared this. With this in your possession, should any of you wish to return, you or your cousins could find your way to the island where the Elder Priestess dwells, and from there with little difficulty to the House of the Clan of the Horned Moon."

Garanwyn carefully placed the token back inside the box. "I don't know what to say . . . not only for the gifts, but also because your kinswoman has chosen to demonstrate the friendship and the trust of your people in such a . . . convincing manner. I am deeply moved," he said.

He wanted to tell her, then, everything that was in his heart: his need to leave and his desire to stay, his confusion and his questions and his uncertainty about the future. But he said nothing. While he remained undecided, it would be wrong either to encourage or deny any hopes she might cherish.

Long before dawn, the rest of the household began to wake. While the others rose and dressed, Garanwyn and Arfondw remained on the steps, exchanging shy, inexperienced kisses and conversing in soft voices.

"There is no need to say good-bye just yet," said Arfondwy resting comfortably in the curve of his arm. "I am going wit you to the island of the blackbirds, and there we shall say our farewells. In any case, we will not be leaving until after breakfast.''

"Of course," he said, though privately he doubted that he could eat a thing. There was a cold hard lump in the pit of his stomach, and he thought how hard it would be to say those goodbyes in the cold hours before sunrise. Partings were always easier under the light of day. Yet he was a little homesick, this morning, thinking of Gwenlliant for the first time in weeks—his poor little sister would be frantic with worry by now, or else past hoping for his return.

Fflergant and Tryffin came downstairs, and everyone gathered around the hearth where Gonwenlyn prepared breakfast. Tryffin and Fflergant naturally consumed a hearty meal, and even Garanwyn ate more than he expected. They ate oatcakes and apples, goat cheese and smoked fish, and washed it all down with a clear golden mead that Arfondwy served from a brown earthenware jug. After they ate, the boys packed up their things and made ready to depart.

They had already expressed their gratitude the evening before, thanking their kindly hosts fervently, but this morning they did it all again. Yet once more Garanwyn wished for some tangible means to express his sense of obligation.

"We'll send gifts later," Tryffin said in his ear. "I am sure there is a way we might do that. My father and your grandfather will know how—and no doubt wish to send something of their own."

With that, Garanwyn had to be satisfied. He put on the blue cloak, Arfondwy's gift, and she wrapped her checkered mantle around her head and shoulders. The Weaver disappeared into one of the little rooms and reappeared a moment later, wrapped in a long scarlet cloak, carrying a second lantern. The young men picked up their belongings and followed the two young women to the door.

On the ledge outside, the air was thick and cold and damp. The sky was overcast, devoid of moon or stars. Garanwyn handed his gear down to Fflergant and Tryffin, then climbed down the ladder. At the bottom, he paused with one foot on the last rung, gazing in the direction of the make-shift stable under the house.

"The men will bring your horses later," said Arfondwy, slipping her small cold hand into his. "They will meet you on the river at sunrise."

Down by the boats, the mist was thicker, even more claustrophobic. It seemed to press on them, slowing their movements, making every breath of air a burden. Fflergant and Tryffin pushed two canoes out into the water, then waded out along with Anwe, and climbed heavily into one of the boats. Arfondwy and Garanwyn climbed into the other and took up the paddles.

As the two boats glided across the water, Garanwyn was very quiet. This journey through the fog reminded him of the day he had first arrived at the House of the Horned Moon. He had been uncertain of his destination then, and more than a little apprehensive. Now he knew where he was going, but that only doubled his dread. Every stroke of his paddle was taking him closer and closer to the house on the mysterious island of blackbirds and a confrontation with the old woman who lived there.

As they neared the island, Arfondwy began looking for a passage among the dying cattails and bulrushes which clustered so thickly in the shallows. Ahead of them, the other canoe made an unexpected maneuver and disappeared from sight.

As they drew level with the place where the other boat had vanished, Garanwyn saw the yellow light of Anwe's lantern issuing from a break in the line of bulrushes, revealing a narrow passage, scarcely wider than a canoe. Arfondwy skillfully turned her little craft and glided in among the brittle brown rushes—in a moment, they were entirely surrounded and Garanwyn, looking backward, was unable to see the place where they had entered.

The fog lifted, or else it had never penetrated the forest of bulrushes. The air was damp but no longer oppressive. Despite his misgivings, Garanwyn felt his spirits revive. Ahead of them, Anwe's lantern suddenly went out, and Arfondwy lifted the lid of her own lantern and extinguished the rushlight. Much to Garanwyn's surprise, they were not in darkness: A soft glow like moonlight illuminated the passage ahead of them.

"Look over the side; look down into the water," said Arfondwy. "Then shall you see a wonder."

Garanwyn did as she suggested. The water here was as clear as glass—no, clearer, for it was possible to see all the way to the muddy bottom without distortion. There were fish swimming there, rainbow-hued salmon moving among the weeds: silver and rose, emerald-green, deep purple and steel-blue. Garanwyn had never seen anything like them before.

"The salmon of knowledge," said Arfondwy. "They do not sleep by night or by day, and they live to a great age. They are the oldest living creatures on Ynys Celydonn."

Garanwyn had heard of these fish. It was said that the man who caught one and tasted of its flesh would gain in that moment superior knowledge. Yet he felt no desire to make the experiment. Knowledge without experience, compassion, or wisdom seldom gained a man anything worth having—at least, not in any of the stories Garanwyn knew.

The rushes and the wooly cattails began to thin out, and a strip of grassy shoreline appeared. Beyond that, the land sloped upward to a rugged escarpment, and above that was a tangle of blackberry vines blocking their view of the house in the center of the island.

The other boat had already landed, and Anwe and the two young princes from Tir Gwyngelli awaited them on the rocky slope above. As he and Arfondwy climbed the slope, Garanwyn looked around him, searching for the source of the light. The sky was still overcast, the moon still hidden. The eastern horizon was just beginning to turn a rosy grey. Yet the island was bathed in the same silvery radiance that had illuminated their path through the bulrushes.

At the top of the slope where was a narrow ledge and a path leading up the cliff to the blackberry thicket. "Follow me closely," said the Weaver, leading the way. "It would not be wise for you to lose yourselves in the maze."

The path was broad and evidently well-trodden, the brambles rarely intruded but formed a natural tunnel around them, yet Garanwyn saw other pathways, narrower and wilder looking, branching off in many directions. He had no desire to explore those byways, nor to lose sight of Anwe or any of the others. He lengthened his stride in order to keep up with them, dragging Arfondwy along by the hand behind him.

He fell into step with Fflergant. "I feel," said the older boy in a loud whisper, "rather like Ceilyn mac Cuel going to confession. I've searched my conscience thoroughly, and found not a single transgression—not anything recent, anyway. Yet I'm mortally certain that I'm about to be called to account for *something*."

Garanwyn nodded; his cousin's words exactly described his own feelings. And Tryffin, walking a half a pace ahead of them, looked uncharacteristically somber, as though he, too, were considering his sins.

The path gradually narrowed, forcing them to walk in single file, winding upward and inward for what seemed like hours. Garanwyn would not have supposed the thicket nearly so vast, the island half so large. He was beginning to feel fatigued, but was ashamed to admit it.

He glanced back at Fflergant, who was now bringing up the rear, and saw that his face was pale, with a line of pain or weariness between the brows. Fflergant was by no means fully recovered from his long illness. There was not much meat on those big bones of his, and right now his breathing was harsh and shallow. Knowing that Fflergant would never admit to any physical weakness, Garanwyn put his own pride aside, saying as plaintively as he could, "May we stop and rest for a little bit? I don't think that I can keep this up much longer."

"It is not much farther, we are nearly there," said Anwe.

There was a sharp bend in the pathway, a place where the ground sloped more steeply than before, and then they were all standing in a grassy clearing atop the tor, with a view of the labyrinth and most of the island below. The shore and the boats looked deceptively near, the path through the blackberries short and nearly level, with few branches or turnings.

In the center of the clearing stood the house, a long low building thatched with bulrushes. The door—a real door, made of sturdy planks and held in place by leather hinges—stood invitingly ajar and a warm glow of firelight beckoned from the other side.

Anwe pushed the door aside and glided over the threshold. After a moment of hesitation, Tryffin followed her, and then the others came, one by one. Arfondwy was the last one through and closed the door behind her.

They stood inside a long chamber lit by torches and tall yellow candles, not very different from the other houses they had visited, with many little rooms and curtained alcoves built along one side, and a narrow staircase leading up to a second floor. The furnishings were, for the most part, simple and familiar: stools and low benches, a trestle table, and a great loom standing in one corner of the room. But in the middle of the hall, instead of the usual hearth of baked clay, there was an enormous slab of weathered grey stone on which someone had heaped a pile of dried branches and set them ablaze. On the floor all around were many rugs and pillows comfortably arranged, and one huge rough-hewn armchair, facing the fire.

Anwe moved in that direction. Arfondwy and the others followed. As they came closer to the fire, it could be seen that the hearthstone was carved with many pictures and other symbols cut deep into the stone. A line of irregular notches, like letters of some ancient script, formed a kind of border around the edges.

Fflergant nudged his brother. "Is it Ogham, do you think?"

"Or something very like it," Tryffin replied.

"You are familiar with the alphabet?" said a high, brittle-sounding voice, and everyone turned toward one of the alcoves where the curtains had been pushed aside and a tiny sexless figure, clad all in garments of tattered brown and a long veil of some thick, cobwebby material, stood in the opening.

The voice was that of a very old woman. Was she veiled for the sake of modesty, Garanwyn wondered, or to conceal some hideous defect? His first impression of the ragged little figure was that she must be a servant or one of the two women who attended the priestess. But then Anwe and Arfondwy made low obeisances, and Garanwyn understood that he was in the presence of the incarnated Goddess, the living spirit of Teirwaedd Morfa: the Elder Priestess herself.

She let the curtains fall together behind her, moved toward the group by the hearth. Fflergant, taking his cue from the young women, went down on one knee and Tryffin did the same. But Garanwyn hesitated. The gods and goddesses of the marshdwellers were not his gods, their customs were not his own, yet he was a mannerly lad, brought up to respect his elders. He knelt, in deference to her age, experience, and wisdom.

She offered a fragile-looking hand for him to kiss, and another to Fflergant, speaking their names and bidding them welcome in a sweet, reedy voice. But when Tryffin would have followed their example, he was knocked nearly off his balance by a stinging slap, delivered with surprising strength.

"That," said the voice, grown suddenly stern, "is to teach you to speak with respect."

Tryffin's face went blank with shock. He opened his mouth to protest, but she forestalled him with an imperious gesture.

"Think carefully," the voice admonished him, "before you deny anything. Think back to your first night in the marsh, and a certain *filthy foreign mudhole*."

Tryffin did think, long and carefully, and then he had the grace to blush. "I did, most certainly, speak discourteously in asking you to spare my brother. I do apologize—but the circumstances, you will admit, were extraordinary. My manners are usually better."

"So I have heard," said the priestess, relenting enough to offer him her hand.

"But still," Tryffin said, under his breath, "you were cruel on that occasion."

"Cruel?" said the icy sweet voice from under the veils. "It was not I who sought your brother's life. Had you not enjoyed my favor then, as now, not even the power of the dragon could have saved either one of you."

Tryffin was properly chastened. "I see that I misunderstood the situation entirely," he admitted humbly. "I will know you better after this."

"Yes, you will know me better," and now there was a suggestion of a threat in that promise. "No need for me to lesson you—you will learn."

She floated past him and sat down in the armchair, which dwarfed her already tiny figure so that she appeared no larger than a child. Garanwyn had a sudden image of Gwenlliant, sitting in a similar chair back at Caer Cadwy, with her pale hair around her like a veil and her feet dangling several inches above the floor.

The priestess bade her visitors take seats around the hearth, then addressed Fflergant in a gentle voice. "Have you come to hear me prophesy? I am afraid I may not do so."

"But we thought . . ." said Fflergant. "That is, we understood that you wished to see us, and we hoped that there would be a sign or a message."

"There is a message," said the old woman. "One which has awaited your coming for a thousand years. But it will require considerable ingenuity on your part in order to divine its true meaning."

She gestured in Anwe's direction, and the Weaver rose gracefully to her feet. Out of a bag at her belt Anwe emptied a pale powder into her hand, and sprinkled it over the fire. The room slowly filled with a pleasant fragrance: like clover and apple-blossom, like beeswax and fresh-baked bread, and other whole-some, homelike odors.

The effect on Garanwyn was overwhelming and almost immediate. He had grown tired climbing the hill, and now he was assailed by a pleasant but irresistible drowsiness, a languor which rapidly spread to all four limbs and made it difficult for him to hold up his head. Even to keep his eyes open required a tremendous effort and he could scarcely prevent himself from toppling over.

"Lay your head in my lap," Arfondwy suggested softly, and Garanwyn obediently stretched out on the rug with his head resting on her knees. Then, with a sigh of inexpressible weariness, he closed his eyes and fell into a deep, dreamless sleep.

• • •

They crowned Finn at Nehemeton, the Holy Place, on the Plain of Stones, proclaiming him King of the Three Tribes. There was great rejoicing, that day, from the lake country in the north to the great bay in the south. Men cheered and women wept, for peace had finally come to them, and a time of healing.

But there was no celebration at Rimini, where Penfyngon was master. The Prince of the Morgai sat in his tent, with envy gnawing at his bowels. And when night fell, he sacrificed a yearling to the gods of his tribe, vowing that Finn's reign would be a short one.

*—From a manuscript preserved at Ystrad Pangur,
   believed to be the record of a more ancient oral tradition*

• • •

In their places on the other side of the fire, Fflergant and Tryffin shifted uneasily. Neither one had been affected by the smoke, but they had watched with shock and surprise as Garanwyn succumbed. Tryffin started to his feet, but the ancient priestess commanded him to keep his seat.

"Do not disturb him. Your kinsman has taken no harm, nor will he. But it is not for him to hear or see any of the things which I am about to reveal to you."

Fflergant and his brother exchanged a doubtful glance. They were in the habit of looking after their young cousin, shielding him and helping him in ways he never guessed. Yet he lay quite peacefully, and apparently quite content, with his head in the lap of Arfondwy, who loved him, and Anwe knelt down by his side, taking his hand into one of her own and stroking his pale gold hair with a look of such motherly tenderness that it was impossible to believe she intended him harm.

"Sit, if you will learn why I sent for you," said the Elder Priestess. And Tryffin, only partly reassured, returned to his place sitting cross-legged at her feet.

"Gaze into the fire. Do not fear to breathe the smoke. It will not affect you—except, perhaps, to help you see more clearly," said the old woman. "Look into the flames, and tell me what you see."

For several minutes, the two young princes gazed intently into the heart of the fire, without comprehending what was expected of them. "Come now," said the old woman, "even untrained children see pictures in the flames, though lacking the clear-sight, such visions are meaningless. But the pictures on my hearth are never so. Unfocus your eyes, allow your imaginations free rein, and tell me everything that you see."

Tryffin was the first, speaking with great effort. "I see a grassy plain . . . a sort of fold between two hills, and a circle of standing stones."

"Very good," said the priestess. "Do you know the place?"

"*Dol Tal Carreg*, the plain of tall stones. No . . . I am mistaken. The stone circle at Dol Tal Carreg is largely in ruins."

"You are not mistaken. You see the circle as it stood in ancient times, in the days when our ancestors first came into these islands. They did not build it, but they had seen similar structures before, and regarded them as holy places. What else do you see?"

This time, Fflergant answered. "A great gathering of men, a multitude of warriors carrying weapons made of bronze. I see banners with unfamiliar devices: a leaping lion, a disk with many rays—the sun, I suppose—and a white winged serpent."

"These represent the three tribes that once inhabited Camboglanna: the Korred, the Camberians, and the Morgai. What further?"

"I see men erecting a great stone table," said Fflergant, straining to see. "I see a long procession, led by men in white robes. The first one, the oldest, wears a wreath of oakleaves and bears a branch of holly. They are escorting a young man with dark skin and golden hair. He stands atop the stone table in the midst of the circle of stones, and the old man places a crown upon his head.''

"Do you see the device on the banner of the King?" Fflergant shook his head. "Do you see it?" she asked Tryffin.

Tryffin breathed deeply, inhaling the smoke. "It is the Lion of St. March. . . . No, it is not. It is the other devices, imposed one over the other: the white serpent in the jaws of the lion surmounting the disk of the sun." Suddenly he cried out, as though pierced by bitter pain. "The King dies with an arrow through his heart, and another man appears in his place. He has no right to stand where he stands. The earth shakes and the stones which support the table crack. The coronation stone tips. . . ."

"Yes?" she prompted him.

"There are signs carved in the coronation stone. God above! *This* is the coronation stone . . . the hearth on which the fire burns!"

"Very good," said the old woman. "You have seen more than I hoped. Rest your eyes for a moment, and I will tell you more. As you have guessed, the hearthstone is the coronation stone. It came here, by means which you or I can scarcely conceive of, brought for safekeeping in a time of great trouble.

"Now turn your attention to the letters of the border, and read them to me. No, it is not necessary for you to leave your seats The clear-sight is still on you: You have only to close your eyes and the words will appear in your minds."

Fflergant closed his eyes. Gradually, as she had promised, the image came into his mind: letters of fire burning behind his eyelids. "The first line . . . I am not certain. *The raven triumphant*, I think."

The veiled head inclined forward. "That is correct. The second line?"

"The secret fire is kindled again."

"And the third?"

"The dragon . . . No, the dragon's fire . . ."

"The dragon goes into the fire," said Tryffin.

"The fourth line?"

Tryffin shook his head, and Fflergant sighed. "The fourth line is fainter—I can't make it out at all."

"A pity," she said. "Is the fifth line clear enough for you to read?"

"The King . . ." said Fflergant. "No . . . *The Green King returns to crown Celydonn's Lord.*"

"That is the sense of it. But the true meaning?"

Fflergant opened his eyes. "The raven must be Rhianedd and the dragon Tir Gwyngelli, but beyond that . . . ?"

The old woman inclined her head toward Tryffin. "Do you know?"

"The secret fire . . . perhaps a gemstone from the mines: The miners say they can feel them burning in the dark places under the earth. The Clach Ghealach . . . No, that's already been re-kindled, and the raven comes first. The Clach Grian, perhaps?"

"It has been said that Ynys Celydonn will never know a last-ing peace until the rightful King holds both the Clach Ghealach and the Clach Grian," said the priestess. "What more?"

"I don't know who the Green King might be."

"That is the Glas-tann. He it was, in times past, who crowned the kings of Camboglanna." She sat back in her chair, as though overcome by weariness or disappointment. "I had hoped you might enlighten me further. But it hardly matters. Doubtless the full meaning of the prophecy will come to you at the proper time."

"But how . . . how do we know that it is a prophecy?" asked Fflergant. "Aren't inscriptions of this sort usually commemo-rative?"

"When this was written there was no kingdom of Celydonn as we know it. There were many kings, many princes, countless tribal chieftains, but even the warrior-kings who reigned in the south saw no further than the union of the three tribes. Cynwal and his sons would not be born for centuries and there was no one, as yet, to style himself Lord of all Celydonn."

"Well, then," said Tryffin, contriving to sound absolutely cool and logical, in spite of his rising excitement. "How do you know that this prophecy, old as it is, has anything to do with *us*?"

Her voice sounded amused now. "What am I to think when two young princes—sons of the raven and of the dragon, distant grandsons of the kings of the south, raised in the New Religion but taught to respect the Old—what am I to think when two such extraordinary young men come to me, by land and by water, through perils they do not even comprehend, to sit in this place and look upon the coronation stone, which no man of their age or their faith has seen before? Am I to think that this amazing sequence of events has no reason or purpose behind it?''

Tryffin and Fflergant exchanged a radiant glance. That they *were* extraordinary they already knew. Since a time before memory, the Hillfolk had assured them, again and again, that they were not like other men, that they had been endowed with certain heroic capabilities and responsibilities which set them . . . not so much above others, but certainly apart, as a man must be if he is to shape events, make a positive impression on the history of his land and his people. That was the birthright of a prince of Tir Gwyngelli, and a fact they had both accepted so long ago that it no longer moved them: neither to excessive pride, nor to wonder, nor to hopeful anticipation.

Lately, however, they had begun to doubt. That heroic destiny promised to them since birth was certainly taking its time in manifesting; events were dragging along at a most discouraging pace. It had begun to look as though they were doomed, after all, to spend the best years of their golden youth doing absolutely nothing of real importance.

But now there was this: their very own prophecy, chiseled in stone some ten centuries before either of them was born . . . and that was far, far beyond even their most confident expectations.

"Where shall we seek the answer?" Tryffin asked breathlessly.

"Seek it everywhere and at all times."

"Is it a geas, then?" Fflergant asked reverently.

Again the Lady of Teirwaedd Morfa was amused. "The Gwyngellach and their geasa! Call it such, if you will. But do not abandon the quest while you both live."

And Finarfon took the King's daughter for his wife, and he lived with her three years in the Land of Youth. All that time passed pleasantly in feasting and hunting and in continual merry-making. But when the three years had ended, Finarfon began to long for his home and for sight of his parents and his brothers and sisters. He asked his wife if he might return to his father's house for a visit.

"I will give my consent," said the daughter of the King, "though my heart misgives me."

She gave him the white steed to carry him back to Celydonn and also a cloak, a ring, and a chaplet of gold, saying, "So long as you keep these three things near you, I know that you will be faithful to me. But if, for any reason, you put one of them aside, then I fear that you and I will never meet again."

Finarfon promised to guard her gifts carefully, and to return to her in three months' time. Then he kissed her and mounted the white horse. As before, the horse ran more swiftly than the wind. Over the sand, over the face of the sea they traveled, and Finarfon clung tightly to the saddle, his golden cloak billowing in the wind behind him. In no time at all, they arrived on the shores of Celydonn.

When Finarfon dismounted before his father's house, Nuala, his youngest sister, came out to greet him. As Finarfon ran to meet her, the golden ring slipped off his finger. In his haste, he neglected to pick it up again.

Then his years in the Land of Youth became as a dream to him, and all memory of the King's daughter passed from his mind.

—From The Book of the White Cockerel

20.

The Rule of Three

Garanwyn woke with a deep sense of well-being, a dreamy impression that he was at home, and safe, and utterly content. But then the room around him came into focus, he remembered where he really was, and he sat up at once, looking around him in bewilderment. On the other side of the fire, the old woman sat silent and immobile in her great rough-hewn armchair. Arfondwy knelt on the rug beside him. But Anwe the Weaver was gone, and Fflergant and Tryffin were nowhere to be seen.

"All is well, Garanwyn," said Arfondwy. "Your kinsmen have completed their business here, and await you down below. Now it is your turn to hear what fate holds in store for you."

Garanwyn shook his head, as though that might clear it. "But I understood . . . Surely she said she was not going to prophesy for us?"

"For your kinsmen . . . no," replied Arfondwy. "Yet your cousins have learned that which may be of service to them. Now it is your turn, and you may ask her any question you wish. If it is not a proper one, she will tell you so. But you need not be afraid to ask."

"No . . . I mean, yes, I see," said Garanwyn, still a little disoriented. But he had already lost most of his fear of the old woman, and there was one question, in particular, which he wanted to ask her.

"Is it possible . . . is it permitted to ask, not about my own future, but about my sister's?"

The old woman leaned forward in her chair. "If you ask out of genuine concern, with love in your heart, and not seeking power over your sister, you are permitted to ask."

Garanwyn considered that. "But if one should seek power over another person, merely to guide their steps, to protect them and spare them pain . . . is that so very wrong?"

"We cannot hope to spare our loved ones from pain all their lives long," said the priestess. "Yet we try . . . oh yes, we try. But tell me this: Do you think you have the wisdom to choose what is best for this sister of yours?"

"No," said Garanwyn humbly. "No, I do not. I don't even know what is the best course for me to take . . . not anymore. The truth is, I have an important decision to make, a difficult decision, which might be easier if I knew what the future holds for my sister."

"And if what I have to tell you does little or nothing to make that decision easier . . . what then?" asked the gentle voice from beneath the veil.

Garanwyn thought that over carefully. "Nevertheless," he decided, "I think I would like to hear it."

The fire suddenly blazed up more brightly than before, snapping and crackling upon the hearth. "Very well," said the priestess. Her voice changed, became clearer and, at the same time, more distant. "Your sister was named *Gwenlliant Branwen*, which in the Old Tongue signify the White Flood and the white raven, which are attributes of the Goddess Celedon, who is one and is many. We worship her under many names, but these are the three by which she is best known: Maiden, Mother, and Crone. And in this wise and by the rule of three, shall Gwenlliant ni Cyndrywyn's life be shaped. Listen, if you will hear . . .

"She will learn about love from three men, all of the same blood.
She will marry three times: once to please her father, once to
*   please the man she loves best, and lastly to please herself.*
She will remain a maid over-long, but she will bear and raise
*   many beautiful children.*
Men will die with her name on their lips.
She will wear a crown and walk barefoot.
She will ascend to a great height and fall down again.
But her blood will flow in the veins of kings."

Garanwyn listened to all this with his eyes downcast and a frown creasing his brow. As the old woman had promised, there was little in what she said to give him ease.

"It is a heavy fate," he murmured. "Widowed twice and happiness only at the end."

"Not so," said the Lady. "Look in the mirror."

Garanwyn looked up and discovered that she was dangling some shining object before his eyes—not a real mirror, but a piece of polished metal, curved like the horns of the moon, dangling from a silver chain. Yet it was not his own reflection or that of anything in the room which met his startled gaze:

A dimly lit chapel, empty save for bride, groom, and priest. A plain golden band changing hands.

A great hall ablaze with light. A fillet of white-gold on Gwenlliant's brow.

A wooded glade. A blood-stained gown. An intricately wrought bracelet encircling his sister's wrist.

Beside her, through everything, stood a tall, fair-haired man.

"But it is always . . ." Garanwyn was thoroughly bewildered now. In every scene, the bridegroom's back had been turned toward him; though Garanwyn thought that he knew him, he could not be certain. "It is always the same man!"

They left the house and Arfondwy led the way down the winding pathway, through the blackberry thicket, to the beach. This time the journey was accomplished quickly, too quickly to suit Garanwyn, and they found Fflergant and Tryffin waiting by one of the boats, Anwe by the other.

He turned to Arfondwy. The moment of parting had finally come, and a feeling like panic rose up inside him. "Tiffaine . . ." he managed, around the lump in his throat. "Tiffaine, I . . ."

"There is no need for you to say anything," she whispered. "This is not our final farewell, Garanwyn. I know that we are destined to meet again; whether in sorrow or in joy I do not know; but that we shall meet I have no doubt."

He knew that she was right, that whatever course his life took after this, he would find her again and tell her all the things he lacked the courage to speak of now. For now, there was nothing he could do but take her in his arms and kiss her one last time.

"They are waiting for us on the river," said Tryffin, when the embrace showed signs of going on forever. "This won't get easier, the longer you put if off," he added.

Garanwyn and Arfondwy moved apart. With many a backward glance, Garanwyn climbed into the canoe with his cousins, and took up one of the paddles.

"What happens now?" he managed to ask, when the island and the young women had disappeared from view.

"They are waiting for us with our horses and their barges, to take us up river to a place near a village where they sometimes trade," said Fflergant.

"I'll not offer you any false comfort," he added, "or pretend to know how you feel when I don't. But we are going *home*, you know."

"I know," said Garanwyn, taking a long deep breath. "And you needn't worry about me. I intend to survive this. And it was such an incredible thing, that Tiffaine and I should meet and love, we who lived in two different worlds—I can't believe that it all happened by chance, without any purpose or meaning behind it. I want to be stronger and wiser because of it."

Fflergant and Tryffin exchanged an amused glance.

"You left Caer Cadwy a mere careless lad, and you return a philosopher," said Fflergant.

Garanwyn cast him an evil look. "You are going to pay for that . . . just as soon as I'm feeling more myself."

"Oh aye," said Fflergant cheerfully. "I begin to hope that I may."

What it was that moved them, so near their journey's end, to pull up the reins and pause just outside the graveyard, Garanwyn and his cousins were not afterward certain. But once they were there, it seemed perfectly natural to climb out of their saddles and allow the horses a brief rest before attempting that last wearying trek up the dusty road to the castle.

The yews and the oaks which sheltered the southern end of the cemetery offered them a place to sit out of the wind. So they tied up their horses at one of the oaks, and perched on the dry-stone wall which surrounded the graveyard.

Their journey across Camboglanna had been accomplished rapidly and uneventfully. But scarcely rapid enough for Garanwyn, who once they had left the marsh behind had regained that sense of urgency which had driven them into the arms of Teirwaedd Morfa in the first place. Now, however, that urgency was beginning to evaporate, and he was content to sit and rest for a while just within sight of home.

He glanced idly around him and his gaze chanced to fall on the two fresh graves, the unmarked mounds at the eastern end of the cemetery. "Now, who do you suppose it was that died while we were gone?" he wondered out loud.

No one thought, at first, that it might be anyone they all knew. Counting the servants, the guards, and the hermit monks living in the outer walls, the castle housed more than two hundred souls. But one fear always followed Garanwyn whenever he was away from home, and that fear caught up to him now, turning him suddenly cold with apprehension. He scrambled over the wall in order to take a closer look.

Tryffin and Fflergant joined him beside the two unmarked graves. "Not a child," said Tryffin, correctly guessing what troubled his friend. "Neither of them was a child . . . look at the size of the mounds."

Garanwyn sat down on a mossy gravestone, summoned up a sheepish grin. "I wasn't thinking. I forgot that it couldn't be Gwenlliant. The Lady prophesied a long and eventful life for her. There were parts of it I didn't care for at the time, but it all strikes me as particularly reassuring right now."

Fflergant inspected the graves with a puzzled frown. "No headstones, no flowers. Odd that there isn't any sort of marker. Even for a beggar, somebody usually puts up a wooden cross."

"Suicides?" suggested Garanwyn.

But Fflergant shook his head. "Not buried in hallowed ground."

Tryffin, meanwhile, had paced out the length of one of the graves. "This fellow was tall—two yards at least, and probably more."

"Now, who do we know—or did we know," Fflergant speculated, "who stood so high as that? I will thank you, Cousin," he added, only half in jest, "not to look at me that way."

Garanwyn, who had been unaware that he was staring, immediately apologized. "I was just thinking . . . the two bodies I saw burned in the marsh, the two men who died violently: One of them was a big man, too. At least . . . I didn't actually see the bodies, only their bloody shrouds, but it was obvious they were both too large to be any of the men of the marsh. Now the first thing that greets us when we return to Caer Cadwy is these two graves—an odd sort of coincidence, don't you think?"

"An unpleasant coincidence," said Fflergant. "And one I would rather not dwell on."

They left their horses at the stable in the hands of two capable young stableboys, and headed for their own room, to change their clothes and clean up before presenting themselves to the Master of Squires. As they crossed the outer courtyard, they chanced to encounter the Princess Diaspad and Calchas, and their usual entourage of dwarfs and wildmen. At sight of Fflergant and Tryffin, the Princess and Calchas stopped dead in their tracks and exchanged a look of utter horror.

"Now, what was that all about?" asked Fflergant, when he and his kinsmen had passed out of earshot. "You would think those graves down below were meant for us after all. Tell me," he asked the others, "do I look such a ghost of the man I was?"

Garanwyn examined him critically. "You've lost a good deal of flesh . . . there's no denying that," he said judiciously. "But your color, if I may say so, is exceedingly good."

"As I thought," murmured Fflergant, opening the door at the base of the Seraphim Tower and passing through. "Exactly as I thought."

Climbing the stairs to the second floor, they met Ceilyn mac Cuel coming down. There was a look on the young knight's face that boded ill for somebody. Garanwyn and Tryffin politely (and prudently) stepped aside, but Fflergant and Ceilyn both bristled like two strange dogs catching scent of one another.

Ceilyn folded his arms, leaned up against the wall, surveying the three boys with a look of weary superiority. "I see that the three of you have finally returned. I only hope you have a good excuse for the delay."

Fflergant stiffened. "If we have, it's not for you to demand it. We don't have to account to *you* for our comings and—" He broke off when Tryffin dealt him a swift, sharp kick on the shin.

Ceilyn scowled at them, apparently weighing the relative merits of boiling in oil and roasting over an open fire.

"It wasn't exactly our fault," Garanwyn offered. "We lost ourselves coming across Walgan, and then we—"

"You lost yourselves?" said Ceilyn. His smile was even more daunting than his frown, if that were possible. "Coming across Walgan? That can't have been easy."

"It wasn't," Garanwyn assured him. "It took us the better part of the night to accomplish."

Ceilyn straightened. "I've no time to waste, listening to such nonsense," he sniffed. "And as for you . . . your sister was in the Solar with the Queen, just a little while since. You'll want to see her at once, of course. God knows, you've caused the poor child anguish enough as it is."

The door at the foot of the stairs slammed shut behind him. Garanwyn turned to Fflergant. "Why do the two of you always *do* that?'' he asked. ''And you . . . Can't you even *try* not to antagonize Ceilyn?''

''Try not to . . . ?'' Fflergant was indignant. ''Now, how was that my fault? I will admit that I've deliberately provoked the man a time or two in the past, but this time I didn't do a thing. And you saw how he was. He is the one who looks like he ought to be out haunting the ruins! I've never seen him like this . . . at least, not since last winter.''

Garanwyn had to agree. ''It does seem,'' he admitted, as he opened the door at the top of the stairs, ''that whenever the days grow shorter so does Ceilyn's temper. And this is only the last week of November. God help us all when winter arrives.''

But Ceilyn and his odd behavior were soon forgotten, as they turned a corner and Garanwyn spotted Gwenlliant.

''Oh, Garanwyn,'' exclaimed the little girl, hurling herself into her brother's arms. ''I thought you were *never* coming back.''

Garanwyn held her close, buried his face in her fine pale hair, and wondered how he could ever have contemplated deserting her.

*And after the storm, the Princess Goewin went down to the
shore, searching for her lover among the rocks and the sea-
wrack. Yet there was no sign of the young man, either by land
or by sea. She sat down upon a rock and buried her face in her
hands, and Goewin wept bitterly, for all that had been, and was,
and never could be.*

*As she wept, one of the seals crawled up onto the beach, one
of the great grey seals of the north, as large as a man. The seal
came to the Princess, all the while crying out in a voice of great
anguish and sorrow. When Goewin looked into the eyes of the
seal, she saw the soul of the man she loved looking back at her.
Then Goewin knew that she had lost him indeed.*

—*From Goewin and Ellwy:* The Death of Goewin

21.

A Circle of Fire

The first snow fell that night, a light powder which melted
away as soon as it fell, but it brought with it a pack of silver-
grey wolves, driven south in search of game by a three-day storm
in upper Camboglanna.

In his bed in the Seraphim Tower, Ceilyn tossed and turned.
The iron bracelet was a band of fire encircling his wrist, the
metal eating into his flesh like silver. Whenever he dozed off,
his dreams were troubled, images of wolves and seagulls dancing in his mind.

But then everything changed. He was in the garden as of old,
kneeling beneath the appletree, the tree which bore fruit and
white blossoms both in the same season. He fumbled with the
catch on the bracelet, frantic to free himself. The iron burned
his fingers and the catch refused to open. *Someone had welded*

it shut and there was no way he could free himself from the agonizing grip of the iron.

Suddenly, his mother was there. She stepped out of the apple-tree, shaking the scented blossoms out of her hair. She carried a sword with a golden hilt—his sword, he realized with a shock. The blade was all tarnished and blackened. Solemnly, Merewyn handed him the blade. *"You know what you must do."*

Ceilyn began to tremble. He did know what was expected of him, but he was afraid. He wept, the hot tears burning his face. "Mother, I can't. Mother . . . help me."

But Merewyn was no longer there. In her place stood a slender white deer with branching silver antlers, staring at him with reproachful dark eyes.

He tightened his grip on the hilt of his sword, raised it, took a deep breath. The blade descended, shearing his hand off cleanly just above the wrist. There was surprisingly little pain, but the dark blood gushed out of the stump, staining the green earth below.

He reached out in panic for the white deer, his mother, but she shied away from his touch, shook her head, and took flight. . . .

Ceilyn woke in a cold sweat. The iron bracelet was still there, burning on his wrist. He threw off the blankets, staggered to his feet, and swiftly dressed.

He prowled among the shadows in the innermost courtyard. A gust of wind carried the scent of one of the guards past him; Ceilyn felt the hairs on the back of his neck rising, the old wildness stirring. It was all that he could do to resist the temptation to throw back his head and howl his anguish to the night.

He slipped through the Gamelyon Gate and into the outer courtyard, past the stables where the horses, catching wind of him, moved restlessly in their stalls. Then he came to the place where someone had slaughtered a calf earlier. Tasting blood in the air, he felt something twist inside him, the agony of the iron burning deeper.

A time of stumbling, sweating, panting confusion followed. When his mind cleared, he discovered that he was standing over the well beside the wash-house, gazing down into the shadowy depths and fumbling, as in his dream, with the catch on the bracelet. But this time the catch yielded, and the metal released its grip.

He hesitated only for an instant before casting the bracelet into the darkness below. There was a tiny, distant splash as the iron hit the water, and then it was gone forever.

In her bedchamber in the Wizard's Tower, Teleri opened her eyes, fought her way free of the dreams which tangled her thoughts. Dim grey shadows moved at the edge of her mind, wolf-shapes prowling outside the gates of Caer Cadwy. All in an instant, she knew that Ceilyn was in trouble.

Quickly, she dressed. She searched frantically for her shoes but could not find them. Abandoning the search, she threw on her long grey cloak, pulled open the door, and passed through.

Her doorstep was wet and slick with melting snow; the stones in the courtyard bit into her bare feet. In the sky above, the dying moon, wasted away to a narrow crescent, lent only a thin, watery light to her search. And well she knew the many hiding places, the places where Ceilyn might crouch unseen—if only he would remain unseen, unseen by others, until she could find him herself!

She passed through the Gamelyon Gate, searched behind the wash-house, the mews, and the rookery. All the little houses where the castle craftsmen lived were dark and she detected no movement in that direction, not even a breath of wind, yet she could not risk missing him if he lay there in hiding—she searched between the cottages until a commotion over by the stable drew her in that direction.

She heard excited voices: ". . . a wolf, I swear it . . . the biggest I've seen in years . . . the same beast that attacked the Marshall last winter?" The horses whickered in their stalls and the wolfhounds in the kennel next door growled softly.

Teleri's blood ran cold. If she could not find Ceilyn before he attacked someone, or before one of the guards thought to release the King's wolfhounds . . . once they spotted him, the huge, tireless hounds would pursue him to the death.

The little gate behind the guardtower stood open, the gate leading into the ruins. Ceilyn might choose that way to go, yes, that was very likely. Into the ruins and away from the sounds and scents of men and dogs, into the ruins seeking a way out of the castle.

Keeping to the shadows, she crept past the tower and through the gate. Cracked flagstones under her feet bit into her soles; thorny branches caught and ripped at her skirts, scratched her legs and hands, tangled in her braided hair and pulled it loose. Teleri went on. She thought she heard a rustling among bushes on the far side of a high stone wall, and searched among the rubble until she discovered a gateway.

The yard on the other side had once been a formal garden, but a century of neglect had reduced everything to dust and decay. Withered vines twined around a pair of crumbling head-less statues on either side of the gate; an ancient oak, as bent and twisted with age as an old man, leaned over a shallow, scum-covered pond. She called Ceilyn's name, but nobody answered.

Teleri sank to the ground, there among the decaying leaves of a hundred autumns, and she called his name over and over again, desperately, without real hope. The shrubbery rustled again. An enormous grey wolf materialized out of the bushes and stretched out on the ground beside her.

Teleri put a trembling hand on the rough grey head. The beast whimpered and laid his head in her lap. She said his name again, but the beast did not respond. Panic caught at the back of her throat. Had Ceilyn forgotten his name so soon?

She closed her eyes, imagined him as she had last seen him: pale face set, determined; hazel eyes troubled; a shock of unruly russet hair. The beast moaned, low in his throat, stirred beneath her hands.

When she opened her eyes, the wolf was gone and she was stroking Ceilyn's hair. She knew that he was crying, too.

At last his shoulders stopped heaving. He took a long, trem-bling breath, and sat up. His eyes were wild, terrified, still the eyes of the wolf, and not of the man that she knew.

"I couldn't stop myself. . . . I had to be free of it. But you were right. . . . To rid myself of the iron, I would have done anything!" His face changed, he stared at her with a look of horror, suddenly recognizing her peril. "What are you doing here? You should never have tried to find me. I might have . . . God help me, I don't know what I might have done. I don't now that you are safe even now!"

"I am not afraid," she said, but indeed, she was afraid. "Anyway . . . you didn't hurt me."

"I still could—I could! And then what would become of me? Do you think I could continue to live if I ever harmed you?"

He was shivering violently, flinched when she tried to touch him. "Don't," he said, between clenched teeth. "Don't. You don't know what I am, what I am capable of doing."

"But I do know, Ceilyn," she said, striving to control the tremor which crept into her voice. "And I know that there is nothing inherently evil in that part of you, for all that you fear it so. And you are not a bad man, not a vicious man. . . ."

Pain twisted behind his eyes. "It is little you know about the things which go on in my mind—even at the best of times. How it all gets mixed up: you and Sidonwy and Prescelli and my mother . . . the loving and the hurting and the wanting . . . until I can't sort it out at all. You don't know and you can't guess, and I can only thank God! Because if you did know me as I really am, you would *despise* me."

"Whatever sins you have committed, whatever sins you have contemplated, I can't believe that any of them are unique," she insisted patiently. "No, truly, Ceilyn, you can't have invented any new sins—the world is far too old for that! You really must stop believing that there is something almost supernaturally *wicked* about you, that you have been singled out for some par-particular punishment. . . . When you think about it, that's dreadfully pre-presumptuous." Her voice caught on a sob "Anyway, you are not suffering for your own s-sins now. . . It is all because of mine!"

"Your sins!" he exclaimed. "By what stretch of that fantasti imagination of yours is any of this your doing?"

"Tampering with things I didn't understand. Dragging yo into them against your will. Exposing you to influences you ha every reason to fear . . . If anyone deserves to be punished, is I!"

He shook his head wearily. "No, this was none of your doing I felt this coming for a long, long time. Don't you remember? told you that I was afraid of losing myself, long before Forgoll wretched bull even arrived here." He sifted a handful of fade leaves through his fingers, watched them crumble into dus "Why, you warned me at the very beginning that this day mu finally arrive. And speaking of presumption! You didn't mak me what I am, and you are not responsible for anything that do. I don't recall that you held any kind of blade to my throat on All Hallows Eve.

"Not that any of it matters . . . the how or the why of it. The real question is: What am I to do now?"

She knew, but could not make herself say the words. He knew also. Glancing up, he smiled wistfully at the disheveled, tear-stained picture she presented. It was going to be hard for him to go, now that he finally knew how much she wanted him to stay.

"What is the use of either of us pretending? You told me that, too, at the beginning. The time has come for me to join the pack, to learn, if I can, what force it is—good, bad, or utterly amoral—that draws me to them."

"You don't think of going tonight?" she whispered. "Now? But surely there is no hurry. After the last time that this happened to you, nearly a whole year passed before—and I will find a way to make the iron stronger, I promise."

He did not tell her what had happened to the iron bracelet, did not have the heart. "Even if you could . . . what would that accomplish, besides delaying the inevitable?"

The air seemed to move and shimmer around him, and then she was looking into the eyes of the great grey wolf. She threw her arms around his neck, buried her face in the thick fur, and burst into tears again.

They remained that way for a long time: her face pressed up against him, moon-silvered hair mingling with grey fur. There was no sound but her tremulous breathing and the soft panting of the wolf. At last she drew away, wiped the tears from her eyes.

"You can leave by the sally port, take the steps on the seaward side. I will open the gate for you. Will you come with me?"

There could be no answer; she could not even be certain that he understood her. But when she rose to her feet and moved in the direction of the garden gate, the wolf rose also and followed obediently at her side.

They arrived at the sally gate all too soon. Teleri struggled with the bolt, threw her weight against the heavy timbers, forcing the gate open a bare twelve inches. It was enough for the wolf, who pushed past her and was gone.

Then came the long, cold journey back to the Wizard's Tower. She pushed open her door, paused before crossing the threshold, and leaned against the doorframe, too exhausted for any more tears.

Dawn was turning the eastern sky as grey as ashes. A long, quivering cry, attenuated by distance, hung mournfully on the air. A moment later, another wolf answered. Teleri stepped inside her bare, silent bedchamber and closed the door softly behind her.